Walking to Israel

EMMA GATES

WELLS STREET PRESS

Copyright © 2014 by Emma Gates

ISBN 978-0-9888906-9-5

Cover design: Derek Murphy

Cover Photograph: Christopher Whitehead

Printed in the United States of America

Walking to Israel

London 1962

ONE

D UNNO WHY THERE'S A BOBBY AT THE DOOR.
Lottie, hiding behind her older sister Nell, studied him: dark blue suit, conical hat, silver badge. He leaned in to peer down at them.

"Is Mr. Arkwright here?"

"Our Dad's back home in America," said Nell.

"Cor," said the bobby, looking at an older, fatter bobby who wheezed behind him at the top of their third floor flat.

"Arsk where she thinks er mum's got to," the fat one mumbled.

Nell stood straight as the young bobby. "Our mother's gone to Israel."

Mommy decided to go *without* them? And she didn't tell Lottie?

Nell added, "She started walking there this morning."

The bobbies looked at each other in the way that meant they didn't want to tell Nell and Lottie something. Lottie had seen that look on Master Rory's face. She knew about keeping secrets.

The fat one wiped at his face. "Is it just the two of you ere, at ome?"

"Our brother Lars is due from Waverley any minute." Nell's voice held the pride of a public-school sister. "They had a gymkhana today."

1

"Well. Er look." The young one shot another glance at his mate. "The thing is, we've got your mum outside, in the lorry. But we need to know if ... everything's all right, for her to come home. "

"S'all right," Lottie said.

Nobody moved.

"I said it's all right! She *can* come ome!" Lottie pushed by Nell and the bobbies, school satchel still flapping on her back, heels clattering on bare wood.

On each landing metal gas-meter faces gaped for coins. She heard their hungry sopranos echo in the stairwell, above the drumbeat of her footfalls.

She reached the ground floor and raced onto the squashed-leaf-smelling road. Autumn lay in the gutters like soggy cornflakes.

There *was* a lorry.

She pressed her face flat against the humid lorry window, smearing it, straining sideways to see if Mommy really was inside.

And she was!

But she looked ... unready to get out.

Lottie shrank back as she recognized the look: Mommy was *in a mood*.

Sometimes they were cozy moods, where everyone stayed home from school, and drank cocoa round the fire, curled like puppies in a basket, no squabbles. Mommy told them about the people who made pearls from a river of molten lava, deep beneath the Earth's crust, or about those who lived in the permanent winter Forest of Firth, or about the grandfather who made Easter flowers out of his grand-daughter's long blond hair. She liked to twist Lottie's never-cut yellow locks during that story.

And sometimes they were funny moods, as when they refused to eat the abysmal rhubarb pudding at lunch. Headmistress asked what had they eaten for breakfast, then, refusing good school food, and they told her cocoa and toast, and when Headmistress sent someone round to find out if this were true, from Mommy, she just said *take*

2

a hike. "Take a hike," she'd repeated to the children after school. "I put that old biddy in her place. Nothing wrong with cocoa and toast. The gall!"

But sometimes they were scary moods, when Mommy, in a deep voice, said *silence,* and if anyone made a sound, even after days, Mommy would pinch their lips together and bring her furious face down into theirs, so that it was more frightening than the pinching, and if Lottie whimpered, Mommy would pinch harder, nails digging in.

But Mommy's face now, white behind the window, didn't look like those moods.

She looks like a bloomin runaway.

Like the boy, Jamie, that Lars had brought home from the park last week, a thin boy with a shock of dark hair; dressed, in autumn's chill, in shorts that showed his sharp scabby knees, a raggedy jersey, and plimsoles with gaps where his toes showed through. He said he was living in a phonebooth because he was afraid to go home. "Mum's drinkin again. She might hit me like she done upon babby."

They'd taken the tube to his flat, further away than they'd ever gone before. They'd each carried bags of outgrown clothes.

Jamie's street was dark, and he'd clung to Mommy's hand tight, hanging back. Lottie could tell he didn't want to go up his dirt-slippery stairs.

His Mum and Mommy had talked in the kitchen, drinking tea, while Jamie showed off his new clothes in front of his two sisters, one in a crib, the hit-upon babby; and the other, in a too-small nightgown, who sniggered at the Arkwright children. Nell helped that one try on clothes but Lottie stood stiff in a corner, shy, not wanting to make friends, not wanting to touch anything.

They'd come back on the last train, past midnight, staggering up the three flights to their flat which looked to Lottie, as if she were seeing it for the first time, much nicer than Jamie's. The next day had been a stay-home day.

3

Hiding now behind the lorry window, Mommy looked like Jamie: someone who didn't want to be found.

Lottie took hold of the door handle.

"Well now," said the first bobby, coming up behind her. "Let's let her come out by herself, shall we, there's a good gel."

But Mommy didn't get out. Her eyes seemed to sink further inside her face as she looked at Lottie through the window.

"She didn't want you to bring er back," Lottie told the bobby.

"She did, though. She knew your address. She'd just lost her way."

"She wanted to keep going to Isreel. You made er stop."

"Why was she going, then, can you tell me that?" The bobby bent down to Lottie's face, but his looming close, his searching eyes reminded her of Master Rory, and she hung her head. "Your sister said it was to do with God. Is that right, then, gel, you can tell me."

"God told er to go." *England's just a halfway point for us, children, a stopping-off on our way to glory.*

"Coo-er," the bobby said quietly. "Why's that, d'you think?"

"It's where Jesus lives," Lottie said, looking for Mommy to get out.

"Jesus?"

Lottie yanked the lorry door open and flung herself inside to Mommy's lap, finally felt those soft hands stroking her head.

"Why didn't you tell me, Mommy?"

"But Charlotte, you knew the time was near. The Father said it could be any moment." Mommy's voice was as dreamy as the light touch of her rhythmic hand.

"But I didn't know it was today!"

"I didn't know either, not until you'd all gone to school, and then I heard the Father telling me." Mommy's voice held the familiar enthralled certainty, the un-arguable awe. "I wrote a note for Lars and Eleanor."

"But Nell didn't tell me! I didn't know til them bobbies came! "

Mommy's hand stilled. She slumped back against the seat.

"I walked halfway across London," she said faintly. "I headed east. They found me in some sort of ... marketplace. I guess I was a little ... disoriented."

"Mrs. Arkwright, Ma'am," the bobby said, leaning in. "Are you quite sure ye're able to look after these children?"

Mommy looked at him.

"I could ring round the social services, Ma'am, even though you're aliens here, they could ... lend a hand, p' raps, with the children."

Mommy's eyes narrowed. Lottie recognized a funny mood pending. English people's mannerisms and expressions often brought them on.

"Aliens," Mommy drawled. "Who d'you think you're calling an alien." Her scarlet-tipped fingers smoothed back her blond hair.

"I mean, seein as you're American." The bobby dropped his hold on Lottie's arm and stood back as Mommy, elegant in her long raincoat and good leather walking shoes, stepped out of the lorry.

"No need to worry about your social services," she told the bobby, cool now, dropping one slim hand briefly on his navy shoulder. "We both know no good will come of that. You leave these children to me. They know me."

The fat one was down by now, watching Mommy and Lottie pass. "Ye're never lettin er just go on in, with only them little gels at ome?" Lottie heard him ask his partner. "She's mad as a feckin atter. Them kids should be in Care. "

Nell was right behind him. She took one of Mommy's arms; Lottie took the other, concentrating on helping Nell get Mommy inside without her tripping on the green velvet bathrobe she wore under the raincoat.

5

TWO

"GO UP," Nell told Lottie. "Make sure the meter's loaded. Then run the bath."

Upstairs, Lottie checked the closed-mouth meter on the landing, and turned on the tub taps as far as they would go. The pipes knocked loudly, musical as the wild Christmas bells they were singing about at school, and Lottie had her usual urge to suck at the raw end of the copper faucet, to taste its sweetish tang, but just as she stuck out her tongue, Nell led Mommy into the bathroom.

At first Mommy was quiet in the tub, but soon she started twisting about so that the bun Nell had tried to fasten began to unravel, blond fronds darkening as they sank into the water, Mommy's head now thrashing back and forth:

"I *tried* to get a start."

"We know, Mum, it's all right." Nell swirled the hot water with both hands, nodding fiercely for Lottie to pour in more of the dishwashing liquid, to make bubbles.

"Ow far is it to Isreel, exactly?" Lottie could not help asking again.

Nell scowled at her.

"Not as far as you'd think, sweetie," sighed Mommy. She seemed soothed, as always, by the bubbles and by Lottie's voice. "Next time we'll all go together. It's a long, long walk, but we'll stop when we get tired and walk again when we're able. There are kind people, all over Europe and the Middle East, you'll see. They'll help us. Our

6

pilgrimage will inspire their sympathy, and they'll help us along."

This was more than Mommy usually said about their journey, and Lottie was encouraged to ask, "An we'll see Jesus when we get there, then, lying in the manger?"

Nell sent her another stern look, but too late, for Mommy started to rear up out of the tub, water streaming from her white flanks, crying, "... in the manger! Charlotte! What kind of ... claptrap are they teaching at that school!"

"The baby Jesus ...?" Lottie faltered. "Away in the manger?" She thought their trip to Isreel, to visit Jesus, was the same as the Wise Men's, in the songs they were practising for the Christmas pageant next month.

Just that morning, Miss Dowd chose Lottie to be the angel, a role always given to a third-form girl. She was to stand on a desk behind the manger scene and sing the last song. "You've a lovely voice, and the proper angelic look," Miss Dowd had told her. "Your mummy can make a costume."

"Lottie, His birth was a long time ago, He isn't a baby anymore," Mommy said, sliding back into the tub. "He won't be lying around in any manger when *we* get there," she declared triumphantly. "He'll be greeting us with the girded Seraphim." She looked up then, as if knowing this sounded incredible, as if the girls could be expected to walk across two continents but not to meet an army of angels, standing behind the living, grownup Christ, once they got to their destination; and she amended, "At least it will feel that way to us, when we see Him."

"Will it be very ot?" wondered Lottie, thinking of the palm trees under construction at school. Bethlehem was not far from a big desert, they'd learnt.

"Not now." Mommy frowned. "It's autumn, and by the time we get there it'll be the middle of winter. We'll have to be better prepared than I was today." Her voice dropped and she hung her head so that all the strands glistened wet. "Today ... wasn't very ... well thought out, girls, I'm sorry."

7

"That's all right, Mum," crooned Nell.

Lottie chimed, "Can't we wait until the pageant is over? Pr'aps we can still get there in time for Christmas? "

"Pageant?" Mommy looked at Nell. "Eleanor?"

Nell swished the water hard. "It's only a stupid play," she muttered.

"It's not stupid! Miss Dowd says it's the most important time of the year! And I'm to be the angel behind the baby Jesus, and I'm to sing Oh Little Town of Bethlehem." Mommy was very unlike the mummies who visited occasionally, bringing sweets for the class, chatting cosily with Miss Dowd, so Lottie continued doubtfully, "You're to make me a costume."

"You're the Angel?" Mommy repeated slowly. "The Angel Gabriel. Oh Charlotte." Her eyes got the dreamy look that signaled an impending mood. "And a little child shall lead them. Daughters. This is a *sign*."

Nell shot Lottie a glance. "Coffee."

Lottie scrambled into the kitchen, which was really more of a stained wall with slender appliances: stove, frig, sink; and shelves above, with a tiny table and four spindly chairs, in the room where Mommy slept in a cot shoved tight in the corner.

She held the battered tin coffeepot under the single spigot: watching its trickle, she felt the familiar tingling in her tongue, the impulse to lick the metal rim, but she turned off the tap when the pot was full. Her wrist wobbled with its weight and she balanced it on the sink's wide porcelain lip: she'd been practising not to spill.

She scooped fragrant coffee into the perforated basket, which fit so neatly onto the long pole nestled into its well at the bottom of the pot. She set it carefully onto the stovetop.

She struck a long wooden match and held it over the ring, frightened as always by the perilous moment between turning the gas knob and seeing the whoosh of flame.

Lars had warned them about the stovetop; just as he'd warned them about the bomb shelter, left over from the war, at the bottom of the garden. It was a stone cube overgrown with ivy and moss. He told them never to shut the door if they went in. The heavy plaster door, once swung shut, could not be opened from the inside. After Lars' pronouncement Lottie and Nell had immediately braved the few dank steps to inspect the shelter and saw a bare iron bedstead, on which rested a canteen covered in mildewed cloth, and one lone stiff boot. "Must be a story there," Mommy mused when they told her about the boot. "A soldier like the ones in the fairy tales, perhaps."

Lottie waited now in the kitchen for the first burble of coffee to appear in the glass cupola. It looked to her like a turret, and she liked to imagine that a tiny princess in a boat would emerge one day behind the glass, coloured wisps streaming from her pointed hat, waving and then setting sail as the geyser of coffee bore her away. Lottie tapped the little tune she'd made up for the princess with her fingers, as if she were playing it on the piano, and hummed the harmony she heard as accompaniment.

"Lottie!" Nell called from the bathroom. "Hurry up!"

The burble wasn't as dark as Mommy usually wanted, and the princess song wasn't finished, but Lottie turned off the gas. She wrapped the dishcloth around her hands so that she could safely lift the pot and pour the cup.

It smelled lovely. Her stomach growled. There had been no time for tea. She glanced hopefully at the cupboard, thinking that perhaps Mommy'd gone round the shops before setting out for Isreel. But there was only the same box of Saltines as yesterday, unaccompanied by any new jar of marmite or tin of Spam.

In the bathroom, Mommy was sitting on the side of the tub in her bathrobe again. She took the cup Lottie handed her with trembling, waxy-looking fingers. Even though Mommy had done her nails, their yellowed ends reminded Lottie that she'd forgotten the Kents, and she reeled back to the kitchen to collect them.

Mommy lit the cigarette and breathed in so the tip glowed with familiar fire.

9

The opening of the front door signaled Lars' entrance. He stood still when he saw them huddled together—the bath was just off the tiny entryway—and apprehension clouded his already stern face.

"Mommy was walking to Isreel but the bobbies caught her and made er come ome," Lottie said in a rush, eager to tell before Nell got a word in.

Lars' satchel slid to the floor.

His mouth drooped as he looked at Mommy, but she wouldn't look at him: she took another big gulp of smoke and tapped her ash in the bath with fingers that were no longer trembling. He looked then at his sisters. Nell gave a grave nod.

Lars' mouth flattened into a thin line. "*Mother.* Your head is like a *sieve.*"

The word sizzled in the humid smoky space.

Lottie knew what a sieve was, they used one for draining boiled potatoes, and Mommy's blonde head was nothing like. Mommy was very pretty, when she wasn't in a mood; bus drivers and shopkeepers were always saying so.

But no one argued with Lars. He was fourteen, 'the man of the house,' Mommy said, since the divorce three years ago.

He bent to pick up his satchel and turned away. "I've got homework, so I'll have to talk to you about this after supper." He looked back then sharply. "There *is* supper?"

"Saltines, from yesterday, but I want some for my tea," Lottie said, feeling grumpy now. She was hungry.

Nell hushed her. "Lottie, it's fine. We'll open a can of something."

"I'll make potato soup," Mommy declared. She rose and tightened her belt before picking up her coffee cup and cigarette. She pushed past Lars. She didn't see the disgusted faces the children made at each other, at the mention of potato soup.

"Just bake mine," Lars said as he walked into his room. "Lots of butter and salt."

Lottie's mouth watered. "Me too."

10

"And I'll make boiled eggs!" Mommy's cigarette hand swooped out to bring Lottie close and she leaned down to plant a kiss on her cheek.

"I'm sorry I worried you," she whispered. "We'll make a better plan."

"We can use a map," Lottie told her. "Miss Dowd as ever such a big one, in the classroom, we can borrow it to see where to go. Then you won't get lost again."

"My smart girl," Mommy murmured, holding tight. "A map. What a good idea. "

"I'll arsk tomorrow," Lottie promised, hugging back with all her might.

THREE

"MY MUMMY SAID I could have you for tea," Wendy told Lottie, next day at school. "Come home with me today, if you think it's all right with your Mum."

Wendy was one of the girls who sat at the front of the class. Her frock was pressed as if she had a new uniform for every day, instead of a wrinkled one for always like Lottie and Nell. The clasp that held back her smooth brown hair shone like gold. She smiled at Lottie, her neat teeth gleaming.

"I dunno," said Lottie. "I'll ave to arsk Nell."

"Go on then, she's right over there."

Lottie trotted across the playground to where Nell stood with her friends. Nell gave her a look as if she'd dropped in from Outer Space.

"Wendy's arsked me to tea," she blurted.

"*Asked*," Nell hissed in correction. "Don't talk Cockney!" Nell craned round Lottie to look at Wendy. "Why's she asking you? Because you're the angel?" Word of Lottie's role had spread quickly through the school. The angel wasn't as important as Jesus' mother Mary, who was played by a girl in Nell's form, but it was assumed the angel would have the prettiest dress as well as the last word.

"Can I go then?"

"How will you get home?"

"Wendy's just down the road from us."

"So you can walk. What time shall we expect you?"

"Um. After tea?"

12

"All right. Now go away."

Lottie stood for a moment, belatedly wondering what would be expected of her at Wendy's tea, thinking that Nell would know, but Nell had firmly turned her back. Lottie wondered, also, if this would be another day when Mommy started walking to Isreel without her. But Nell couldn't tell her that. And Mommy would wait, she was sure, for Miss Dowd's map. Wouldn't she?

She plodded back over the asphalt, oblivious of the wheeling girls and shouting boys, wondering what would happen if she didn't come home with the map right after school today.

Wendy smiled again when Lottie told her she could come. "Smashing."

After break, Lottie went to Miss Dowd's desk and waited until she was noticed.

"Charlotte?"

"Yes, Miss," Lottie began. "Can we borrow your map?"

The thin white brows rose.

"That one." Lottie pointed.

Miss Dowd looked at the side wall where the wide world spread out.

"We need it to make our plan. For getting to Isreel."

"Isree- yel," corrected Miss Dowd. "But that map's quite large, and we need it for Geography. Perhaps a small Atlas instead?" She reached into a drawer on the side of her desk and took out a book, slim and bendy, with folded plastic pages. "This should do. Mind you, I'll want it back, but you can get one like it in a bookshop or at the lib'ry."

She flipped through the book, opened it out, and pointed to a jigsaw of different coloured countries like the one on the wall. "This is Europe and the Middle East." Mommy said those countries last night, during that bit about the helpful people. She handed the book to Lottie. "Are you planning your holidays, then? You'll want a guidebook, really, as well as a map. Israel's quite far. I

13

should think you'd fly direct to Tel Aviv, or perhaps Jerusalem."

"We're walking, Mommy says."

"Oh, a walking holiday? Christmas in the Holy Land—that sounds lovely, you'll see the Little Town of Bethlehem, just like your song." She smiled then, sweetly, and Lottie felt easier. If Miss Dowd thought they could go, then God must be telling Mommy the right thing. "Did you tell your Mum about the costume?"

"Yes, Miss," Lottie said slowly. "We didn't make it yet, though."

That afternoon, Lottie realized she wasn't the only one asked to tea. A gaggle of four girls clustered tightly round Wendy in the cloakroom, and Lottie stood back, until Wendy tugged at her hand and said, "Come on, Lottie, we're leaving now."

There was an actual tiger skin lying on the front hall in Wendy's house. "My Grandad shot him in Inja," Wendy commented carelessly as they all trod past, wary of his open mouthful of white teeth. "You needn't be frightened."

The table in the kitchen was set with six matching plates and flowered napkins. There was a platter of cakes and one of buttered toast slices. A blue pot held red jam.

"Cor, Wendy," said Lottie. "Is your tea like this every day?"

"We don't always have cakes. Mum and I made them specially for today."

"I elped Mommy make the boiled eggs yesterday."

"Those are nice for tea as well," said Wendy's Mum. "I don't know your Mum, Lottie, did she come to the last Parents' Meeting?"

"She don't go to meetings at school."

"Oh, is she working then, during the day?"

"She's writing a book."

"She must be clever," Wendy's Mum said approvingly. "Fancy writing a book when you've got

14

children! Your Dad must be quite a help round the house."

"E's in America."

"Oh." Wendy's Mum looked at Lottie a moment longer. Then she took off the tea cozy. "Wendy, you can pour out, but mind the handle."

Smiling with importance, Wendy carefully maneuvered the teapot to the dainty cups, and allowed a steady thin stream of tea into each.

"Good on you, Wendy," Pamela told her. She was another front-row girl, with hair as yellow as Lottie's but in a neat chinlength bob. Lottie knew Pamela had expected to play the angel. She usually ignored Lottie, but had turned to give her a bit of a crooked smile, when Miss Dowd announced the roles yesterday.

"I've been practising," Wendy said. "Mum said I could have a tea on Fridays, like this, once a month, if I'm good at lessons and clean my room."

"Can we see your room?" asked Jenny. She sat next to Lottie in class, and sometimes shared her 'elevens' snack with Lottie, who always brought Saltines. Lottie thought she was pretty, with twinkly green eyes, apple cheeks and shiny black hair.

"I've seen it, lots of times," Pamela told her.

"Can I come to tea, on the Fridays?" asked Lottie. She hadn't seen such delicious-looking cupcakes since they came to England.

Wendy tilted her head, her mouth curving in a little smile. "P'raps," she said, considering Lottie. "If you mind your manners."

"I shall invite you to my tenth birthday party, Lottie, in January," Jenny declared. She looked round the table. "You're all to come."

"I'll be ten in January too!" Lottie exclaimed, excited until she remembered. "But ... we might be in Israel."

"Israel?" asked Pamela. "Whyever would you go there?"

"It's where Jesus lives," Lottie said. Without thinking, as she took a cake, she added, "God told Mommy to go see im."

The way they stared made Lottie duck her head again. She crowded her mouth with cake, so much that she couldn't even taste it. She balled the flowered napkin tight in her other hand, under the table.

"Is your Mum a saint, then, like the Catholics have? They're always being told to do things by God. It's quite interesting," said Ursula.

"She's writing about a saint." Lottie looked into Ursula's eyes, friendly behind their little spectacles. "Er book is about Saint Paul." He was the one who changed his name on his journey to some city, Lottie forgot the boring bits; it wasn't as thrilling a story as the Forest of Firth.

"Are you *Catholic*?" Wendy asked.

Catholics didn't say prayers at Assembly but stayed in a separate room. Lottie had learnt the prayers right away, chanting along every morning and singing the hymns. She loved the tunes. "If we were Cat'lic we wouldn't go to Assembly."

"Where do you go to church?"

Lottie remembered church in America: crayoning pictures of Jesus holding lambs, talking to children, or looking up at the sky, where sunbeams shone down on him. On Easter they had worn new pink dresses, and flowered straw hats; the band bit under her chin. "We used to go to Sunday school, in America, but we don't go ere."

Here, they had Scripture every day after Sums, when Miss Dowd read stories from the Bible. They were learning a psalm about the Lord being a shepherd, who made them lie down in green pastures, beside still waters. The still waters reminded Lottie of the Thames River, its mucky banks and sluggish tides, where they went walking once a month, when they went into the City to cash the check.

16

"I don't believe you," Pamela was announcing. "It's because you're the angel, you're just saying that."

"No, it's true, we are going to Israel. I arsked Miss Dowd for a map." Lottie pulled the Atlas out of her satchel. "Ere."

"Why're you talking Cockney?" Pamela folded her arms in front of her chest.

"Mommy says it's because I didn't come to school at first, I only played with the neighbors." She talked just like Stevie next door. *I need you to keep me company, little Lottie, we can get used to our new country together,* Mommy had told her, after they came to England last January. *School can wait.*

"Well you *should* be talking properly by now," said Pamela, frowning.

"We shall teach you," said Wendy.

"Mommy's already got me a teacher for that."

"Well she isn't doing a very good job," Wendy said, her tilted smile taking the sting out of her words. "You sound a right urchin."

"E's my piano teacher as well. E mostly ... teaches piano."

"Jolly good!" Jenny approved. "Mum says we're getting a piano for Christmas, at last, and I'm to finally start lessons. Who's your tutor?"

"Is name's Master Rory." *I'm not your master. I'm your slave.*

"You should have your Mum call mine. We can have lessons together!"

Lottie stared at Jenny, seeing her planted on his lap, his warm slender hands roaming up and down, up and down, threading through her black hair, his slow whisper soft in her ear. *Turn your head, darling, give us a kiss.*

"What's wrong with that, Lottie?" Jenny looked hurt. "Right then, don't, you can have your old master."

"E's not mine. I don't like im." *You like the way this feels, don't you love.*

"My tutor's ever so difficult," Ursula told them. "I'm to practise two hours a day, she said, and Mum won't let me watch the telly until it's over! It's so boring!"

"Two hours! That's torture," said Pamela.

"I wouldn't mind practising," Jenny said. "I want to be a great concert pianist."

"That's what Mommy wants me to be, ever since I told er how I'm always earin music," Lottie said glumly. "That's why I have to see im all the time."

"Why don't you like him? Is he a grumpy old man?" Ursula asked. "I had a very old one at first, he was practically blind, and I didn't learn a thing." She reached for another cake. "And he smelt funny, like mothballs, as if he only came out of the closet to tutor piano!" They giggled, all but Lottie. "Maybe he's yours?"

"E's not old. E doesn't smell like mothballs." He smelt like a fresh Christmas tree, like a tree you'd want to stick your nose in and breathe deeply, until you got jabbed by the sharp needles. But she didn't want to talk about him. *You must keep this secret, darling, nobody would understand our love. They'd call you a bad girl and lock you away in a special school.* She slid the flowered napkin into her pocket.

When she didn't say more, the girls lost interest and started to talk about the telly programmes they watched. There was one about a secret agent and one about cowboys.

"Did you know any cowboys, Lottie, in America?" asked Wendy.

"No." In America, the Wonderful World of Disney was on Sunday nights. "But we watched Mickey Mouse, when we lived at Nana's."

Mickey wasn't on the telly here, but the girls had seen him at the pictures. They were well into a spirited discussion of who was the preferable character, Mickey or Donald Duck, when Wendy's Mum came back into the kitchen. "It's past five thirty, girls, you'd best be off."

18

Jenny and Lottie stood for a moment outside Wendy's house. The sky was blazing orange and the chimney tops poked into it like dark fingers into paint.

"See you tomorrow, then, Lottie."

"Cheerio."

FOUR

LOTTIE WALKED HOME ON AIR.

Cor! Tea with Wendy every month and Jenny's birthday party as well. I'm in clover now! That's what Stevie's Da said, when one of his races went well, in clover, or in the money. Sometimes, after a win, he'd give Stevie half a crown and Lottie and Stevie would run down the shops to buy sweets.

Lottie always chose the melting vanilla smoothness of caramels. Stevie favored gobstoppers. *More for the money, see, larsts all day like,* he'd inform her, gobstopper swelling his cheek like the big marbles Master Rory put in Lottie's mouth, to teach her how to talk like him and not like Stevie.

Funny, though, Stevie talked like himself even with his gobstopper lodged the day long. And Lottie liked the way he talked. He sounded tough and clever.

Lottie turned the corner onto her own road and stood for a moment, puzzled. It didn't look the same. The red brick building next to her was unfamiliar, as was the grey one across the way.

Blimey, it ain't me road. I've bloody gone and lost me way.

She gnawed at the inside of her cheek. She had a little ridge chewn away there that helped her to think.

She looked down at the pavement, and then turned all the way round. If she'd gone wrong from Wendy's door then she had only to retrace her steps, like Hansel and Gretel when they used stones instead of breadcrumbs, that's what Mommy always said when she lost anything at home, *just retrace your steps.*

20

Only she had neither stones nor crumbs, she'd been wittering on to herself about Wendy's tea and Jenny's party and she hadn't paid any attention to where she was going. Now nothing looked familiar.

Bloody feckin ell.

That was Stevie's worst, said in a fierce whisper, but she'd heard his Da shout it plenty of times when the race didn't go. Bloody feckin nag, that meant the horse; when he snarled it at the radio Stevie and Lottie would get out of there, because it meant he was right bloody pissed off.

Retracing her steps didn't make any difference because she couldn't find Wendy's house. *I'm lost now, I am, good an proper.*

She ambled along, kicking at small piles of leaves with her thick school shoes. A few notes filled her head for the swirling leaves, making them dance in the pink light. She let her fingers dance as well, finding the tune, before she stuffed both hands into her cardigan pockets, to keep them warm.

In her pocket was the crumpled napkin she'd taken from Wendy's. It would make a lovely kerchief for her best friend, Pollyanna. She'd seen Polly standing bravely alone in a shop window and pestered Mommy until she gave in. *All right, Lottie, we'll get your doll. But it means no uniform blazer. I can't afford both.*

Lottie didn't care. Polly was so much better than the stiff wool blazers Nell and Lars wore. Polly was the one she talked to, late at night when Nell was snoring away on the bunk above her; Polly always listened. Her glassy blue gaze on Lottie was bland and comforting, not like other peoples' too-hungry stares. And Polly's curly yellow hair was like Lottie's would be, she was sure, if Mommy would ever let her get it cut.

The blazer would have been nice just now, as the wind kicked dry leaf bits up into Lottie's eyes. The notes in her head got louder. And it was getting dark.

Nell would be furious. *She'll tan me arse,* Lottie thought, liking the confident Stevie sound of the phrase, although she'd never been struck by Nell or anyone.

21

Lottie bit harder on her cheek and kneaded the napkin. The dim streetlamps seemed to be leading her astray. The pavement in their neighborhood curved round inside itself, winding long, except for the one straighter road which led to the shops and the tube station and the big park where Stevie and Lottie ate their sweets.

She could see, beyond the batch of chimneys ahead, treetops feathering against the last line of crimson in the sky: mightn't that be the park? She hurried toward it.

"Ullo, lit'le gel, where you off to?"

She whirled. A tall boy was loping behind her, older than Lars but not as old as Master Rory, dressed in narrow black trousers, short boots and a dark jacket. His smile seemed friendly, but his hair was slicked back in 'teddy' style.

Lottie had been warned about 'teddy boys' by Stevie. *They take kids to the park, see, and strangle em in the loo there. Appens all the time.*

She turned her back and kept walking toward where she'd glimpsed the trees.

"Ow old are you, then, out all alone loike this?"

She hurried faster but he was just as fast.

"Off to the shops?"

Would he not go away?

He knew the shops were near, that was good, she could find her way home from there. But if he stayed with her? She glanced at him. His jacket had a Waverley badge on the pocket. *P'rhaps e's alright, then, p'rhaps e knows Lars.*

"Are you in the twelfth form?"

He looked down at her. "No. I left school last year, well shot of all that rubbish." He said it as if one could choose to be shot of it. He followed her gaze to the Waverley badge. "Nicked this off a posh public schoolboy." He laughed. "Right stupid, wa'nt he, leavin it on a bench like that!"

22

The road opened up to the familiar bank of lit windows. There was the tube station, there was the park, darker than she'd ever seen it.

"Just your luck, ducks, they aven't closed yet."

She went into the greengrocers where the sweets were, hoping he'd leave. But he came right along inside and greeted the shopkeeper, Mr. Moore.

"Ullo, Ralphie, look what was wandrin the streets all by erself."

Mr. Moore shot her a keen look. "Everything alright at ome, Lottie?"

She nodded.

"What'll it be then love, packet of caramels?" Lottie prided herself on not being the crying sort, but the kindness of Mr. Moore's voice brought heat prickling behind her eyes and she shook her head. She had no money. She just wanted to get home.

"I think she was lost," the teddy boy said.

"She knows her way from ere, don't you, Lottie?"

"Yes."

"I can see er ome."

"Don't try anything on," said Mr. Moore to the teddy boy, who jolted back, face horrified.

"Cor blimey, she's only a lit'le gel, what d'you bloody well take me for!"

Mr. Moore leaned over the counter to hand Lottie a packet of caramels.

"I don't ave any pence on me," Lottie began, but Mr. Moore waved her off.

"If Jeremy ere, or any other bloke, is ever anything less than a perfect gentleman, you just kick im hard, and then scream as loud as you can, and then run away."

"Crikey, Ralph, you must be barmy. Who'd muck about with a lit'le gel like er?"

"There's summat might. She should know, if she's wandrin round alone."

Kick? Scream? Run away? Less than a gentle man? Master Rory was gentle, except when he hugged too tight. What would he do if she kicked and screamed, next time

23

he tried something on, next time he started muckin about?

She and Jeremy walked to her flat in silence made companionable by consuming the caramels. He came all the way up with her, and stood as she knocked on the door.

Lars opened it right away and Nell crowded behind him. Lottie could see anger and fear in the way they stood, staring from her to Jeremy.

"I got lost coming from Wendy's tea and this, this lad Jeremy, e brought me ome safe from the shops, it's alright, Mr. Moore knows im."

Lars seemed to sum up the situation quickly, and extended his hand to Jeremy in a formal gesture. "Thank you. We were ... worried."

Jeremy looked down at him, eyebrows raising, and then shook his proffered hand. "S'alright," he said. "I'd've worried as well, if she was my lit'le sisteh. Your parents, are they ome then?" He looked into the empty hallway.

"Our mother's resting," Nell said stiffly. Jeremy's eyes narrowed on her and he looked suddenly more like a grownup to Lottie.

"Ah, restin, is it?" He nodded once. "Right then. I'm off. Don't get lost again, Lottie, arsk the way next time, before you leave the tea party."

"Ta," she thanked him, wondering would he give her the last caramels.

He reached into the pocket with the Waverley badge. "Ere." He produced the final two and pressed them firmly into her hand as if to ensure the others wouldn't get even a taste. "Brush y'teeth after now, gel."

"He doesn't *sound* like a Waverley boy," said a bewildered Lars, closing the door after Jeremy. "I certainly don't recognize him."

"E nicked is blazer," Lottie told him, mouth full of caramel.

" ... 'nicked it!' You mean he stole it?" Lars stared at her, fury winning over worry. "How'd you find him,

24

anyway!" He spun round. "Nell, what's she learning from that guy Rory? He's been here twice a week for more than a month, and she can't even play Twinkle Twinkle Little Star, and she still sounds like a ruddy teddy boy!"

"Maybe Twinkle Twinkle Little Star isn't an English song," Nell said. "And I'm not here during her lessons, how d'you expect me to bloody know!"

"Nice," fumed Lars. "Now even you're talking like them."

"So did you, you said ruddy," Nell snapped.

Lars sighed.

Nell sulked.

Lottie looked from one to the other, chewing noisily.

"Oh go to bed," Nell told her.

Lottie went to the kitchen to wake Mommy. "I've a good map," she told her. "Miss Dowd give me it."

"Gave it to me," Mommy said, drowsy, hugging her.

"She gave me her map. It is a very nice one." If she talked properly, perhaps Master Rory wouldn't have to come so often. "Now we can find the way to Is-ree-yel."

"Lottie, you're so smart."

"Clever, that's how we say it here in England, I'm clever."

Mommy laughed and hugged Lottie tighter. "Clever girl."

"And I can learn piano with my friend Jenny. I needn't see Master Rory alone no more." Oops. She knew 'no more' wasn't right.

But Mommy wasn't listening. "Master Rory is a prodigal, terribly sought after; we're lucky he isn't playing fulltime with the Symphony this season. You should be grateful." She sat up in bed, looking at Lottie, disapproving now. "You weren't here when he came today. Charlotte, that can't happen again. We have to pay for every lesson, whether you're here or not! That was my arrangement with his agency."

"But Wendy arsked me to tea, it was my first tea ever!"

25

"And he's correcting your speech, too, which is very kind of him. I've told that boy next door not to come over, since I know he's the one with the Cockney accent, but he will persist."

"Stevie's my friend!" Her best friend, after Polly.

Mommy took Lottie's face in both hands. "My darling. Your kind heart makes you a good girl and a loyal friend." She kissed her forehead. "But I know you have the ability to be a fine pianist, and Master Rory's the only person we know who can help you with that." She lay down again, pulling the covers up round her chin. "And he's getting you a costume, and he's going to help you practice your song for the pageant!" She smiled at Lottie. "I told him all about it, sweetie," she said, yawning.

Cor blimey, Master Rory gettin me an angel costume? Bloody feckin ell. She'd never be well shot of him and his rubbish now. She went to her bunk and curled up with Polly, recounting for her the entire afternoon, from Wendy to Jeremy, tying the napkin round her springy plastic curls.

26

FIVE

MASTER RORY WAS THERE when she came from school several days later, sitting in the kitchen with Mommy and drinking a cup of coffee. He always brought Mommy's special coffee with him, and sometimes a tin of biscuits. Once he'd brought fish'n'chips wrapped in newspaper. She wondered had he brought anything good to eat this time, perhaps in the bag dangling from the back of his chair.

He turned round and saw her rooted in the doorway.

"Charlotte. I have a surprise for you." His voice was as quiet as a radio host, well, not Stevie's Da's radio host, who did the races, but one from the slow music station that Lars listened to.

He reached into the bag and unfolded a swath of cream-coloured velvet. It was a long dress with gold smocking across the bodice and pointy sleeves that looked, if one squinted, a bit like wings. The gold thread was like sparkling sunshine on a field of new snow. She remembered snow like that, in America.

"Come here, love, try it on," he told her.

She didn't move.

"Charlotte, say thank you, it's a beautiful dress!" Mommy leaned forward to put her hand on top of Master Rory's. "You're so good to us, Rory. Where did you find it?"

"It was my sister's. She was in a Christmas wedding one year, as a flower girl, and the theme was medieval. The bridesmaids wore dark green dresses like this."

"It must have been so lovely."

27

"Quite." Still holding up the dress, he stared at Lottie.

"I can just picture the church." Mommy went on, "dark greens with red bows, tall white candles, the scent of incense, the hush of Christmas Eve, the happy families gathered in the pews, the sense of wonder ..."

If Stevie'd been there, he'd have rolled his eyes and he and Lottie would've escaped. He liked Mommy, she always gave him a chocolate biscuit with tea, when they had biscuits, but he saw through her wittering as Nell and Lars did, he knew when a mood was coming on and he knew to get well shot of it.

Polly would've whispered, *just go away quietly, she won't notice, she's only dreaming.* Polly's voice used to have an American accent but lately she'd been sounding more like Miss Dowd.

Master Rory slid his hand away from Mommy's.

"Time for our lesson, love," he whispered. He stood noiselessly and left the kitchen, propelling Lottie forward with a tight arm round her waist.

The piano was in Lars' room. It was a shiny upright with a gold 'Steinway' label emblazoned in the center of the music stand.

Mommy'd had a big squabble with Nana about the piano, the time when Nana visited; the children heard a lot of hissed whispers about the cost of their school and the cost of the piano. Nana thought Mommy wasn't *good with money.* She was *lucky to be getting any alimony at all, after taking these children out of the country; she shouldn't waste it. A piano is not a waste,* Mommy said fiercely in her *silence* voice, but Nana wasn't frightened. Mommy didn't know *how to manage a budget,* Nana said, she needed to *learn or else come back home.*

Master Rory closed the door behind them and turned the lock. *We mustn't be interrupted during lessons,* he'd told Mommy. *She can't be allowed to think of anything but what we're doing, whether it's playing the piano or improving her speech.*

He hung the dress on the lamp next to the piano. He sat backwards on the bench, stretching out his long legs into the room, and folded his arms across his chest. He always wore a black jacket and trousers like the ones the musicians wore on the Ed Sullivan show, back in America.

He looked at Lottie. He waited. After what seemed like forever, with Mr. Moore in her head telling her to give him a kick, to scream, to rush to the door and unlock it and run away, and bloody ell with is feckin special school, she walked toward him and sat beside him on the bench, but facing the piano.

"Now," he said.

She opened the lid and started doing her scales. She could tell she was getting much stronger in her fingers, flexing them out the way he'd taught her, leaning her whole self to the right and left to reach the very highest and lowest notes.

The keys still looked like black and white teeth to her, like a gollywog's wide manic grin, a gollywog who hadn't been to the dentist in much too long, but she was beginning to know where all the grinning secrets were, the strange black flats and sharps he'd shown her hiding behind the Cs, and the broad octaves who marched up and down, a tribe of perfect brothers born exactly eight years apart, like a Bible story.

When she leaned to the left she leaned into him, but she soon stopped taking notice of his too-closeness. She finished her scales and put up the sheet for the song he'd brought her last time, the 'Claire de Lune.' She peered closely at the music, picking carefully through the notes. She only made three mistakes.

She folded her hands in her lap.

Now she looked at him. She waited for him to speak.

He was still facing the other way, eyes closed, arms still crossed. After the first time with each new tune, when he showed her the notes on the page and on the keys, he never watched her play. *You have to know it, and make it yours. You have to play by hearing it. I can't make your fingers work.*

He nodded. "Again." She could tell he didn't like it.

29

She played more slowly, watching each note, trying to make her hands into the web he'd talked about, the web cast over the span of the piano like wings. This time it was perfect, if a bit stilted. He would like it better now, she knew.

"Yes." His whisper right into her ear made her shiver. "You've been practising, haven't you darling?"

She nodded.

"Well done. Let's hear a bit more."

She let her eyes close as her right hand wandered up into the high notes, trying to make them sound as light and airy as he did. She turned to look at him when she finished. He'd like this as well, she was sure, he always liked her improvising.

"Lovely," he said quietly. Was it time to give him a kiss? *Well done! Give us a kiss,* he'd say, smiling, *come a bit closer*—as if he were the jolly rag-and-bone man who roamed the streets once a week, smiling and calling to all the girls, 'Give us a kiss, then, love!' when he wasn't shouting 'Old rags and bo-ones, old rags and bo-ones!'

But Master Rory's eyes were still closed now, although he was smiling.

"Can I learn 'How Many Flowers'?" she asked. They'd sung it at school that week and she loved the tune,

How many flowers can you find in an English country garden?
How many something something else, those you miss we'll surely pardon?

It was one of the sweetest songs she'd ever heard. She started humming it to herself, trying to remember the 'somethings' in between a long recitation of hollyhock and roses and buttercups—

"—in an English country garden," he sang, opening his eyes, before breaking off and laughing in a dry way. "Really, Charlotte, I think we can spare you that sort of nonsense."

"But I like it."

"Oh all right then. Watch me."

30

He swung round to the keyboard and played slowly, so she could see each note.

"How many flowers can you find in an English country garden," he sang, in a lilting voice, just as if he were the English country gardener. He glanced at her and played it again. She put her hands on top of his, to follow his fingers, as he'd shown her once before at the beginning of their lessons.

He swung back on the bench, facing away from her: "By yourself, now."

She played it through twice, surer the second time, singing from what she'd learned from him of the words, liking it when he joined her in a soft harmony.

When she finished, she nudged him slightly, to get on with the lesson.

His arms came round her in the cuddling that seemed comforting at first, like Stevie petting his cat. She closed her eyes because it scared her, the way he looked at her during this bit. It made her feel *suffocated*. That's what happened when babies were held too tight, Stevie's sister Rita said, they suffocated to death.

He pulled her so she was facing away from him. His right hand curled under her skirt, his left under her jersey. She waited, tense and rigid, for the tickling to be over; pretending she was immobile as Polly, holding her breath, trying not to squirm, or to giggle, since the quicker this went, the quicker they got back to the piano.

He pushed his fingers down and drummed them, as if playing a fast tune, and their movements seemed to catch up, suddenly, to her racing heart, her pent-up shallow breathing. All at once she felt more than suffocated. All at once she had to let out the huge cloud of air he'd been trapping inside her. She felt herself lurching forward, clutching onto his knees that gripped around her legs, panting as if she were running relays, out of breath, bursting with a shudder of some unkown sort.

Sudden heat splashed from his fingers all the way through her, shocking as the first scalding gush from the

31

raw metal spigot when the meter was full, and the sweet taste of copper flooded her mouth.

She sagged back against him, her heart pounding, dragging huge gulps of air, suddenly weak, reverberating with what he'd done to her.

His laugh warmed her cheek. "Yes, angel, at last."

Her head was so heavy she couldn't stop it from lolling back on his shoulder. He lifted her and carried her to Lars' cot and lay down next to her. Before she closed her eyes she saw again the dress, swinging slightly on its hanger. Its golden smocking glittered in the lamplight.

Polly seemed to be scolding her in her dream, sounding now like Jeremy from last night. "Get out of it! You're only a lit'le gel and he's a great big boy! He shouldn't be muckin about with a lit'le gel, it's nasty." She didn't recall that word, nasty, except for Jenny saying it once when one of the boys at school was chasing a girl into the loo. Nasty. *But Polly, he was ever so warm, I never felt anything like.*

SIX

A LOUD KNOCKING ON THE DOOR stirred Lottie to sit up. Master Rory was asleep beside her, his dark hair fanning onto the pillow. She poked him awake.

"What is it, Mrs. Arkwright?" he said, stifling a yawn.

"It's Jenny, I'm Lottie's friend, I've come to visit."

He looked at Lottie. "We haven't finished our lesson."

"Mrs. Arkwright said I could watch."

Master Rory sat up, as Lottie climbed out, and caught her by the wrist. "Remember." His fingers dug in.

His eyes were like the black puddles of ice that formed in the gutters last winter, water bubbles trapped underneath, tempting walkers to crunch into them in spite of the thrilling frigidity they knew would quickly seep into their toes.

Receiving her stare, he loosened his grip so his hand held her gently now. "Charlotte," he whispered, his lips lifting in ever so small a smile. "I love you."

Then he stood.

He ran his hands through his hair, and smoothed Lars' blanket tight over the cot.

She whirled away from him to open the door.

Jenny's grin was as bright as the white keys, as full of promise. "Isn't this grand, we can have lessons together, my Mum said she'd ask your tutor, and your Mum told me to come in!"

Lottie was happy to see Jenny, but so confused as well by her strange dream, and by the feeling Master Rory had given her, that she slumped against the doorjamb as

33

if she were still asleep, blocking it so Jenny couldn't even come inside. "Hullo Jenny, this is Master Rory." She flapped one hand in his direction.

Master Rory put his hands in his pockets. He tilted his head to one side and looked at Jenny. She was looking past him, at the dress.

"Is that your costume? It's ever so pretty, Lottie, aren't you a lucky girl!"

"Perhaps you'd like to try it on?" Master Rory asked Jenny. "Charlotte isn't quite ... sure she wants it."

E's not being fair! Just because I wouldn't try is bloomin dress on in the kitchen—I don't want im to see me in me knickers!

Jenny looked at him, a confused wrinkle on her forehead. "But ... but it's Lottie's dress, sir, she's to be the ..." she trailed off as he kept looking at her. She seemed to be as transfixed by the black ice as Lottie had just been.

Mommy entered their silence with a cheery trill. "Tea! Tea and chocolate biscuits for everyone." She set a tray on Lars' desk, moving battleships aside. "Rory, Jenny's mother asked about your tutoring fees. I took her telephone number so you can chat later. I told her what a fine job you're doing with Lottie."

His small smile appeared again.

"Did she come upstairs, your Mum?" Lottie asked Jenny. Perhaps another grownup would break the spell Master Rory was holding, the way the prince slashed through a hundred years of thorns to Sleeping Beauty's castle, thorns neither Mommy nor Jenny seemed able to see—even though they were digging right into their eyes.

"No, she didn't stay. She just brought me here. She'll collect me in an hour's time, if it's all right with you, sir." Jenny looked at him from under her lashes, shy. Lottie felt like kicking her.

"If it's all right with Charlotte it's all right with me. She's my star pupil just now and her lessons are going ... splendidly. In fact, Jenny, I'm not sure I could take on another pupil, although you seem to be a charming girl.

34

Excuse me for a moment, ladies." He walked out of the room, gliding soundlessly, and they watched him go.

Then Jenny stared at Lottie with round eyes. "He's ever so handsome! He looks like one of the Beatles!" She took a cup of tea and sat down on the floor.

"A matinee idol, we'd have called him when I was your age, girls," said Mommy, sounding girlish herself. "And as talented as he is cute." She sat at Lars' desk.

"Whyever don't you like him, Lottie?"

If she told Mommy and Jenny what he just did, how she just felt, right there on the bench, would they believe her? If he was nasty, then so was she. She *belonged* in the special school. Puzzling it out made her head hurt. She chewed her cheek.

"Dunno," she mumbled finally.

Jenny twisted her mouth in a dubious pout.

Mommy was frowning, probably wondering how Jenny thought Master Rory, prodigal, could possibly be disliked? How could he possibly be anything but adored?

Then he was there again in the doorway, quick and silent as a snake, looking at her with those black pools, and she had no chance to speak, even if she could find the words to begin.

He strode over and put his arm round her. "She doesn't like me, Jenny, because I make her work so hard." He smoothed her hair. "Isn't that right, Charlotte, you don't like our lessons. But you did well today."

"Everything has a price, dear," Mommy said, stern. "Every accomplishment comes from practice. All the great musicians suffered for their art, Tchaikovsky, Mozart, and look at Beethoven!"

Jenny listened, watching Mommy, politely reaching for a biscuit, munching it quietly. Occasionally she asked a question in her piping voice.

Lottie looked at Master Rory. He slid his hand under her hair where Jenny and Mommy couldn't see, and he touched the curve on the back of her head, down to her neck, in a rhythmic stroking that seemed to make her puzzle go away, and yet become more confusing. His

35

smile grew until she half expected him to kiss her again, right in front of Mommy and Jenny.

As if he sensed her alarm, he dropped his hand and walked to the piano. He laid his fingers on the keys and began to play softly, a mere brushing of notes, a minor-key waterfall that made her think of Mommy's sad story about the pearl-making people, far underground, their skin burnt rust-red from the lava that flowed through their cave.

She stood next to him to study the way his hands moved. He'd told her that when she read music more easily then she could play anything ever written. But Master Rory played with his eyes closed as if making it up as he went along. He wasn't reading, he was remembering; or he was creating, as soon as his long fingers hit the keys.

She wanted to listen to him forever.

She wanted him to leave and never come back.

She wanted to be able to play the way he did.

When he stopped, and laid his hands in his lap, Mommy and Jenny clapped. Master Rory opened his eyes and turned to look at Lottie with his suffocating stare. But she could not seem to make herself move away from him.

Mommy said, "Now let's hear 'Oh Little Town of Bethlehem,' since Lottie needs to practice."

Master Rory glanced back at Mommy, perhaps as surprised as Lottie by her tone, the tone of a mother in charge.

"Go on, Rory, surely you know it?"

Indeed, he began to play, and Lottie began to sing:

Oh little town of Bethlehem, how still we see thee lie,
Above thy deep and dreamless sleep the silent stars go by.
Yet in thy dark streets shineth the everlasting light
The hopes and fears of all the years are met in thee tonight.

She thought it a very odd song. Its tune was slow, and its words strange, so it hardly seemed to fit the jolly mood

36

Christmas was supposed to have. And she didn't want to go to Israel, now that she was finally making friends at school, and this song would remind Mommy of the pending trip. *Stupid Bethlehem, stupid little sleepy town to be so blind to baby Jesus being born right in its middle in a mucky old manger.*

She didn't like it, in fact, and she suddenly wondered it if mightn't make her look *all wet*, as Stevie's sister Rita would say, to have to croon it above everyone, on a wobbly table, the night of the pageant. And wearing that dress!

She'd stopped singing several seconds before she realized everyone was looking at her: Master Rory with his little smile, as if everything was so bloody feckin funny, as if he could keep on playing with her like Nell played with their one puppet, jerking it about on long strings; Jenny with wide eyes; Mommy with a serious frown that Lottie wanted to answer, to shout like Stevie would, to deepen the frown on Mommy's face so that she really would become that taking-charge Mum she'd sounded like just now.

"It's the wettest song I've ever heard in me loife! I'm bloody well dast if I'll sing that standin on a table in a dead girl's dress!"

The piano lid crashed down.

Master Rory's footsteps, clattering down the wooden stairwell, echoed in the silence that followed his departure.

Lottie looked round, defiant. "We're well shot of im," she said. "I'm not takin any more of is bloody lessons." She put her hands on her hips like Rita did when she scolded her husband Jimbo. "E's *nasty*."

"You'll take lessons as long as you're told to, young lady. And your language!" Mommy was staring at her as if she'd never seen the like. "You must apologize next time you see him. That was inexcusably rude. And cruel. I'm surprised at you, Charlotte. I'm sure he doesn't like to be reminded of his sister's death, he'd probably prefer to think of her as she was ... when she wore that, for

37

example, when she was in the Christmas wedding." She looked at the dress. "It's perfect for your pageant."

"How did she die?" asked Jenny in a whisper.

"She drowned," Mommy answered briskly. "She was at camp, and there was a boating accident. You should always wear life preservers, girls, when swimming."

Jenny was staring at the dress, fascinated as if the sister were still inside it, dripping. Then she looked over at Lottie. "P'raps she's an angel now Lottie, and it's right you should wear it as the Angel Gabriel, and sing for her."

Angel my arse, Stevie's Da would snort. As if a dead girl could hear anything! A dead girl was no use to her. His sister, if alive, might kick Master Rory good and proper, that's what Lottie'd do if she ever caught Lars muckin about with some little gel.

"That's a beautiful sentiment, Jenny," Mommy nodded, approving. "Wear it in that spirit, Lottie, and you won't have any qualms."

Qualms sounded like psalms, of the sort with the Lord and his still waters, and also like palms, of the sort round the manger.

Well. P'raps.

P'raps if Miss Dowd changed the song.

"But I'm not avin Master Rory come to the pageant," she warned them.

"We'll see." That was Mommy's answer when she didn't want to answer.

SEVEN

MISS DOWD HAD NO INTENTION of changing the song, she informed Lottie the next day. "It's a quaint old song and people love it," she said. "If you don't want to sing it then another girl can be chosen. You're not the only one with musical talent, dear."

"No it's all right, I'll do it," Lottie told her, thinking of how Mommy's face would look if she went home and told her that Pamela was going to be the angel, after all, because Lottie didn't like the stupid song or the bloody dress.

"On another subject, Lottie, did you look at the Atlas I lent you the other day?"

"I showed me Mum it."

"Showed it to my Mum. Did you work out a route, then, for your trip to Israel?"

"Not just yet, Miss, we're still in need of it, thanks ever so much," Lottie hedged, having no idea of where Miss Dowd's nice neat Atlas might've fetched up in the jumbled mass of things at home. Mommy'd been up late the night before, writing, and her book was all over the kitchen.

What's happening in the story now, she'd asked Mommy, so she could tell the girls from Wendy's tea. She'd had to ask twice before Mommy paid attention. *Is it still St.Paul?*

Yes.

Can you read me some?

Not right now.

Mommy, it must be a jolly good story.

39

Mmm.

Mommy?

What, Charlotte, what is it, can't you see I'm busy!

I only said ... I'm sure it's jolly good.

Thank you. Now it's time for bed.

So she'd taken two more chocolate biscuits—the tea biscuits had served as supper—and curled up with Polly. When she told Polly about Master Rory, about his fingers on her this time, she felt a funny tingling between her legs, and she rolled on top of Polly to make it go away. She rubbed so hard that Polly's kerchief got twisted off.

"Lottie?" Miss Dowd's voice brought her back to the classroom, just after break. Miss Dowd was holding out a tissue. "Lottie, what's wrong? Are you crying?"

"Course not!" She never cried.

Miss Dowd patted Lottie's cheek with the tissue. "Perhaps you're getting a little cold, dear, perhaps you should go home this afternoon."

"I'm always cold."

"You do look tired. Did you get enough sleep last night, and a proper breakfast?"

Lottie couldn't remember breakfast. Mommy had been asleep when Lars woke Nell and her, and they'd hurried out to get to school on time. She shrugged.

"I'm sending you home. I know your Mum doesn't have a telephone, but I'll tell your sister. You can walk by yourself, it isn't far." Miss Dowd patted her shoulder. "Go home and have a good nap, and tell your Mummy to make you a nice big tea."

"Master Rory might come back."

"Who is he?"

"My piano tutor."

"Your Mummy can tell him you're resting today, no more lessons."

"Really? Will she do that?"

Miss Dowd took off her spectacles and studied Lottie. Her eyes were the misty grey of the Forest of Firth, as if she'd been reading fairy tales for a long time,

40

and knew them all to be true, even the frightening ones. "Is everything all right?"

Lottie chewed on her cheek. She didn't know how to answer. "I have a costume," she said finally.

Miss Dowd unclasped her hands, and smiled.

"Very good. You can bring it in when you're feeling better."

As Lottie walked slowly away, she heard Claire de Lune in her head, its beat matching the fall of her footsteps. She tapped the keys with her fingers, over and over, trying not to look at them as they played the cool breeze.

The sun was shining and the grey squares of pavement glittered. A stray marble was lying in one of the grates outside the school, where children always played marbles, and she picked it up. *Coo-er!* It was clear with a thin blue twisty streak, only a little scuffed on one side. This one would make the seventh marble she'd found, enough to finally play a real game with the others instead of having to just watch from the sidelines. What luck!

She put it into her cardigan pocket, and found the chocolate bar she'd nicked from the cloakroom earlier when she'd rifled through the coat pockets, looking for snacks. The check was late again this month so Mommy hadn't been able to pay for the school lunch. They were supposed to be taking their own lunches.

"Ta, love!" Stevie suddenly swooped past, and snatched the chocolate from her hand just as she was going to take a bite.

"Gimme it back!" She chased after him until he stopped short, so that she crashed into him. She burst out laughing. Stevie always made her laugh.

"Ere." He broke it in half. "Why're you out early?"

"Miss Dowd says I'm sick. Why're you?" Stevie went to the comprehensive school a bus ride away, where they didn't have to wear uniforms and they had outdoor play every afternoon. Lottie'd wished she could go with him, until Wendy's invitation.

41

"Alf day. Whooee!" Stevie ran off, and again she chased him.

"Let's build our Guy!"

"Don't you ave your bloody pianer lesson?"

"I'm not avin em anymore."

"I want me dinner first, come ome wi' me."

At Stevie's house, his Da made them egg and baked beans on toast, with a rasher of bacon, washed down with mugs of sweet milky tea.

"Park that round ya and then bugger off, me program's on at one thirty," he told them, tapping his long fag ash into his cup. Stevie's house always smelled comfortingly of fried eggs, fags, and a hint of ale. Lottie ate so fast she nearly choked, she was that hungry. "I've a tenner on Lucky Star in the third. Ow's she sound to ya Lottie?" He always pretended that she could call the races' outcome.

"Loike a winner, Mr. Avery," she said, her mouth full.

"Bloody roight she does."

She told him about finding the lucky blue marble, her seventh. "Well done, Lottie, I'll be looking for marbles and seven! Ta, love."

Outside, Stevie dragged the baby buggy from where they'd hidden it under the back stairs. Lottie had wanted to hide it in the bomb shelter, where nobody could ever find it, but Rita advised against it. "One o' you lot would get locked inside, and we'd never ear from you again."

Wheeling the buggy to the park, they picked up bits and pieces of rubbish, mostly old newspapers, and piled them in.

"Tell me again, about the Guy?"

"We make im outta this lot, put old clothes on im, wheel im round the night of Guy Fawkes' next month and get lots and lots of money!"

"Why'll people give us money?"

"We arsk em for it! Say 'penny for the Guy,' Lottie, that's ow it's done."

"Penny for the Guy!"

"Then we bring im round to me back garden where Jimbo'll ave a big bonfire goin. E'll ave fireworks as well, it's to be a huge party." Stevie elaborated, "All is mates are comin round, and me Da's mates as well. Mum and Rita're doin up a big supper, sausages an ever so much ale. Let's nick us a bottle!" His wicked grin flashed across his face, crinkling up his brown eyes and brightening his already red cheeks.

"Then we throw the Guy on the bonfire!"

"And watch im burn! That's why we only keep the rubbish that'll burn, Lottie, not no metal nor rubber. That's wot e gets, see, for tryin to blow up Parliament."

The pickings were slim: neighbourhood children had been out scavenging for weeks. The buggy was only halfway filled by the time they got to the park.

Stevie threw some of the newspapers onto the hard ground and flung himself on top of them. He sprawled back and folded his hands under his head. Lottie followed him. They looked up at the spiky treetops, to which a few brave leaves still clung.

"I got lost the other night," she told him. "Only found me way by them trees."

"Wot was you doin out ere alone?"

She told him about Wendy's tea, about the tiger and matching plates. She didn't confess nicking Polly's kerchief. She told him about Jeremy, the teddy boy.

"E sounds a roight bloke," Stevie approved.

"E didn't strangle me in the loo, anyroad."

Stevie rolled to his side and looked at her. "Y'know I was only pullin your leg about that, I eard it from Rita." It sounded just like one of Rita's dreadful yet fascinating newspaper accounts. There was usually a satisfying end to the criminals in her story, which she always claimed to have read that very morning.

"*Tis* true, Stevie, it's roight ere in the *Mirror*." She'd hold it out, knowing he would never read it. "Look! They found his fingers all over London!"

"Shut ya face, ya rabbitin on again, you'll frighten them children," Jimbo would tell her. Lottie had used to

43

love being frightened by Rita, she and Stevie would giggle wildly with delicious fear, but lately the gruesome stories didn't seem funny anymore.

"Stevie," Lottie blurted, "if a bloke, an old boy like Jeremy, if e was trying anythin on with a gel my age, wot would you think?"

"Tryin anythin on?"

"Loike, kissin er. Loike that."

Stevie stared at her, grimacing, and made a gagging noise. "Kissin! Wot a nasty idear, Lottie, you been listenin to Rita's orrid tales again." He twisted up and pretended to retch. "Disgustin." He turned to push her. "Shut up. Go find us some conkers."

Lottie scrambled up and ran to the nearest stretch of bushes where, hidden on the ground, some last conkers lay. She was lucky enough to find two of the spiny green spheres. One for each!

As she approached Stevie, still on the ground, she heard again what he'd said. *Nasty. Disgustin. Horrid.* That's what he'd think of her: *a gel wiv a bloke muckin about.* She scuffed her shoes, slowing herself down.

"Ere." She hurled one of the conkers at him and it glanced off his cheek. He glared up at her, astonished. Red streaks appeared where the spines had grazed him, next to his eye and, dismayed, she saw small beads of blood welling up in the streaks.

"Bloody feckin ell, Lottie, that's done it, I'll beat you daft!"

She got a good head start, since she was already on her feet, but he was stronger and faster, and he caught up with her by the bushes. He slammed her into them and she fell, scratching into the dry shrub bones. He sprang after her and pushed her further down, shaking her until she screamed, "Uncle! Sorry then Stevie!"

"Wot's all this?" A stern grownup voice made Stevie whip round.

A bobby stood nearby, arms folded, grumpy look on his face. It was, Lottie recognized, the younger of the bobbies who'd brought Mommy home.

44

She didn't want to see him again! She knew what they thought of Mommy. She rolled away, under the bushes, and wriggled out on the other side of the copse.

She stumbled up and ran down the pavement toward home, running as fast as she could, not noticing that the conker flew out of her saggy cardigan pocket and then the lucky seventh marble as well, bouncing so hard behind her that it cracked in half on the gritty pavement.

EIGHT

BAD LUCK, SHE RAN SMACK INTO MASTER RORY as he was getting out of his car, in front of the flat. The wind had picked up, and the piles of music sheets he carried flew in every direction when she careened into him.

Lottie raced toward the largest bunch, thinking madly of the Guy who still needed building, wondering if perhaps she could spirit away this batch, *more rubbish for our bonfire*. But she wouldn't really want to burn music, would she? All those notes in the air? She pictured them on fire, the little round bits and the long stems, pluming with delicate orange and blue flame like the kitchen matches. How would they sound?

Master Rory was standing still, watching his music fly, keys dangling from his hand. His hair blew round his face so she couldn't tell what he was thinking. She brought the pages she'd captured and held them out to him.

"Ere. Sorry."

He rolled them into a cone and tapped it against the palm of his other hand.

She looked at her muddy shoes, and saw his neat black boots pointed toward her. Mommy had told her to apologize. *Bloody ell if e deserves it*, but she told him, in a sullen mumble, "Sorry about yesterday, as well, Master Rory."

She knew he was still upset when he didn't answer. She supposed she had been rather unkind, saying that about his dead sister's dress. She shifted from foot to foot. She was glad when Stevie ran round the corner,

46

even though she could tell that he, too, was furious with her.

"Oy! You bloody well left me alone to 'ave a lit'le chat' wiv that copper!" He stood, panting, the smears of blood on his cheek blending, she saw with a pang, into a trickle of tears. He fisted them away carelessly. "I'm bloody lucky he ain't sendin me to reformatory. Me Da'd tan me arse proper, he would."

"I'm ever so sorry, Stevie, I never meant it!"

"An I ad to leave the pram behind! I was afraid e'd say I nicked it!"

"We must fetch it back." She started in the direction of the park, but Master Rory's hand caught her arm.

"What's all this, Charlotte, Steven? What's this about a policeman?" *E's thick as a grownup.* "Steven, you're bleeding, how did that happen?"

"She did it." Stevie jerked a sulky head toward Lottie.

Lottie saw, out of the corner of her eye, Master Rory's surprise. *Prob'ly thinks is 'angel' as turned into a proper devil now.* She yanked her arm away from him, roughly. "Lemme go! I wanna fetch that baby buggy before someone else gets it!"

"Baby buggy?"

"Our pram, Master Rory." Stevie explained, "For the Guy."

"Penny for the Guy, that's right, in a fortnight." Master Rory nodded slowly. "Where did you leave it?"

"At the park."

"Shall I drive you over there? We can put it in the boot."

"Would you?" Stevie grinned at Master Rory. "Smashin!"

Lottie felt like stamping her foot when she saw Master Rory's uncommon wide smile answer Stevie's. "Come along, then, let's be quick about it."

Stevie sat in front, Lottie behind. "Go fast, Master, pretend we're at the Grand Pree, me Da eard it on the radio last year. E won five bob."

47

Still smiling, Master Rory complied, and the buildings and cars and busses flew past until Lottie felt dizzy. Stevie whooped in laughter, and Master Rory laughed with him. At the park, he left the motor running and leapt out. The buggy stood next to the last of the newspapers scattered about. He dragged it away and lifted it into the boot.

"Coo-er, Master, you are a one," Stevie told him. "Ta."

"You're welcome, Steven."

"Wouldja like to come to our bonfire, then, on Guy Fawkes's Day? We're avin ever such a big party. There'll be lots of people your age, me sister Rita an all."

No! E bloody well can't come!

Master Rory shot him another smile. "Thanks for asking me, but I've a concert that night. I shall be playing some of that music I brought, Charlotte, I thought your mother might like to hear it."

The music that was now fluttering to the four winds, all over west London, except what she'd managed to catch? He followed her glance out the window and smiled at her, finally, in the rearview mirror. "I don't need the sheets to play. It's all right."

Lottie slumped back in the seat. She felt in her pocket for her marble and her conker. Her chin dropped further onto her chest when her fingers came up empty. *E's dead wrong.* Nothing was all right.

Stevie was looking at Master Rory curiously now. "I thought she war'nt avin no more lessons wiv you?"

"Is that what she said?" Lottie heard his dry little laugh. "She wishes our lessons were different, perhaps, but there are bits she likes very much. Don't you, love?"

She didn't look at him.

"She's playin all the time, I must say, she sounds roight grand."

"She's a natural musician. It's why I like to teach her."

At the flat, Master Rory heaved the buggy into its hiding place under Stevie's stairway next door. He took a big shopping bag, with a greasy bottom that promised

48

fish'n'chips, out of the boot, and carried it up to Lottie's. She and Stevie trailed behind.

Nell answered his knock.

"Hello, Eleanor," he began, but she dashed past him to fly at Lottie. The sound of her slap resounded in the landing. Lottie's face burned, then stung, and she covered her cheek with her dirty hand. She looked at the floor. She knew why Nell was angry.

"Ere, Nellie, wot you on about, wot's she done to *you!*"

"Eleanor, surely that's uncalled for?"

"She did it again! She got herself lost, or delayed or something stupid, and she lied to Miss Dowd about it!" Nell was shaking.

"Lied?" Master Rory lifted Lottie's chin with a steady finger. "Charlotte?"

She twisted her face away. "Miss Dowd told me to come ome, as I was sick, an she said she'd tell Nell." She felt hot pressure behind her eyes and she dug her nails into her palms. She wouldn't cry. "Only I dint come ome, see, I run into Stevie an we was gettin our Guy ready."

"You're so thoughtless! You didn't even care that I'd worry about you, the second time you've gone missing, especially after what happened the other night! You're beastly!" Nell took a deep breath. "And I'm *sick* of taking care of you!"

"What happened the other night?" Master Rory's voice was very quiet.

"None o your bloody beeswax!" Lottie snarled, suddenly recalling this aggressive-sounding Americanism, beeswax. "Take a hike!"

He ignored her. "Eleanor?"

Nell was crying. "Our m-mother—she started to walk—"

Lottie kicked Nell's shin, harder than she'd meant to, as hard as she'd hit Stevie without meaning to. "It's NONE OF IS BLOODY BEESWAX!"

Mommy's voice came from the kitchen, her writing mood voice, the one just preceding *silence*.

49

"Charlotte. How often do I have to tell you, *lower your voice.*"

Master Rory frowned, as rare a look as the wide smile he'd given Stevie.

He marched Lottie into Lars' room and sat her at the bench. "Scales," he snapped. He left, closing the door behind him.

She didn't start her scales, though, she was listening to his low voice in the hallway. Nell's sobs sounded right heartbroken. Lottie's lower lip trembled and she dug her nails harder into her balled hands. She heard them troop into the kitchen. Heard the crackling that indicated the fish'n'chip supper, from his shopping bag. Heard Mommy's exclamation of pleasure and, after a bit, Nell's wobbly post-crying laugh. Even Stevie joined in the feast, the traitor, she heard his guffaw.

The door opened. She could tell from the quality of the silence that he was just standing there, watching her, and she put her hands quickly onto the keys. She slowly sounded out the wistful little song they'd done that morning at school, and sang along in as brave a voice as she could muster:

*I left my love at Woolich pier, beneath a big crane standing,
And all the love I had for her, it passeth understanding.
Took her sailing on the river, flow sweet river flow.
London town was mine to give her, sweet Thames flow softly.*

She picked out each note as she heard it, in her head, and sang it round twice, although she could only remember one verse. Then she let her hands drop into her lap. After a moment she heard the door close. The room felt empty again.

He'd left her alone. Finally. *About bloody time.*

She didn't know why, when it was supposed to feel right, his leaving her all alone, now, should feel so much worse than everything else.

The tears she hated came burning, it felt like scraping, out of her eyes, blurring the keys in front of her.

50

NINE

WHEN LARS CAME HOME she was obliged to leave his room. She used one of his model-ship rags to mop her face, leaving battleship grey streaks on her hands and cheeks.

"Go wash your face, Lottie, you look a fright." He dumped his books on his desk. "There's supper in the kitchen. They saved some for us."

The hallway was quiet, the kitchen empty. The last of the fish'n'chips sat on the table on their white wrapper, looking cold and heavy, next to a half-filled bottle of brown liquid. "Where'd they go?" she asked Lars, while his door was still open.

"Rory took them out," he said without turning round. "I guess he has money to burn, from all your lessons."

Money to burn? She pictured pound notes flaming in the air along with the musical notes she'd imagined earlier.

She went to the bath to wash her face. With no one to interrupt her, she drank right from the spigot and sucked at the metal rim as long as she liked, chewing at the soft copper, liking the marks her teeth made, like a sign of the sort they saw carved into trees at the park. John loves Mary. Sally + Ian 4ever. Rory loves Lottie.

She turned on the hot tap and sat in the bath, watching the water creep up the sides, sat until her fingers wrinkled and the water cooled and her eyes felt better. She put on a clean nightdress and her slippers.

In the kitchen, she rummaged until she found Miss Dowd's Atlas. She tip-toed into Lars' room where he

51

frowned over his books, studying, and lifted the white dress from the lamp stand. She took them both into hers and Nell's bedroom, hung the dress on the hook behind their door, and crawled into her bunk with the Atlas. She tucked Polly under her arm, to show her the pictures. The room was cold but she was too tired to bother making a fire. She wrapped the covers round her tightly.

She looked at the page Miss Dowd had unfolded for her the other day.

She recognized England, an orange blobby cat shape with what looked like its toy ball of blue wool unraveling off to the side. The wool was Ireland.

To England's right was yellow Holland, where the Little Dutch Tulip Girl in one of their storybooks came from, and the Little Boy who held his Finger in the Dike to stop the flooding. She wondered how that would feel, right bloody frightful, *cor blimey, just one finger between me an the ole bloomin sea.*

There were other shapes and colours and she could read the letters of some of them, not every name. France was below England. Miss Dowd had just started telling them about France, and Germany above it.

Pink France had a piece like a mitten reaching into the grey sea.

Green Germany had the rough shape of the snow angels they used to make in their backyard in America with Daddy.

She didn't know the others yet, but she could count how many were between England and the tiny yellow dagger shape of Israel. At least ten, as well as some squiggly bits that hardly looked big enough to matter. It was a lot of countries.

She looked again at the map of England.

LONDON was down in the corner near the top of France.

It took them half an hour on the tube, then twenty minutes on the bus, to get to the bank in the City where Mommy cashed Daddy's alimony check every month. The walk afterwards, to Wimpy's for their monthly

52

hamburger treat, took another fifteen minutes. Lars was always telling them hurry up, *we've only got an hour before the last bus*. He had a watch to keep them on time.

At that rate, walking to Israel would take years. They'd need to find some tubes and busses on the way. And what about the water?

They'd come to England on a big ship, tall and brightly-lit as the building where Grandfather's office was, in Chicago.

Lottie had been afraid to swim in the swimming pool, since she thought it was part of the sea, but she'd liked the movie theatre and the gift shop. She liked the bell for their dinner seating and the man who sat next to them, who poured them all a little sip of Champagne, a fizzy drink, and winked at Nell and Lottie. She liked having everyone smile at her, then, all the waiters and grownups, their stares hadn't felt suffocating.

The sea between America and England was the same distance, on the Atlas, as between England and Israel. That trip took five days. Mommy had woken them up very early, the last morning on board, to point out the window at a brown patch in the distance. "That's France, children. France! That's the direction we're going, to get to Israel."

Only five days, on a ship, to go all the way from New York to Southampton.

P'raps we can take a ship to Israel, then, be there and back in time for next term.

But there wasn't enough water in the map to make a straight line, like there was between America and England, they'd have to sail all the way down past France and the shapes beneath it, into a crocodile's-head-shaped grey bit, that started out 'M E D' and went into a difficult-looking word.

She put the Atlas down and turned off the bedside lamp. She curled into the blankets and chewed, thoughtful, on Polly's hand, which had a pleasant consistency and a fresh rubbery smell. She would have to

53

learn to read better, so she could speed confidently through, as impatiently as Lars, for example, would do.

Should she show Lars the Atlas? He was the most sensible of them and would know immediately how far away everything was.

Nell, on the other hand, was touchy these days. It wasn't just minding Lottie, and Mommy wandering off, it was the looming 'Eleven Plus' exams at school that would determine, Nell said tearfully and often, her *entire future*. She'd even stopped taking ballet lessons so she could study more.

"She'll drive erself right round the bloody bend with them exams." Stevie was a year older than Lottie, and would face the Eleven Plus next year, but he was more philosophical about it than Nell. "Me Rita never bothered about em. She did roight well gettin her job down the pub, it's where she met Jimbo."

Lottie thought it would be jolly to work down the pub. It was a lively place, with a lot of laughing people, a dartboard, a billiard table; and packets of crisps and bottles of ginger beer given by Rita, who always winked at Stevie and Lottie as cheerily as the man on the ship. "Op it now, ducks, gotta earn me daily bread."

The door opened, spilling light into the room. She stopped chewing Polly's hand. Nell always made fun of her doing that.

But it wasn't Nell, it was Master Rory who walked toward her, holding a little paper bag, bringing in the scent of the windy night.

"I bought you a treat, Charlotte. I know you've had a difficult evening."

He knelt beside her. "*After that there was no stopping*," he sang quietly, the refrain from the song she'd been playing before. "*Sweet Thames flow softly.*"

He unwrapped a cornet—a square of vanilla ice cream—and put it into its rectangular cone. He held it toward her mouth and put his other arm round her. "Here, darling, your favourite. Have a bite."

He smelt like ale. She wriggled away to sit up and take the cornet from him. The ice cream was cold and sweet.

He took her again in his arms. "I want a taste." He loomed in to lick her mouth. "Mmm. Vanilla ice cream and sherry, delicious."

Nell's entrance made him straighten up and let her go abruptly, although he started laughing.

"Thanks ever so much for the treats, Rory," she told him, coming close.

"You're welcome, Eleanor."

Lottie leaned out past him. "I didn't mean to hurt you."

Nell looked at her. "I know. You aren't as beastly as all that," she mumbled. "Mother has to take a bit more notice, that's all."

Master Rory stood. "Perhaps I can help, at least on the days I'm here with Charlotte," he said. He went to the fireplace, checked the flue, loaded in two logs and lit them with a scratching flick of a match. "Eleanor, make me a list of things I can bring in my car, things that might be difficult for your mother to carry from the shops."

Nell frowned. "That wouldn't be right."

"Of course it's right," he said, as he fitted the firescreen back into place. "I'm part of your family now. You must know how I adore Charlotte."

Nell made a dubious face, as if to say, she might not be as beastly as all that but she's still bloody annoying. "Maybe it's okay," she answered, still a bit hesitant. "We're always running out of potatoes, and coal and firewood, and we're always behind on the meter, sometimes we can't have a hot bath."

"Charlotte can bathe at my flat, then, she can see what a grand piano is like." He turned from the fireplace to smile at her. "You'd like its sound, darling."

"No!"

"Lottie, that's enough." Mommy stood in the doorway. "Rory's being extraordinarily helpful." She came winding up to Master Rory and put her arms round him. Lottie felt funny when she saw how Mommy smiled at

55

him, and how she leaned into him, to kiss his cheek. "Thanks again. We all needed this little outing. You're just a living doll." Her laugh was one Lottie hadn't heard before.

In the firelight, she saw how he looked bashful, for the first time ever, how he blushed. He looked down, letting his hair slide over his face just like Lottie did when she didn't want people looking at her.

"Goodnight now, girls." When Mommy kissed her, Lottie smelled the same pub scent as Master Rory had.

Mommy took his arm and left their room, closing the door behind her. "Play something for us," they heard her say. "Something pretty that the girls can fall asleep to. And let's have another sherry. I haven't had such fun in I don't know when."

"I can't play well when I've been drinking."

"Oh just a little something quiet, come on, don't you know any Cole Porter?" They heard, again, that unaccustomed laugh. "Surely even an English pianist, even one as young as you, has heard of Cole Porter?"

After some time they heard a soft tinkling of keys, then a rippling, then a long cascade, all very light. They must have put Lars at the kitchen table.

"Mother likes him, I can tell," Nell said as she put on her nightgown. She looked at herself in the mirror, something she'd taken to doing often. "He's a lot younger than her, though, don't you think it's kind of icky?"

Icky as anything, ducks.

Nell kept studying herself, twisting her head this way and that, playing with her long red-brown hair. "He's real cute, but he's way too old for me. There's this boy at school—" she broke off when she saw the way Lottie was staring at her. "Why am I telling you, you're just a baby! What do you know about anything!"

Lottie turned away from Nell and curled up with Polly.

56

TEN

MOMMY DECIDED THAT THEY SHOULD DO A PLAY. "The English always have plays at Christmastime!" She beamed at them, brightly, as they sat for supper at the kitchen table one night. "They call them pantomimes. I've told your Dad to send an extra big check. Lars will compose the score, and Nell will dance, and Lottie can play the piano. We can invite the neighbors, and your friends, and we'll serve drinks and snacks. It will be such fun!"

"What play, Mommy, the Forest of Firth?"

Mommy smiled at Lottie. "How about the Twelve Dancing Princesses? We can use your dolls for princesses."

"Oh, yes!"

"You don't have twelve dolls," Lars pointed out.

"We can use the animals, then, and some of your toys too, Lars." Mommy poked him playfully, but he sat up stiffer, leaning away from her. "It'll be modern art. Let the audience use their imaginations."

Lottie thought even Lars' best battleship didn't look anything like a princess. "P'raps we can use some of the check to buy more dolls," she suggested hopefully. She knew how lonely Polly was getting, with no dolls her age to play with, only a few floppy baby rag dolls whose faces were worn off.

"Or, you can invite your friends to join in, Jenny and Wendy, and the others you've talked about, and they can bring their dolls too. It's a way of thanking them for having you."

Wizard! Who'd have guessed Mommy could come up with such a brilliant idea!

"What'll you use for the princes?" Lars asked.

"Why you, of course, and Rory, and maybe you can bring some friends from school too."

Lars stared at Mommy with such a mean look, Lottie was surprised. "Mother, grow up. First of all, I'm much too busy with exams to take part in some stupid play—"

"I've got the Eleven Plus soon, but I'll help out," Nell put in, with a snooty glance at Lars. "I'd love to do a dance. It'll be like Recital."

"—second of all, I'd never want my friends here, and third of all, there's barely room to swing a dead cat, let alone have troops of girls storming in."

"You're just like your father, always harping on the negative," Mommy said sadly. Then she poked him again. "Don't be such an old man. Live a little! Rory can help you write the music, you'd like that. It's good practice for your composing work."

"I really don't like that guy," Lars muttered.

"I can do the music. I'm improvising ever so well," Lottie announced.

"We can build a cardboard stage set, simple yet evocative, a sort of haunting blue background with some draped gauze. I have it all figured out. We'll draw a curtain across the alcove in the girls' room, where the bay window is, and that will be the stage."

"Stevie can help build too, he's clever at things like that." She used her proper pronunciation so Mommy wouldn't be reminded of Stevie's Cockneyism.

"We can stand behind the curtain and dangle the dolls over, like a puppet show," Nell said. "But we still need twelve princes."

"How about Lars and Steven doing their voices, unseen behind the curtain—a *suggestion* of princes. And Rory can play the piano, in the background."

"I am *not* helping you, Mother, get used to the idea." Lars stood and clattered his dishes into the sink. "I have to study." He left the kitchen.

"Teenagers," Mommy said, waving him off with a careless hand.

"Can I have my friends to tea, to tell them about it? And then can they come after school, until we have the play, to rehearse?"

"Of course, Lottie."

"So I won't have piano lessons! We shall have to have snacks, as well, and Mommy—you shall have to be awake in the afternoon, and help me. That's what Wendy's Mum does."

"Certainly! I wouldn't miss it."

Cor. Now this was more like.

"And you won't start walking to Israel without us," she finished, wanting to have it all perfectly clear.

Mommy looked at her, still, her deep blue eyes seeming to grow larger as seconds passed. When she spoke, her voice was quiet and serious. "I promise. We have the map, and we'll make our plan, as a family. I've been thinking, the Father would want me to wait until Nell's and Lars' exams are over. We should go when next term is finished and the weather is better."

"That's good thinking, Mother." Nell's relief was so apparent that Mommy looked at her with a raised brow.

"Really, Eleanor, it wasn't that bad, it was more like a trial run, actually, the way marathoners have to practice. You and Lars shouldn't have been so exercised. It wasn't as if I'd abandoned you without warning, I left you a note. You over-reacted!"

Nell stood, slung her dishes into the sink the way Lars had, left as he'd done.

"Adolescence," Mommy said, and she hugged Lottie close. "At least you're still my pal, hmm, sweetie, you'll keep me company."

"But we have to give the map back to Miss Dowd," Lottie said, muffled into Mommy's soft sweater, smelling the Kent and perfume scent she loved. She put her arms round Mommy and rested.

"Dowd shmowd," said Mommy. She tightened her hug and kissed Lottie on both cheeks. Lottie, eyes still

59

closed, suddenly felt the kisses like Master Rory's, like the way he started, so soft. She stiffened. "You're my darling angel," Mommy crooned, rocking her slightly, more tightly, and Lottie felt suffocated.

She twisted out of Mommy's arms.

"Are you getting too big for cuddles?" Mommy smiled. "You're turning into such a beautiful girl, you look just like I did at your age, and everyone stared at me wherever I went just the same way they stare at you." She stroked Lottie's hair back. "Wear your beauty with pride, darling, it's the Father's gift, His mark of goodness on you. You were *meant* to be the angel!"

The suffocated feeling grew. "Shall we talk some more about the Twelve Dancing Princesses?"

"Invite the girls! We can begin right away."

ELEVEN

TWO AFTERNOONS LATER, Lottie felt comfortably surrounded as she, Jenny, Wendy, Pamela, Agnes and Ursula trooped home together. Stevie was waiting for them, as she'd asked, and she introduced the girls to him.

"Allo ducks!" His broad grin spread as he took in their lavender uniform dresses, purple blazers and purple felt cloche hats. "Ever so nice to meetcha."

"Lead on then, Lottie," said Ursula.

They sat on the floor of Nell's and Lottie's room. Pamela and Ursula took doll inventory, and Stevie measured the lengths of string they would tie round the dolls, from a ball in the shoebox of sewing things Mommy had collected for the play.

"We'll need to raise this curtain so the dolls show below," Jenny said, indicating the sheet Mommy had strung across the small bay alcove. She and Agnes pulled it this way and that.

"This is just what I'd hoped for!" Mommy cried from the doorway. "A hive of creative activity!" Lottie was happy to see her looking alert and pretty, with her hair fixed and her lipstick on. She held a tray of tea mugs and biscuits.

"Rory hon, give me a hand. Help me pass these out," she told Master Rory, who was behind her. He took the tray from her and brought it into the room.

"Allo, mate!" Stevie said. "Me fellow prince!" Brothers in arms, his tone implied; he'd taken a familiar approach since Master Rory's retrieval of their Guy rubbish.

61

As they clustered round close to him, reaching, a look of alarm grew on Master Rory's face. He set the tray on the floor and backed away, to perch on the edge of Lottie's bed, stooping slightly to fit his long frame under Nell's bunk.

"Hullo, Master Rory, thanks for helping us," Jenny told him, with a shy smile.

"Hello, Jenny."

"Are you the tutor, then, did you make up the tunes for the play?" Ursula asked.

"Er ... play?"

"I didn't get a chance to warn you, we cooked up a plan to put on a show! The children are already underway." Mommy stood next to him and put a hand on his shoulder. "Since you're such a brilliant pianist, we thought you could compose the music—with Lars, of course, he needs the experience." She introduced the children.

"Didja not ear, we're to be princes," snickered Stevie, preening. "Where's me crown, then, gels, and where's is?"

Mommy put both hands in a circle above Master Rory's head. "He can have a halo or a crown." She held up her fingers behind his black hair as if making points in a diadem, and wiggled them, laughing. He glanced up at her and pulled slightly away.

"Nobody's supposed to see the princes, they don't need crowns." Lottie moved between them, and pulled Mommy's hands from his head. He slipped his arm round Lottie's waist, drawing her to sit next to him.

"If you didn't make up the music yet, we'd best get on with it," Ursula said briskly. "It's only a few weeks to Christmas, and we've got the school pageant as well."

"What sort of music?" Master Rory asked her.

"We're doing the Twelve Dancing Princesses. So you'll have to make tunes that go with the story," she informed him. "There are four main bits. When they decide to go dancing, when they're crossing the magic river on the boat, when they're actually at the dance, and when they're discovered at the end, by the King."

"Right after the prince comes to visit the one he falls in love with," Jenny added.

"And his magic cloak falls off, and he becomes visible to her," Agnes finished. She sighed. "It's ever so romantic," she told Master Rory. "You must play love songs."

Master Rory stared at her as if he was hearing the story for the first time. Agnes ducked her head, blushing, and her dark ringlets bounced.

"Serves him right, to be made visible," Pamela declared. "He should never have been creeping about in their bedroom in the middle of the night anyway."

Lottie added the thought that suddenly occurred to her. "When he's found out, he loses his spell over her." She shot Master Rory a look, to make this point clear, but he was watching Agnes.

Agnes protested, "But she falls madly in love with him as soon as she sees how handsome he is. We should make it so she convinces her father it's all right to go dancing. Then they all cross the river again, and he gets his powers back."

"That's not how it goes, Agnes, we can't just change it," Ursula chided.

"But it's to be a Christmas play. We must have a happy ending."

"You have the artistic license to alter the plot slightly, to suit your own production," Mommy said. "But the greatest interpreters stay true to the original scripts, at least in spirit."

"So ... it's a tragedy," Master Rory concluded.

"Well, nobody *dies,* but the king prohibits his daughters from ever dancing again, once they're caught out, and the prince who's in love with the youngest gets banished," Pamela told him. "The ending is rather boring, actually."

Stevie looked crestfallen. "I thought there was fighting. I thought it was a soldier ad the magic cloak, an a great silver sword, given im by the old witch, and e fought the dragons to get to the princess."

63

"That's Sleeping Beauty," Pamela said scornfully. "You've got it all mixed up."

"There is a soldier—" Mommy began.

"It's one o these ere," Stevie said, pulling the worn fairy tale book from the shelf. "Nell used to read it out, before she ad to study the Eleven Plus."

"I suppose I shall have to look it over," Master Rory murmured.

"We need more dolls," Jenny announced, looking up from the toy shelf. "We can't use these pathetic rag babies. Lottie, where's that one you talked about, your favourite, with the red dress?"

Polly was lying in her usual place, on Lottie's pillow, covers to her chin. Master Rory pulled her out. "D'you mean Pollyanna?"

She bit her lip to stop herself shouting, "Don't touch er!" and clenched her fists to stop herself from reaching over him to snatch Polly away, which she knew would look odd to the girls. *Ow does e know er name, e must've eard me talking to er. E shouldn't touch er!*

"I say," said Wendy, studying Polly as Master Rory held her up, "that looks awfully like one of Mummy's fancy tea napkins. What's it doing on her head?"

"I ... brought it ome in me pocket, by mistake," Lottie mumbled, feeling hot in her cheeks. Master Rory took off the kerchief, folded it into a neat square, and handed it down to where Wendy sat at his feet.

"I daresay she forgot all about it. I've been making her practise ever so much," he said smoothly. "If you need dolls, my sister had quite a collection, clothes for them too. They'd lend themselves beautifully to your play. And Polly, here ..." He looked at her matted hair and rumpled dress. "Why, she could have a new dress and hat." He examined her hands, with their chewed-off fingers. "Perhaps ... a pair of gloves.

"You can have any of my sister's dolls you fancy, Charlotte. I'll take you some weekend soon to see them, at my parent's house in Devon. There are shelves of them."

64

What a stupid idea, she didn't want any of his dead sister's dolls. And she certainly didn't want to go off alone with him.

"Can I come to see them too?" Jenny asked eagerly.

"And me," Agnes chimed in, looking up at him. He returned her gaze, lips curving up in his little smile, not answering.

If they all went, it might be fun, at that. Polly would like new clothes.

"I thought there was a soldier," Stevie kept grumbling. "I don't care about dolls."

"Shan't we begin, then?" Ursula reminded them.

TWELVE

NOVEMBER WAS FLYING PAST, fast as the final meager leaf piles were swept away by the colder winds, fast as Lottie's fingers flew on the music she was helping Master Rory make for the play.

Stevie and Lottie, skills honed on their new venture into stagecraft, put a stodgy Guy together and collected ten shillings each from their Penny for the Guy buggy tour round the neighborhood. They watched their Guy burst into satisfying flames afterwards in the bonfire in Stevie's back garden. Lottie ate so many sausages she felt too ill to share more than a sip of Stevie's nicked bottle of ale.

The pageant details were concluded at school. In Miss Dowd's class, they were learning everything about India. Lottie was reading more, and faster, every day.

The play rehearsals progressed at home. The scenery was taking shape behind the draped curtain in the alcove, and the story was being worked out to everyone's satisfaction; well, to Mommy's, who spent more time on it than any of them and who stayed awake for hours each night revising the script, painting the scenery, and sewing different costumes for Polly and the dolls collected from Lottie's friends.

"Let me take Charlotte to Devon, Althea. You could save yourself all this doll clothing work, she could have her pick of twelve dresses in five minutes," Lottie heard Master Rory tell Mommy one afternoon when Lottie came home from school.

66

It was his first visit in a fortnight. When she heard his voice, she didn't go into the kitchen where they were drinking coffee. "I can see you're exhausting yourself with their silly play, Althea."

"It's not silly. This is something I have to do for them. They're growing so fast, away from me, and it's good for Lottie to have this. She's been a little behind, at school. This is a way for her to share a project with her new friends."

"She's getting behind now at piano."

"She's keeping up her practice, Rory, I hear her doing the script music every night, and she plays for hours on the weekend. You could give her a lesson again ..."

"I'm sure Charlotte's been surrounded by the others every day. There's been no opportunity for me to give her a private lesson."

"I'm sorry we haven't been able to pay you, this month's check's been spent—"

"Do you think I care about *money*?"

Lottie shrank against the wall. She'd heard him warning, about what would happen to her if she told their secret, and she'd seen how he banged the piano top down that day when he gave her the dress, but she had never before heard him raise his voice.

"I *care* about Charlotte. I see enormous potential in her. She needs to be nurtured, to be looked after, in order for that talent to grow. I could do so much for her."

"You've done so much for us already, Rory, don't think I'm not grateful." Lottie suddenly had a recollection of hearing Mommy talk to Daddy in this same way; the wheedling way she herself talked to Nell when she was losing at a game.

"Let me take her for a weekend. I'll show her my grand, at my flat, and I'll run her down to Devon so she can have some new dolls. Or, if that doesn't suit, let me take all of you. It'd be a lovely change, you'd like the country."

67

There was a short silence. Then Mommy said slowly, "You know, I *have* been thinking about Thanksgiving dinner."

"Thanks-giving?"

"It's an American holiday, quieter than Christmas, more humble, with simple foods and prayers of gratitude. There's a moving story behind it, of the first Pilgrims—"

"I recall the story. What about it?"

"I'd like to make you a nice dinner, but this kitchen is so ... inadequate. I'd like to cook a real Thanksgiving dinner for you, since you're our best friend in this country. You're helping us to survive our first winter here just as the Indians helped the Pilgrims that first Thanksgiving."

"Mmm. Why not come to Devon, then, Althea, we've a large kitchen there, and my parents would be delighted to meet all of you, and delighted to think of themselves as red Indians hosting starving Pilgrims." She heard a chair scrape and his dry laugh sounded louder. She realized he was leaving the table, coming into the hallway.

Caught!

She only looked up at him for a second before he pulled her close. She smelled his fir-tree scent, heard his heart thudding against her ear as he clutched her, felt his lips plant a kiss on her head. Then, arm round her waist, he led her into the kitchen.

"Look who was listening behind the door."

"Would you like a wonderful treat, Lottie? Rory's planning one for us!" Mommy poured out two little glasses of sherry. "Here's to the first Thanksgiving!"

"No." She tried to twist away.

"It's really for your mother," he said, holding her against his side. "It's to give her a bit of rest from all the work she's been doing on your play. Don't you want her to have a holiday?"

"I want my tea."

He let her go.

She poured out a cup, stood against the far wall, sipped while she stared at him.

68

She'd heard Nell and her friends when they talked about boys one day, talked in hushed tones about what men did to women to get babies, and it had sounded awful to Lottie, so unbelievably nasty that she wondered if it could really be true. But before that final thing, the girls said, there was a lot of hugging and kissing and touching, of the sort Master Rory liked, and it was supposed to feel nice. They had giggled about which boys they would let kiss them, not now of course, boys were such rude 'gets,' that was a scornful English word for idiots, but when they were teenagers, or if it were one of the Beatles. They all agreed they'd like that.

The conversation made her feel unsorted, *all at sixes and sevens* as Stevie would say. She wondered would it feel nice to kiss Stevie, the way Master Rory kissed her, or touch Jenny the way he did last time, the way she'd begun to touch herself every so often when she was lying in bed at night with Polly, to feel that shocking warmth.

"I can tell you're thinking about our lessons, darling, I'm sure you've been missing them as much as I have," he said quietly, watching her, beginning to smile. "Come along, we can fit in some quick scales now, those others aren't here today, are they, and Lars isn't home yet."

"No." She meant to say, no I don't want no more bloody lessons with you, but she couldn't seem to finish her sentence.

"Have a sherry with me first, while she finishes her tea, and then you can practice away!" Mommy handed him the glass. "Thanks for this, Rory, and thanks for the groceries." Lottie saw two big bags on the floor next to Mommy's chair. Mommy clinked her glass with his and they drank. The liquid was golden brown, like ale, but looked thicker. It gave off a sweetish scent. She wondered was it like ginger beer.

"Come here, love, have a taste," he said, catching her eye again, leaning back, waving his glass.

"When she's sixteen," Mommy said firmly.

"You Americans. Such Puritans." He smiled at Mommy and poured her another glass. "Pilgrims still, eh,

69

wandering the world in search of ... redemption, was it, religious freedom, or some such? Following Columbus?"

"Columbus was looking for a route to India. America got in the way." Mommy leaned toward him, returning his smile. "It was just a side trip."

"Like England is for us," Lottie blurted. She clapped her hand over her mouth, but Mommy was laughing.

"A side trip?" he asked, his smile widening to amusement. "On the way to where? France? The rest of the continent, perhaps?"

"Israel," Mommy told him brightly.

"What!" He laughed in the way she'd only heard that day getting the Guy with Stevie, a real open laugh, like a boy. The boy he must have been, not so long ago, with a lively white grin and a sparkle in his black eyes, a boy who might have been as much fun as Stevie. "Jolly good, that, I think you've gone a bit out of your way!"

"Charlotte is right. This is a stopping off place, en route to the Holy Land."

He regarded them for a moment, eyes moving from one to the other, smile fading. "Surely you're joking."

Lottie clunked her cup into the sink and ran next door into Lars' room. She began hammering on the piano in a harsh cacophony.

Above her noise she could hear Mommy's troubled query in the kitchen, Rory's answering reassurance. He came in, locking the door.

"Charlotte. Charlotte." He sat next to her on the bench and caught her hands. "You've worried your mother, she was ready to rush in but I told her I'd help you, I'd find out—what is it, darling, what's wrong?"

She struggled to wrench free, jerking her hands from his with such force that his wrists were flung onto the keyboard in a jarring clang. She scrambled up but he caught her fast, spinning on the bench and locking her in front of him.

"Tell me." His stare held her still. "Then we'll have a lesson."

70

"It's a secret," she spat out, pulling her face as far away from his as she could manage. "You know about secrets, Master Rory, you know I *mustn't tell!*"

She hoped this would upset him, but he just smiled. "I'm sure it's not a secret like the one we have, that nobody else will ever know as long as we live." He stroked the hair down her back. "Why are you so angry? Was it this talk about going to Israel, love, you can tell me. I know your Mummy's ideas are a bit ... odd." His hand slowed into a rhythmic circling. "You know you can tell me anything, and I'll never breathe a word." His eyes got darker as he whispered, "I'll keep all your secrets."

She felt her lips begin to tremble as she stared at him. She pressed them tight.

I don't WANT to tell him God talks to Mommy!

She'd told Stevie and the girls at school without worrying what they would say. But Master Rory was practically a grownup; like the bobbies, he might think Mommy was mad. "Mad as a feckin atter. Them kids belong in Care," the fat bobby had said. Master Rory might think they belonged in Care too.

"There, love." He cradled her head onto his shoulder. "Shh. Shh." He began to rock her, swaying on the bench. She lost her footing and fell into him. He lifted her, carried her to the bed.

Be like Polly. Still as Polly. Be stiff plastic, eyes squeezed shut, no heartbeat, no breath, no insides at all, a cold pink shell: feel nothing.

But she couldn't: black spots were dancing scarily inside her eyes, so she had to open them, and he was smiling, as her held breath gusted into that shivery heat she recognized from before.

"I missed you," he whispered. He pulled her on top of him. "We need more time alone." He kissed her, tongue wet as new bubble gum and as sweet: she tasted the sherry.

She managed to push him away, to roll and stand up, although her legs were shaky, and stalk toward the piano.

71

She sat. When her breathing slowed she put her hands on the keys.

"Now," she said out loud, trying to make her voice steady, trying to tell herself as firmly as he usually did. She began her scales. Behind her, from the bed, she heard his low chuckle.

THIRTEEN

OUTSIDE LONDON, the road to Devon took them through endless fields, brown in spots, white in others where an early snowfall dusted the tops of the highest hills. Lars sat in front with Master Rory, who was telling him how a Mini worked.

"Here, take the wheel." Master Rory reached over to put Lars' hands on the wheel. "See how you can feel the engine? You've only to keep it steady."

Mommy leaned forward from between the girls in back. "Rory, he's never driven, it isn't safe! Please don't let him!"

"He's fourteen, that's when I started learning. It's fun eh Lars?"

Lars' grin was so rare that it looked odd on his face. He nodded.

"Now here's a bit of a curve ahead, I'll let you turn the wheel on your own, just to get used to the feeling ..."

Everyone seemed to let out a breath when the curve turned straight again.

Lars laughed out loud.

"Well done, lad." Master Rory ruffled his hair and Lars' hands wobbled on the wheel. The car swooped sideways. "Steady on." Master Rory laughed, and covered Lars' hands with his own again.

"Can we hear the radio?" Nell asked.

He switched it on. "From Me to You" was playing, the song all the girls liked, by the Beatles. Nell sang along:

I've got arms that long to hold you, to keep you by my side,

73

I've got lips that long to kiss you, to keep you satisfied ...

"I thought you only liked classical music," Lars said, staring fixedly at the road.

"Call me Rory, Lars, we're mates now." He glanced at the backseat through the rearview mirror. "You too, girls, no more 'Master.' I'm twenty four, not forty."

"Rory, I'd prefer they still see you as an adult, that's why I told them to call you 'Master'—"

"But Althea, darling, I'd prefer to be their friend."

Mommy sank back.

"Do you like the Beatles, Rory?" Nell asked.

"Very much. They're rather raw, as musicians, but they've got enormous energy, and such a unique sound. It's impossible not to like them. I know a fellow who's been their pianist at times."

"You do?" Nell bounced forward on her seat. "Can you get me their autographs?"

"Certainly. Just remind me."

"Coo-er!"

"But you mustn't swear, Eleanor love, it isn't ladylike."

"That's what I'm always telling her," Lars said.

"No Beatles autograph if I hear any naughty language, then." His voice was teasing as he smiled at Nell in the rearview. "And Charlotte, you too, no dolls if I hear a single 'bloody' out of you this weekend. Although your pronunciation has improved quite a bit. You don't sound like a little Cockney anymore."

"Thanks to you," said Mommy.

"Thanks to Jenny, probably, right Charlotte?" he answered, giving Lottie a wink. "And Wendy, and Pamela, and Ursula, and who's that smallest pretty one? Curly hair?"

"Agnes," groaned Lars. "I'm sick of them all. I don't know how you can stand them, Rory, it's like a flock of silly geese! And Agnes is the worst, with her mooning around, whining about the princes, quack quack!"

"Not as bad as all that. She's really rather charming."

"You've only had to practice twice. I have to hear them nearly every day."

"You've done well with the music, Lars. You'll soon be ready for Conservatory."

Lars didn't answer. Mommy had said there was no money for any more special lessons. Nell wouldn't be returning to ballet, and Lottie was only having Master Rory because he 'volunteered' his time now. Whatever that meant. The big Christmas check had almost all gone into the play, Mommy said.

The road narrowed and seemed to rise higher as they got deeper into the darkening afternoon. He'd said it was about 150 miles southwest of London. Lottie took Miss Dowd's Atlas out of her satchel and looked it up. DEVON. It was an easy word.

She'd told Miss Dowd that the Atlas had gotten lost.

"But, Charlotte. I told you I'd need it back, dear." Her misty eyes looked at Lottie with disappointment. "How could you have been so careless?"

"P'raps my neighbor stole it," Lottie mumbled, feeling only the slightest twinge of conscience toward Stevie as she said this. She looked at her scuffed shoes and knocked at the desk leg with the left. The toes pinched; the little kick hurt. "He steals everything. Only he calls it nickin."

Miss Dowd leaned forward on her desk. "Do you suppose he's getting into our cloakroom as well? So many things are going missing lately, nobody can remember where they put their snacks, and a number of favourite pens have been lost."

Lottie could feel her cheeks burn. "Dunno," she said. Polly had helped her hide the little things she'd taken home, and she'd eaten the chocolate bars quickly, in the loo, with the stall door locked, and flushed the wrappers down in a tremendous whoosh.

"Tell your neighbor it's very wrong to steal, because it hurts other people's feelings to lose something they like," Miss Dowd said quietly. "Tell him all the stealing in the

75

world doesn't make up for what might be missing inside of one."

Lottie didn't look up.

"Or hurting one."

The bell rang and Lottie turned to go to her seat, but Miss Dowd reached out suddenly and held her arm. Lottie twisted away, roughly. *Don't touch me!*

"You look so tired these days, dear, what time do you usually go to bed?"

"Dunno." Lars had the watch and he never took it off his wrist. He woke Nell and Lottie up before he left for school.

"I think it's time I had a chat with your mother."

"She's working, she can't come to school." Mommy had, indeed, kept up her non-stop schedule of sewing and re-sewing the doll dresses. She said she just couldn't get them right; she'd do them at night and then rip the seams all out again the next afternoon. She'd sip the sherry Master Rory brought and snip away at the miniscule stitches, giggling to the girls that it was just like being caught in a witch's spell.

"Very well." Miss Dowd told her to go to her seat, but Lottie could feel her steady grey gaze on her all the way, itchy as a hand stroking up and down her back.

In the car, now, Lottie flipped the pages back and forth. Their plastic edges were getting a bit worn where she'd chewn them. They were sharper than Polly's hand, more satisfying to work her teeth against; she could bite through them as she could never seem to manage on the spigot no matter how furiously she gnashed away at it. Her teeth were aching all the time now, it seemed, and gnawing was the only relief for it.

"Hungry, Charlotte?" Master Rory's eyes seemed to watch every move she made. "Take out what's in the lunch basket, love, have a sandwich."

She dropped the Atlas and stared out the window.

Low clouds hid the tops of the hills now and a deep slow thunder of tune sounded in her head as she watched

76

them creep. The woods loomed close, trees thick together as gateposts, dark as the forests in the worst fairy tales.

"I'd like one," said Nell, reaching to tug the basket out of Lottie's lap.

"Hand me something, Nell." Lars' eyes were still glued to the road.

"Ham or roast beef?"

"Ham."

"Lovely sandwiches, Rory, ta," Nell thanked him.

Lottie remembered picnics long ago in summertime America, when Daddy would be at the wheel, top down, Mommy's hair in a kerchief, Nell's and Lottie's flying free so they screamed with laughter as the whipping strands flew into their mouths. Lars used to laugh then too, at least until Mommy and Daddy started arguing. But on picnic days they never did. The sky then had been as blue as a swimming pool, the clouds, if any, big puffy cartoon clouds, far away. Whenever she thought of America she saw that limitless high blue sky and heard its bright brassy fanfare.

Outside, here, the clouds seemed to push in at the window, grey mist blotting out the light and air like gloved hands pressing over her face.

"Desolate," Mommy said. "Looks like good ghost story scenery."

"There are a million of them in Dartmoor. Druids, witches, pixies. The folk round here are quite fanciful."

"Dartmoor?" Lars asked. "That's where we're going?"

"Mmm, my house is in a little village just outside the moor."

"Isn't there a famous penitentiary there? The boys at school were telling me about it, some horrible legend, or escape—"

"There was, yes, some time ago. But the moor is lovely, if you like walking and climbing. It's a royal park."

"What horrible legend?" asked Nell.

He glanced at her. He shook his head.

"What's a penitentiary?" Lottie asked Mommy.

77

"It's a prison, a place where people who do very bad things are locked away, so they can't get out and do any more damage," said Mommy.

"Like … a special school," Lottie murmured to herself.

Mommy heard her. "Yes, something like that."

"Tell us the ghost stories, then, Rory, if you aren't going to tell us about the prisoners who got out and murdered all those little girls," Nell said, peeking sly at Lottie. "The ones they cut up into pieces, after they—"

Lottie didn't even bother to smile. "I heard that story already, Rita told me it." She chewed at the Atlas again, surreptitious, ducking down so he could not see her through the rearview.

FOURTEEN

BY THE TIME ALL THE SANDWICHES WERE EATEN, Rory was driving up a long gravel road toward a building on a hill with a lot of windows and turrets. To Lottie it looked like the Tower of London, a penitentiary, she now knew, where the little princes had been locked away before they were killed. England seemed to be full of such stories.

"Good Lord, Rory, this is where you live?" Mommy laughed, but Lottie could hear the uncertain surprise in her voice.

"It's where I grew up. It's only my parents here now."

"You never told us you were royalty."

"It's a drafty old heap of stone. Good for playing hide and seek." He smiled back at the girls. "And for ghost stories, that too."

He stopped in front of the house and they piled out. Mommy stood, stretching, taking in deep gulps of the air. "Oh, it's so fresh here! It's so good to breathe!"

"Yes, away from the smog." He opened the boot and took out their meager collection of satchels and the suitcase Mommy had brought from America. "Lend a hand there, Lars, good lad."

A woman came out of the house, grey-haired, wearing a brown tweed skirt and a cardigan as baggy as Lottie's. Her face was crinkled up in a broad smile.

"Rory! Darling!" She enveloped him in an embrace that rocked him against her slightly. Watching this made Lottie's teeth hurt again and she clenched them tighter.

79

"Hallo, Mum, these are the Arkwrights. Althea, this is my mother Evelyn."

"Hello Althea, children!"

A large dog bounded out and leapt at Rory. He laughed and swatted it down. "Happy. Jump on these children. They're your new friends."

"It's so good of you to have us, Mrs. Eswyth, we really appreciate your hospitality—"

"It's Evelyn, dear. Lovely to meet all of you. Rory's talked of nothing else all this autumn. Now which of you is the prodigal pianist that has him so excited?"

"My daughter Charlotte." Mommy's voice was proud as she put a hand on Lottie's head.

Mrs. Eswyth looked closely at Lottie. "Oh. Rory. Her hair is the colour of Sara's."

He nodded. "I know."

After what felt like a long time studying her, Mrs. Eswyth led the way into the house. They traipsed after her, Happy the dog alongside. It looked a bit like Wendy's house only much bigger. Lottie stayed close to Nell. She didn't want to get lost in here.

Mrs. Eswyth stood in the middle of the biggest room. "Now let's get you settled. Our Mary's in the kitchen putting the finishing touches on dinner, so if you want to get in a quick walk it's best to do so now."

"I thought Lars would enjoy Colin's room, if he isn't coming down?" said Rory.

"He might be, just to Sunday lunch with Lucy, not to stay."

"Colin's my elder brother," Rory said. "He's a camera maniac, Lars, with ever so much equipment and photographs stashed in his room."

"Smashing!"

"Althea, I'm sure you'd like the rose room," said Mrs. Eswyth. "And the girls can choose between Sara's and the yellow room." She smiled at them. "I must say, it's nice having children in the house again."

"You're very kind," murmured Nell, suddenly acting like Mommy.

80

"Right, then, Rory, show them up. We have drinks about five thirty, does that suit?" She turned into a nearby hallway. "I'll just see to dinner."

"I'm in a novel," Mommy told Rory, taking his arm. "A forties novel! Mythical moors, dogs named Happy, rose rooms and yellow ones, kindly mothers and handsome sons, drinks at five-thirty."

He laughed.

"Can we live here, please?" Mommy teased.

"I think you'd find the local schools a bit … sub par."

"How were you educated?"

"We had tutors, here, and then later we were at boarding school. Come along, Charlotte, I'll show you the famous doll collection, and we can put paid to your mother's tireless efforts at becoming a couturier." He said this as if he was joking, but Lottie didn't know what he meant. He reached to hold her hand. "You'll think you're in a toyshop, and Polly will think she's in an orphanage where she can adopt any sisters she likes."

She took her hand back. Orphanages were for children who had no parents, no-one to look after them, like being in Care. She didn't want Polly anywhere near. But she followed him upstairs with the others.

Lars was left crowing about the big room he was in, and Mommy exclaimed over her pink bedspread, curtains, chair and rug. Rory opened the door next to it and stood in front of an all-yellow room, with windows that looked over a garden. "Would you like this one, Eleanor?"

"It's perfect for me!"

Lottie moved to go in with Nell, but he held her close.

"I've a special room just for you, Charlotte, where the dolls are." He took her hand again and led her down a long carpeted hallway. He opened a door into an all-white room, so dazzling it looked like snow, with a view out the window of endless grey-brown ground studded with whitish rocky bits.

"Look, darling."

81

As he'd said, there were shelves of dolls, in a glass-fronted case. There were dolls in dresses of every colour, baby dolls wrapped in bankets, a boy doll in a kilt and another wearing an army uniform, and ones dressed in costumes of different countries. There was a doll with a bicycle and one pushing a pram. There was a bobby.

Lottie stood close, inspecting every detail, feeling delight spread through her.

"But there isn't anyone like Polly," she said, turning to him with a smile she could not contain.

"Well, of course not. There could never be another Pollyanna. But look." He opened the case, and took out one of the bigger ones, dressed for winter in a long velvet cloak. "Polly can have this one's gloves. She'll never miss them, it isn't winter inside, and I think they'd fit Polly's hands perfectly, don't you?"

Lottie untucked Polly from under her arm, where she'd been lodged all day, and took the winter doll. As she tried to get one glove off, the doll slipped from her hands and fell to the floor. Lottie froze. What if she was one of the porcelain ones, like Wendy had, which could break? Would he get angry again?

But he was already retrieving the winter doll, already going to sit on the bed. He patted the space beside him. "Come here, love, let's kit Polly out. Would she like the cloak as well, d'you think?"

Lottie clambered up next to him and took off the gloves.

"How about the boots, then, they're 'cute,' as you Americans say."

She pulled the velvet gloves over Polly's hands. Polly had no fingers anymore, so the gloves stuck out on her hands like rooster combs. The winter doll's face looked haughtier and haughtier as she was stripped of all her clothes, and Polly took on a somewhat stuffed air as she became padded. "Look at her now, Master Rory, she looks ever so fat!"

He laughed with her. "Lottie," he said then, using her nickname for the first time, "please, won't you call me

Rory? We needn't be so formal with each other, we're close friends now, aren't we love?"

She stopped playing and looked up at him, looked to see if the gleam was there in his eyes, ready to scramble off the big soft bed and run down the hallway. She suddenly wondered why she had to stay here all alone, anyway, far away from Nell and Mommy. She'd never slept alone in a room by herself in her life. She shifted away from him.

But he was smiling at Polly. "She still needs a hat, wouldn't you say, let's find one for her." He waved his hand toward the glass case. "Pick one out."

It seemed funny to her suddenly, a boy who liked dolls. Stevie wouldn't have been caught dead. *Not bloody loikely, mate.*

"So this was ... Sara's room?"

"Yes." He looked at her.

She looked back for a long time, wondering should she say something, wondering was he sad, to be reminded of his dead sister.

His eyes got darker, the way they did, but he didn't move. The now-naked winter doll lay loosely in his hands.

"How old was she?"

"When she died? About your age. She was in a boating accident at camp, the summer before last, and she wasn't a strong swimmer."

"Do you ... miss her very much?"

He nodded slowly, still staring at her. "But I miss her less, since I met you."

"Mas—Rory," she began, feeling shy with him all at once. "I am sorry, about what I said that day, when you brought the dress. It was unkind."

"It's all right. Nothing you could ever do would bother me."

She felt uneasy again then, but he sat still, only his look reaching out to her.

Nell came in. "Good grief!" she exclaimed when she saw the dolls. She was always coming home with funny new phrases, these days. "It's like a museum!"

83

"If you see one you like, Eleanor, take her. You can have any of them. And let's be sure to collect as many dresses as you'll need for that blasted play."

"You swore!" Nell rounded on him, laughing. "You have to be punished now!"

"No, that isn't bad, blasted, it's just a saying—"

Nell pounced on him suddenly, pretending to wrestle with him as she did with Lars sometimes, and he fell back on the bed, taken by surprise perhaps, chuckling. "Come on, Lottie, let's get him, let's tickle him to death."

Lottie looked at the way he was sprawled under Nell, the way they twisted together, laughing, the naked doll slipping to the floor, fatter Polly bouncing as they wriggled on the white counterpane.

She felt a sharp stabbing in her teeth and she realized she was clenching them so tightly that one was cracking, she could sense the jaggedy point poking into her tongue. She tumbled off the high, fluffy bed and ran down the hallway.

"Mommy! Mommy!"

Mommy came out of the rose room, her face frightened.

"Lottie, you're bleeding!"

She led her into the bath, behind a door in the rose room. In the mirror Lottie could see a trickle of blood running down her chin. "Rinse out, let's see." Mommy peered into her mouth, once Lottie had spat. "It's okay, honey, it's just a lost tooth."

But Lottie couldn't stop crying now, shaking in Mommy's arms.

"Charlotte," Mommy said after a moment. "You never cry, why are you so upset? You've lost teeth before. You have all the tooth fairy money. What's wrong?"

"There isn't any tooth fairy," she sobbed. "Even I know that."

"Are you afraid she won't find you here, away from home?" Mommy kissed the top of her head. "I promise, she'll come visit you tonight."

"I want to sleep here with you."

"But you have that gorgeous white room all to yourself, with so many dolls keeping you company, as if it was made just for you!"

"How do you know?" Mommy hadn't come in to see it.

"Rory told me about it." Mommy gave her a pat. "He thought you'd love it, and I don't think we should disappoint him, he's gone to so much trouble for us."

She sniffed, and washed her face, and let Mommy brush her hair and dab a little of her perfume behind her ears. Rory and Nell were standing outside the rose room door, awaiting the verdict, and they exclaimed over her lost tooth and put their arms round her.

"Father's a vet, he knows teeth. He can have a look, love, make sure all's well."

"And he can be sure to alert the local tooth fairy," Mommy added.

Lottie let them witter on as if she was a ruddy great bloomin infant. It felt rather nice, after all, being a baby again.

FIFTEEN

"I'LL GIVE YOU A DENTAL CHECKUP worthy of my horses tomorrow," Mr. Eswyth told Lottie, handing her a tiny glass of sherry. "But don't try to say my name," he added, with a smile just like Rory's infrequent wide one.

Why not? "Mithter Ethwyth," she tried, and he laughed.

"That's why, Miss, you'll have that charming lisp for several days now, until your mouth adjusts itself."

They were sitting in a room with a lit fireplace. The flowery curtains were drawn, shutting out the grey mist. Drinks and snacks were set out on low tables. Lars and Nell each had a sip of sherry as well, and a little bowl of crisps.

"Cocktail hour!" Mommy exclaimed. "Civilization!"

Mrs. Eswyth smiled at her. "London life can be awfully rushed, I always find. And you must be so busy with these active youngsters! It's a wonder you get a moment to yourself, to catch your breath. And Rory tells us you're a writer? How ever do you manage that?"

Mommy's voice lost its brightness, shifting to a tentative low tone. "I write while they're at school, and sometimes all night." She shot a glance at Lars. "I'm not usually even awake in the mornings. Lars gets everyone up. He's so reliable, I don't know what I'd do without him. And my Nell makes sure Lottie gets back and forth safely."

"I think the creative life, the artistic life, is quite a challenge. We've seen it take its toll on Rory." Mr.

86

Eswyth patted his son's shoulder. "Ever since he was a lad, it was the piano, all hours of the day and night. And it's that way still, whenever we visit him, he can only spare an hour or two before he has to rush to some performance or practise or lesson. Worth every moment of course, we're tremendously proud. But I don't know when he'll find the time for family life, once he's married."

"His wife will, no doubt, be very understanding." Mrs. Eswyth said. "In any case, he has plenty of time for all that."

Rory smiled. He sipped his drink and turned the glass in his hand, this way and that, catching the firelight that flared and shimmered next to him. Lottie tried it and her sherry slooped about, a little golden puddle.

"My husband didn't understand my writing," Mommy confided, to Mrs. Eswyth. "He wanted a spotless house and dinner on the table. He didn't care about art."

"Perhaps he had other qualities?"

"He was a lot of fun, when we first knew each other. We went out all the time."

"But it's different, isn't it, with children."

Mommy leaned closer. Lottie leaned too, following this conversation. "It all became quite impossible."

"How long have you been divorced?"

"Three years."

"Isn't it hard, raising them on your own? Was your husband able to help, in America?"

"We moved in with my parents, in the same town, so they stayed with him on weekends, sometimes, before we came here."

Lottie remembered. Some were ordinary weekends, when they did chores like painting the shed in their old backyard, and had a cookout with their old neighbours.

Some were more special, when Daddy took them into Chicago, to the museum with big stone lions in front. Mommy was wrong—Daddy did like art, his favourite was the section where people made of thin ink strokes stood on whitish paper screens, looking at each other with secret smiles "It reminds me of Japan," he told them. He'd been to Japan during the same war that produced the forbidden back garden bomb shelter at their flat in Hammersmith.

He liked driving with the top down, taking them to movies at the drive-in, getting them hamburgers at the new restaurant he drove right though called McDonald's, and practising baseball with Lars. He didn't talk with them the way Mommy talked. But when his Air Force buddies came over, and they sat late in the kitchen or the backyard, there were a lot of stories.

"Was there no way to make the marriage work?" Mrs. Eswyth wanted to know.

"His expectations, of me, just weren't realistic. I wasn't cut out to be a wife."

"So you've no plans to marry again, then?"

"No. I decided to follow my own way, a way that became clearer and clearer to me as time went on and my writing took shape."

"Well. That's admirable. And how did you decide to move to England?"

"Oh, I was told to come, last year. I heard the Voice."

"You were … following your way? "

"Yes, the way I'm supposed to go."

"Still … a shame they have to be so far away from their father now," murmured Mrs. Eswyth, peering into her glass. "Perhaps Rory's filling in, a bit, d'you think?"

"They have their heavenly Father."

Mrs. Eswyth looked up, startled. "I meant … your husband."

"That's not a shame. He's remarried since we came here. I'm sure he and his bride don't want to be saddled with all of them right now."

His new wife looked very happy, in the photos he'd sent of the wedding; her smile shone on Daddy like the sunbeams on Jesus, in the Sunday school booklets. The children had gotten a letter from her. Her name was Bunny, which Nell thought was silly and Lottie thought was sweet.

"Children do put rather a damper on romantic life. Especially when there are a number of years between them, as in your children, five years is it?" Mrs. Eswyth spoke quietly. "We felt a bit the same, Sara was such a late surprise! We'd gotten used to the boys being independent. Rory was already ten when Sara was born."

Mommy said, low, "I was sorry to hear about your daughter. I wanted to tell you. We're very grateful for Rory's friendship, and I hope in some way his closeness to my Lottie can ease a little of his loss."

"Perhaps that's why he seems so attached to her? He felt Sara's death deeply, of course we all did, but in a way ..." she looked across at the grouping around the fireplace, where Rory was laughing at something Lars said. "It's shocking to say this, I know, and I'm not sure that Rory would agree with me, but I do feel that God's will was evident when he took our Sara."

Mommy's eyes grew wide. She was an expert on God, and Lottie expected her to answer this with some pronouncement, but she stayed still.

"I don't know if Rory told you? Sara was very ill. She was born with a number of ailments, poor mite, I was much too old to have a healthy child at that age, nearly fifty!

"We did our best. But she was getting worse, often in hospital. I was forever eaten up with wondering should I perhaps find a special school for the handicapped, and worrying about what would happen when Miles and I ... went on, whether she'd have to go into Care. Rory was absolutely devoted to her, but his career was becoming demanding even when he was still at home."

Special school! Handicapped meant retarded. Backwards. Slow.

"Is that why she couldn't swim?" Lottie asked through her lisp. Both women looked down at her with expressions that said they'd forgotten she was there.

"That's right, love, she had very poor lungs. And the boating instructor didn't realize she had managed to unfasten her life jacket. She never liked to be restrained."

"She's an angel now?" Perhaps Jenny had been right.

Mrs. Eswyth smiled. "Just so, darling." She looked at her watch. "Shall we move into the dining room?"

SIXTEEN

IT WAS AS GRAND AS EATING ON THE SHIP. There were separate utensils to use with each new dish, and there was a lot of talking about the food and the different wines that Mr. Eswyth brought out. Mommy was laughing more than Lottie had ever seen, as were Nell and Lars, each served a half glass of wine. It was like the cheery atmosphere at Stevie's house, only sparkly, and the Eswyths didn't use jam jars to drink out of.

"You have jolly dinners," she said to Rory, who was sitting next to her.

"Can you eat without your tooth?"

"Mmm." There were mashed potatoes, Yorkshire pudding, and roast beef sliced so thin it was like eating wafers, and little peas that had to be chased round the plate.

"Lottie, I've been thinking about your progress. I've been wondering if you feel ready to give a recital."

"D'you mean ... on the piano?"

"Think of it as a way of testing your skills. You're comfortable with the keys, you're putting yourself into the music, and you're reading well for your experience level. I'd say you're ready, love."

She looked up at him. He gave her a tiny wink.

"I know we haven't seen much of each other lately, but your mother says you've been practising. This weekend I'd like to hear how you're sounding."

She didn't even want to sing Oh Little Town of Bethlehem in the pageant full of other children for two

91

minutes, how could she possibly play a set of tunes all alone in front of grownups? *Wot a bloomin daft idea!*

"The Conservatory holds open slots one Sunday afternoon a month just for young musicians, and there's a very friendly group who come to listen regularly."

"I'm not very good," she whispered. Didn't he know that?

"Nonsense."

"But Mas—Rory, I've only been playing since September."

"You're extremely talented, Lottie, you must believe me."

She looked closer at his eyes. What was he up to now? He nodded, still smiling, and leaned to whisper, "Don't stare at me like that, sweetheart, not here." When he sat back he said, "You can try playing tonight."

After dinner, in the room next door, stood the biggest piano in the world, shaped like a lake, its keys a beach on the shoreline. Its lid was held up with a long wooden pole and she stood on tiptoe so she could peer into its intricate heart.

From behind, Rory's arms lifted her so she could see even more deeply. It was like looking into another world. It made her skin tingle. Mommy should make up a story about a grand piano's insides, where all the hammers fell on their strings, like the line of ballerinas in Swan Lake. Nana had taken them to the ballet in Chicago. Lottie could picture their graceful skirts settling as they folded their arms over their heads; she could hear the notes rippling in descent as they glided down, one by one.

"Go on, love, sit down, see how it feels," he told her. He sat facing away from her, as if they were having an ordinary lesson. "Now."

She let her hands wander over the gleaming keys. They responded with a deep, rich sound that reverberated inside her like the giant iron bell at the top of Nana's church, and as she began to play her scales the clapper swung heavily round and round inside the bell in a cadence that made waves of beauty crash onto the keyboard beach.

She stopped once, thrilled by her power, and then plunged on. She played until her fingers shook and she sagged against Rory without even taking notice of him.

There was a silence, and then a smattering of applause. She turned around.

Mommy was beaming.

Lars and Nell both grinned and clapped.

"Bravo!" said Mr. Eswyth.

"Such talent!" Mrs. Eswyth cried. "You sound just like Rory did, at your age."

Rory clasped his arm round her briefly. "You're a marvel," he told her. "You're quite ready for Recital." For the first time, she didn't feel suffocated by his stare. She smiled at him.

"It's your turn now, Rory."

He took charge of the enormous instrument as if he were taming a massive ship tossing on a stormy sea, a sea that grew ever louder, more chaotic, more frightening, and then he made it slow down and become calm just like Jesus making the waves go away when he was out fishing on the Galilee with his mates.

Lottie watched his fingers fly. He glanced up at her once with a wild grin.

"Isn't it fun, Lottie."

But he seemed to forget about her after that, and he kept on playing, and when she got tired of sitting up straight on the bench, she sank into the nearest armchair. Mrs. Eswyth passed a tray of little cakes and she put two in her pocket for later. She was too sleepy to eat them now.

93

SEVENTEEN

SHE DIDN'T KNOW WHAT WOKE HER. She was lying under the covers in Sara's room, her nightdress on, Polly snuggled beside her. She barely remembered being carried to bed. Had the cakes gotten squashed?

She climbed down and looked for her dress. In the moonlight she could see quite well, and she found the dress on the back of a chair, cakes still in the pocket, a bit squashed but still edible. She ate them, savoring the creamy sweetness. Then she got herself a drink of water from the little bathroom in the corner. Fancy having a bath right in one's bedroom! *Coo-er. I'm right well in clover now, Stevie, I wish you could see this!*

Back in bed, she hugged Polly, and began to tell her about the day.

Polly wasn't listening. Her eyes kept being drawn to the window, where the mist had dissipated and moonlight was streaming in, where if she looked outside she would see nothing but undulating grassy hills like water. Perhaps it was water, of the sort Lottie was always remembering, from when she'd been on the big ship. When Polly wasn't looking at the window she was looking at the closet. She hadn't seen into the closet earlier in the day, and it had a look that somehow didn't sit well, as if the doors were not completely closed.

"Lottie," she said, but the daft girl was wittering on about sherry and Yorkshire pudding and her everlasting precious Master Rory, who she now was calling 'Rory' and praising his playing as if he was one of the bloody Beatles. Polly didn't like Master Rory. She'd seen what he

94

did to Lottie, and it made her want to hide under the covers. If he ever tried to touch her like that she'd bite off his feckin fingers.

"Lottie," she said louder, "shut the cupboard doors."

Lottie looked over at the corner cupboard.

Funny, she hadn't noticed it before.

It was massive, with scrolls all over it, writing or decoration; like something out of the big fairy tale book, like the closet the princesses went down into before they crossed the magic river to go dancing. It looked a bit ... queer, in the moonlight. But she didn't want to let her bare toes touch the suddenly treacherous soft white carpet to shut it. Something under the bed might snatch at her ankles!

Polly wouldn't shut up about it. "But you need to close those doors. Close them tight. You don't know what might be in there, what might come out of it."

Lottie wasn't afraid of some beastly old cupboard. She was tired. She was a big girl now; she could put herself back to sleep. She snuggled into the soft puffy covers and pulled Polly down. *Go to sleep Polly, there's a love.*

But ...

... if there were water all around, like on the ship ...

... the way the wind was howling, the water would rise, whipped into peaks like they'd seen on board one morning, when the First Mate kept the children away from the railing. "You don't want to get too close during a heavy sea, young maties," he'd said. "You can look, but stay away from the railings when the deck is wet."

The waves would wash up higher and higher. Polly and Lottie would see them breaking at the window in little crests of foam, and the power of the water would rock the house back and forth, gently at first, the way he rocked her at first, but then it would soon get rough, as rough as the storm-struck Galilee, as rough as his wildest playing. Lottie felt seasick just imagining it.

No wonder Sara couldn't bloody well swim, she thought suddenly. *Who'd bother trying to learn, in such heavy sea? Especially if she was as retarded as all that.*

95

Don't think about her! Lottie threw the blanket over her head.

But it was too late.

Now the idea of the dead girl was right here in the room.

If she dared take the covers down, if she dared look, she fancied big empty eyes would be staring down at her, long hair dripping in seaweedy fronds about grey shoulders, mouth black as a nightmare, gaping like a fish.

I've come back, Sara would say in a voice like the bottom of a well, *get out of my bed, get out of my room, get out of my house.* Her speech would be garbled, like children would talk in the special school, if Lottie told of their secret love and was sent away.

Polly piped up. "She'd ask for the doll clothes back as well, Lottie, don't forget to take my gloves off, and all this other white velvet rubbish, it's bloomin ot."

And leave my brother ALONE! Sara would boom. *I'M his favourite, not you!*

Polly tried to set her straight. Her voice came out sounding just like Stevie's. "But he doesn't leave *her* alone, see, you've got it backwards."

Lottie tried to shush Polly, shoving her deep into the covers, terrified that her blathering would anger Sara. She could just imagine the cupboard doors creaking open, one by one so slowly there could be no doubt it was bad magic, and all the drowned things Sara was used to, at the bottom of the water, would come sliding out, slithering over the cupboard threshold and plopping wetly on the carpet, sliming toward her like the snails in Stevie's back garden.

Lottie began to cry, foolish child, leaving Polly to try to work it out with the dead sister. "We never asked to come ere, see, her Mum's a bit loony, it isn't her fault." Polly couldn't imagine ghostly Sara the way Lottie seemed to be able to, but she went on, "Just let her sleep. She'll run away in the morning and you'll never see us again."

"Lottie?"

She very nearly screamed.

96

But it wasn't Sara's hollow voice, nor Polly's Cockney one.

It was Rory's.

She sat up, sobbing with relief, watching as he shut the door behind him and approached the bed. "Lottie, what is it, a bad dream?" He wore striped pajamas like Lars. "I'm meant to be the tooth fairy, don't be frightened of me."

"Tooth fairy my great-aunt's arse! Who wouldn't ave bad dreams in this bloomin ouse, with im creepin about in the middle of the night, an is dead sister gibberin and slobberin at the bedside! Bloody ell!" Polly wished she could talk out loud instead of just in Lottie's head; she'd tell him to sod off. Lottie's elbow shoved her aside.

"I thought it was Sara! She came in the window, or out of the cupboard, it was horrid!" Lottie didn't want him to see her cry, but she couldn't help it.

"Shh. Shh. There, love, calm down, you were just imagining things." He sat next to her and she threw her arms round him, hugging tightly, comforted by his familiar scent of Christmas and the solid feeling of his body, warmer than ever, in his pajamas.

His arms wrapped her close. "Listen, Lottie. Sara would never have frightened you. She'd have loved you just as I love you. It's all right now, darling, I'm here, you're safe with me." His soft laugh reverberated through her. "I've brought sixpence to put under your pillow." He took it out of his pocket and slid it under where Polly was.

She rocked with him until she could breathe again. "In ... the cupboard."

"That old thing, Sara didn't like it either, not at night." He went over to it and opened it wide, showing her that it was stacked with blankets. Then he shut the doors firmly until she heard a little click. "Hear that? Locked up tight. Now you can go back to sleep. Good night." He kissed the top of her head, and turned toward the door.

"Don't go."

"No? Shall I sleep here with you then, love?" His chuckle made her shiver. But she didn't want to be alone again.

"Yes, please."

"All right, sweetheart."

He opened the covers and lay down next to her.

His eyes were black as his hair, his face white, his smile only just visible in the moonlight. She closed her eyes so she could feel how gentle his cuddle was, and his kisses, and the way he smoothed her hair back. "I'm happy to comfort you, darling." His whisper smelt like toothpaste. "I knew you wanted me here."

"Mmm."

He began to stroke, slowly. "You like this, don't you, you like this quite a bit now." It was a hypnotic murmur.

Polly suddenly shouted, from deep inside the covers. "Tell im you don't! Tell im it's more frightening than Sara's ghost! Tell im!"

But he'd put Lottie under his bad spell again, the wicked wizard with his magic hands, and she was getting lost again in the maze that was supposed to lead away from his enchanted dungeon, like every stupid princess in all the obvious stories, going backwards instead of forwards, left instead of right. Silly goose!

"Lottie." It was the barest whisper. "Here, love."

His hand brought hers to show her what he wanted. She felt him sigh deeply, hot breath in her ear, just before she fell asleep.

EIGHTEEN

WHEN SHE WOKE, she was alone. Sunshine was streaming in the big window as the moonlight had done the night before. The case of dolls smiled brilliantly at her from their perches. She looked over at the cupboard. Locked up tight.

Nell came bounding into the room. "Wake up, lazybones, Rory's taking us to see the ponies! Get up right now!" She threw herself on top of Lottie and the bed jumped, making Lottie laugh. They bounced on it together, shrieking, flinging the covers about.

"Steady on, girls, you'll frighten the horses." He was there in the doorway, grinning, still in pajamas.

Nell hurled a pillow at him. "Dare you Rory! Pillow fight!"

He laughed and tossed it back, and the tussle ensued. For a few mad minutes there was a whirl of bedclothes and pillows and twisting bodies. Lottie ended up on the floor, watching as Nell sat on top of him, pummeling his head with the last pillow. He flung her off easily after a moment, and sat up.

"They leave for the higher moors in an hour, we must go quickly if we want to catch them." He stood. "I'll wake Lars as well. You all ride, I hope?"

Ride?

"I've ridden," announced Nell, surprising Lottie. "A girl at school showed me, when I visited her at the weekend. And Lars had a class at Waverley."

99

"Right then, we're off." He turned once, at the doorway. "Shall we wake your mother, won't she want to come along?"

Nell looked at Lottie and they shook their heads. "She sleeps in the mornings."

"Oh. Well, put on your warmest clothes."

Nell scrambled up and went out with him.

Lottie bundled into two jerseys and her trousers, an old pair of Lars' that she had to roll up at the bottom. The thick socks Mommy had packed made her toes ache inside her scuffed shoes. She hurried down to the room just outside the big kitchen, where coats hung on pegs and boots stood about on the floor. Rory was handing out mittens and hats.

"It's like dressing Polly," she told him, as he gave her a wool cap.

"Er. Right." Didn't he remember playing with Polly yesterday? But he was turning aside to inspect the others.

Out in the barn, he showed them how to dress the horses, who had enormous long faces looming with big teeth. Lottie stayed away as Nell and Lars quickly finished, mounted, and stood waiting. The horses' breath plumed out like smoke from their wide nostrils.

"They look like they're smoking," she said when Rory turned to her.

"Come along, Lottie, finish up with your horse, we can't waste any more time."

"I don't know how."

"You don't ride?" His unfamiliar impatience made her feel shy.

She shook her head.

"Right then, you'll ride with me."

"She could come with me," Lars said, as his horse seemed to dance about on the ground in eager little steps.

Rory studied the way the hooves on Lars' horse were moving. "Thanks mate, I think not, this time," he said. Then he picked Lottie up and set her on top of the biggest one, and swung himself up behind her. "Hang on."

100

The sight of the ground so far below, the snorting smoke, the rocking motion made her feel seasick, as she'd been the first day on the ship, and she stiffened so abruptly that she pushed him back.

"Steady on, Lottie!" His firm arm came around her waist, pulling her against him. "Don't look down."

Now she felt like the wooden lady lashed to the prow of an ancient ship. She closed her eyes and wrapped both her arms round his on her tummy.

"Take a deep breath, and look out at the moor." She opened her eyes, just a bit, to see what he meant. "It's lovely today. This is as rare a sight in November as you'll see in all of England." He kept talking like that, as they went, picking their way over rocky outcroppings and the waving grasses. She could hear Nell and Lars talking behind them, laughing as they got used to their horses.

"Now, see there?" He stopped his horse, and Nell and Lars stopped beside them. Just beyond the rise ahead they could see shapes in the tall grass, shapes like dogs, but as the shapes moved further away she saw that they were tiny horses.

"Oh!"

"Shh, Lottie, don't make a sound, you'll frighten them," he whispered.

They watched as the animals meandered this way and that, nibbling on the grass, nudging each other, watched until the small herd, no more than five or six, suddenly seemed to fly away up the hillside as if they were a flock of little birds. She heard his soft laugh in her ear. "Aren't they nice?"

"Smashing, Rory," Nell said, with the coy voice that she used on her friends. He laughed again.

"Are they ponies? Where are their parents?"

"Lars, they aren't ponies. They're miniature horses. It's like a glimpse into our past, they haven't evolved into a bigger species yet, but they've been on these moors since anyone can remember."

101

"There are little horses like this in America, on the coast, I read about them," Lars continued, turning round and heading back the way they came.

Rory made their horse follow. "There are a number of places in the world they exist, and all sorts of fascinating theories about how they got there."

As he and Lars carried on, she felt his low voice through her back, and she settled easily now as she leaned into him, getting used to the horse's walking motion. His hand was spread wide on her tummy, warming her. She closed her eyes again.

"Don't go back to sleep, Lottie, you'll fall right off!" Nell's sharp voice jolted her. "You have to pay attention, on a horse!"

"I'll never let her fall." His hand tightened, reassuring.

"She's such a baby, Rory, you should have made her try it on her own instead of clinging on to you like a rag doll!" She didn't know why Nell was being so shrill.

"Later, perhaps," he said. "I didn't want to spend the time this morning."

"I'm not a baby!"

"You are! You're afraid of everything lately, you've become such a ninny!"

She struggled up, furious. "I'm NOT!"

The horse flung his head back and took an extra step, it probably felt like a little step to him but to Lottie it felt as if the entire earth were rearing up. Rory's arm dropped from her waist and she flew up, striking his chin with the top of her head. He grabbed her again as the horse surged forward, gathering speed.

Lottie bounced helplessly, smashing down on the saddle with every other leap. She dug her hands into the horse's flying mane and hung on tight; but when she did, he gave a furious sideways snort, rolling his eyes at her as if he hated her, and ran even faster. His hooves rang out when he struck the white patches of rock and thudded deep when he pounded the grassy moor.

"Let go of him, Lottie, hold onto my arm!"

She couldn't let go! It was too frightening, being tossed about, she could feel the earth disappearing so far below it was like being right next to those slippery wet railings. She could feel everything sliding away out from under from her.

But his arm clutched her close to him, tight, so tight she finally felt herself lifting and falling with him, somehow matching the rhythm of the horse.

"Whoa! Whoa!" Rory wrapped the reins round one shaking hand; she could see his veins standing out, pointing straight to his suddenly prominent knuckles. The horse finally slowed to a bouncy trot before easing back into an ambling walk. The earth's tilting began to right itself.

"I want to get off now," she whispered. "Please let me down."

"We're just home."

Indeed, the barn was at the bottom of the hill. Mr. Eswyth was raking at a hay bale there, and he leaned on his rake and watched as they came to a stop.

"Rory! What's the matter?"

"He took a bit of a spook. Wanted to run off with us. I had to pull him up short."

Rory slid from the horse, dragging her down with him as if he had no strength left to lift her properly. She crumpled in a heap on the hay bale and watched as he led the horse back into the barn. She noticed his arms trembling.

"How's that missing tooth today? Can I have a look?"

Obediently she opened her mouth as Mr. Eswyth stooped to examine her.

When he stood back, his frown surprised her. "Come with me, lass, let's have a better look." She followed him into a room fitted with a big white table and a lot of shiny tools, like a doctor's office, in the corner of the barn, where he had her sit on a stool in the corner, and turned a bright light into her mouth.

"Do you grind your teeth?" he asked abruptly.

"Dunno."

103

Should she tell him about chewing on the spigots? It seemed such a babyish thing to confess in front of Rory, who had finished with his horse and was leaning on the doorjamb, watching them, arms crossed on his chest. His hair was tossed and he was still breathing heavily.

"You've got very thin enamel on your molar surfaces. You must be grinding at night when you're not aware. You'll want to see your dentist about this, love, I'll tell Althea."

He stood back and looked at her. His eyes were bright blue. His face wasn't like Rory's smooth one, it was crinkly with lines that she somehow knew came from laughing.

"It isn't grinding," she whispered. "I like to chew the waterspout."

"The ... waterspout?"

"I like how the metal tastes."

His kind face leaned down to consider her further.

"What does it taste like, to you, when you chew on it?"

She thought. "Sweetish, like. A bit ... salty?"

He nodded. "You know, Lottie, you might be doing that because you need to be eating different kinds of food. Do you know what vitamins are?"

Vitta-mins? She'd never heard that word. "No."

"Do you eat plenty of vegetables, at home?"

"We have ... potatoes." Those were vegetables, weren't they?

"Hmm. Well, lass, I'll have a chat with your Mum, perhaps a visit to the doctor is in order, as well as the dentist." He smiled the way Miss Dowd did, encouraging. "You want to keep your pretty teeth healthy. By the way, did the tooth fairy pay a visit?"

She nodded over his shoulder at Rory. "He brought me a sixpence."

Mr. Eswyth looked round, and saw his son. "A whole sixpence! What a generous tooth fairy we have in Dartmoor. Or should I say a tooth fairy emissary." He smiled again at Lottie. "Tell me, is the London tooth fairy as generous?"

She leaned forward to tell him, "Mr. Eswyth, there isn't any real tooth fairy. It's just a story."

"Good gracious me! Really?" His face looked surprised, but she had a feeling he was joking. She giggled anyway, liking the idea that a grownup would still believe.

He smiled back, and reached out as if to pat her cheek.

She jerked away.

His smile faded and he brought his hand down slowly.

"Whatever did you think I was going to do, child?"

She stared at the floor. There were bits of hay and dry mud even in the office, and the feeling of horses everywhere. She didn't like horses, she decided, even if Pamela was going to get a pony and put him in her back garden to give them all rides. She wouldn't take a ride. They were horrible, snorting, too-strong.

"Lottie?" Rory's voice came from behind his father. "What's wrong?"

"Tell! Tell NOW!" It was Polly's nagging voice. "Tell Mr. Eswyth, you can trust him. He won't blame you. He'll know what to do about the special school!"

Tell Mr. Eswyth that his son is nasty?

She looked at Rory, who was staring at her, still white-faced from their wild ride. *Was* he so nasty? He wanted her to do a recital. He cheered up Mommy and brought them food and bags of coal. He retrieved their Guy, he said they were close, he gave her the best room, told her she could have any doll she liked, hugged her and stayed with her when she was afraid, and didn't let her fall off the horse. *I love you, Charlotte.*

Polly. If I tell, I'll never see him again.

"You're a right bloody FOOL! He's doing something wrong with you!"

The warm thing? It feels nice, Polly, it puts me to sleep.

"You're a stupid bloomin ninny! Just like Nell says!"

She couldn't stand any more noise.

105

She leapt off the stool so fast that it fell over, and she pushed past father and son in a headlong rush to get out, away from their concerned stares and the cloying stench of horse, out of the barn and up the hill where the grass waved long and swished loud and smelt so sweet.

She careened down the hill, around the first set of tumbled-looking stones, into a strange rock shape where she could hide. No stares, no voices, no touches, nothing but Lottie breathing alone.

She didn't realize she was crying until her trousers felt wet on her knees, where her head was digging in. She fell on her side to curl into the deep forgiving grass that held no secrets.

NINETEEN

CLOUDS SLOWLY COVERED THE SUN. The sky turned from blue to grey, from windy to wet. She could see the spitting raindrops from where she was hiding, just under the lip of twisty white rock.

She heard people calling for her: Mr. Eswyth. Lars. Nell. Rory. But she didn't budge until she heard, at last, Mommy's voice.

"I'm ere, Mommy! Right ere!"

Mommy's anxious face looked over the top of the stone mound. Her bright yellow hair, so like Lottie's own, billowed about in the wind. She didn't say anything, just stared as if Lottie were as frightening a sight as the night-fancy of dead Sara.

"Mommy."

"You're here!"

"I'm ere, but I don't want them others. I was waiting for you."

Mommy crept into the small dark space under the stones. She wrapped Lottie in her arms. "Most of us thought you'd gone back to see the ponies."

"They're little orses." As if she'd want to see any horses again, after this morning's disaster!

"But Rory told me where to find you. He said he used to hide here himself."

"Mommy!"

Mommy rocked her tight. "Lottie, Lottie," she crooned.

She let herself slump completely into Mommy. Her stiff trousers and jerseys warmed up at last. Even her feet

107

went limp, easing the pressure at the toes of her shoes. She yawned.

"We've got to get you inside for a hot bath."

"No. I don't want to go in. Can't we just stay here?"

"It's too cold for us to stay."

"Don't care." Lottie's thumb, forgotten since she was about five, found its way back into her mouth.

"But the turkey is cooking! It's almost ready, it smells so good, and we're going to have such a delicious dinner. You've been out here all morning. Rory said you didn't even have breakfast because he wanted to get to the horses in time." Mommy stood as best she could, crouched under the rock, and took Lottie's hand. "Come on, honey."

"I don't want to go back there."

"But Lottie, why? What's wrong, sweetie, what is it?"

"I want to go home."

"But it's ... so *nice* here. Everyone is kind, and there's plenty to eat, and interesting things to do, and talk about, don't you like it?"

"I want to go home."

"But our home in London is so ... grim." Mommy stared away, and Lottie followed her gaze to the edge of the moor, rimmed by cloudy sky. "I thought it would be different. I thought the Father would show me a true sign, a clear path. But maybe there never is one, maybe that's the lesson, we have to make our way on our own."

"We can go to Israel *now*. We can go there instead of back to London. I looked on the atlas, Mommy, we're further west than London now, but we don't have to walk the whole way. We can get some tubes and busses to Southampton, and from there we can take a ship down to the Mediterranean." She had learnt how to pronounce this from Ursula, and she put Ursula's firmness into her proper English voice. "We'll get a ship that goes right to the edge of Israel."

"You've thought the whole thing through." Mommy's gaze returned to her.

108

"And there will be kind people on the way, that's what you said Mommy, and there will be interesting things to do, when we change from the tube to the bus to the ship," Lottie went on, hopeful. "This isn't the only good place, Mommy."

Mommy's eyes were getting wide with moodlike intensity. "And a little child shall lead them." She leaned her face so that it was right in front of Lottie's and she stared close and took Lottie's cheeks in her hands. "Oh Charlotte." Her fingertips were cold and a little shaky; a sign that she wanted a Kent.

"We can leave right away. We even have our satchels packed!"

"Charlotte. I think the Father is speaking through you."

Lottie didn't hear Him talking the way Mommy did, but it was as good an explanation as any for the urgency she felt, rushing through her as strongly as the fear had rushed this morning, when the horse was running away with her and Rory.

"Althea!" It was his voice. "Althea, is she there?" Mommy's moody expression brightened into one of alert relief.

"We're here, Rory!"

"No Mommy! Don't let him find me!" Lottie twisted out of Mommy's clasp.

"Lottie, honey, Rory told me you were frightened about the horse. And he told me his goal, during that wild ride you had, was not to let you fall. He was as scared as you! He loves you so much!"

"I don't *want* him to love me!"

But Mommy gathered her up in her arms and staggered out from the stone pile, bent over. The air outside was cold and the wind raged round like a biting dog.

"Althea, let me take her."

She saw him as if for the first time ever: slender pale face with black wings of eyebrows and hair, pink lips

109

tense, coal eyes staring into hers as if theirs were the only eyes in existence.

"Thanks, Rory," Mommy said, handing her over.

He wrapped a thick blanket round her and hugged her to him. She felt him galloping down the hill with her as the horse had done, his boots thudding on grass and striding on rock. She heard Mommy panting alongside.

She gave up struggling. She flopped against him, numb.

TWENTY

THEY TOOK HER INTO THE KITCHEN, where Mrs. Eswyth and her helper, Mary, made a fuss over her while Nell stood by.

"Lost and found, eh, missy?" Mary spoke in a broad twang that sounded so comforting Lottie would have liked to sit safe beside her in the warm kitchen the rest of the day. "So the moor dinna keep you today after all. The pixies let you go, as they let our Rory go, ever so many a time when he was a wee lad."

Mary put a bowl of thick barley soup in front of her at the table.

"Ay, he'd run off for hours just as you, missy, lookin for a hidie hole, runnin away from his tutor, so's he could collect his thoughts, I reckon, or hear the music of the moors." She reached over, to where Rory was standing, and ruffled his hair. "Did you hear it then too, lass, did it sing to you?"

She thought of the singing noise the grass made, over her sobs, the sighing of the wind when it curled into her stone tower, peeking at her and then whirling out again, flinging itself away as if disappointed when she wouldn't play. She nodded.

"That's right, missy, but you've got to look sharp for them pixies, ye're naught but a wee lass yerself, you've no idear what ye might have gotten yourself into." Mary handed her a slice of hot bread smeared with butter. The fragrance of roasting turkey and the heat of the oven made her feel sleepy. She yawned.

111

"Time for a hot bath now," Mommy said. "Evelyn, do you know how to make dressing?"

"Dressing?"

"It's made from the bread I set out to dry, you cut it into cubes, and add different spices, I brought some with me. I'll get them after I give her a bath."

"I can take a bath on my own." She knew Mommy wanted to show off her cooking to Mrs. Eswyth, she'd been talking about making dressing for the week leading up to this visit, and packing and then re-packing the spices she'd bought with the last of the Christmas check.

"Are you sure, honey, sure you're all right?"

Lottie nodded.

"I'm sorry about the horse, Lottie." Rory's eyes still had the hollow look as when he'd met them on the moor. "You must know, I'd never have let you fall."

"I know."

"Lottie, come and watch TV with us after your bath," Nell said. "We're going to watch Little Noddy!" Little Noddy was one of Stevie's favourites. He was a long-nosed elf, a bit like Pinocchio, who drove a car and always bobbed his head up and down.

"Mmm."

She went by herself up the staircase, down the long carpeted hallway, into the white room. She ran the hot water and watched it flow down, splashing and gurgling, but for once she didn't feel like wrapping her mouth round the spigot. She got into the water and let herself sink until she was completely covered.

When she came up to take a breath, she noticed a bottle of pink liquid on the side of the tub. 'BUBBLE BATH.' She poured in half the bottle and ran the water again, letting the pinkish-white foam billow up and up, until it covered the whole tub, like the story about the Magic Porridge Pot, which overflowed with porridge, eventually burying the entire village and three counties beyond.

She remembered her dream last night, about the water rising round the house, and the slithering things

112

coming from the cupboard, but instead of stiffening her with terror, the memory made her yawn again.

It was just an odd-looking cupboard.

And poor dead Sara was never coming back. *I hope you can have a bubble bath like this in Heaven, Sara, with the other angels.* Their wings might get wet, but perhaps they were like birds' wings, which kept the water from touching the birds' skin. She could just picture a flock of angels twittering and fluttering round a big white bubble-birdbath, on a puffy cloud, up there in Heaven, their voices joining in 'Ye Holy Angels Bright.'

Her fingers played the tune on the frothy surface of the water and she sang along, "And through the realms of light fly at your Lord's command, assist our song, or else the theme too high doth seem for mortal tongue." Lovely.

When the bubbles flattened she got out of the bath and put on clean clothes.

Time for another look at those dolls.

She was sitting on the floor by the bed, surrounded by them, all in varying stages of undress, when a tap came at the door.

"Hallo," she called, thinking it was Nell come to fetch her for the Little Noddy Show. She didn't get up. She didn't want to go downstairs.

The door opened and Rory came in. After she saw who it was, she went back to playing. The bride dolls were changing clothes with the ones from different countries. He closed the door and sat the floor beside her.

"Can I talk to you?"

She was having a difficult time unwrapping the brilliant scarlet cloth from the doll with the red dot on her forehead. The cloth was called a sari, which was from India, Miss Dowd said.

"I've said I'm sorry." But he didn't sound sorry. He sounded a bit ... sulky.

She finally got the sari untwisted.

"Look, Lottie, if you're unhappy with me about the horse, I understand. We needn't go riding again. But is

113

something else bothering you, about me, or about our ... our secret lessons?"

Why was he *talking* about it! She felt heat rise in her face.

"I mean to say ... I know you've liked it, especially these last times, and that makes me very happy." She dropped her chin, so her hair swung forward and covered her face. "No, love, you've nothing to be shy of. It's just ..." Out of the corner of her eye she saw him push back his own hair. "Other people wouldn't understand, about the way we love each other. They'd think we were doing something wrong."

His hand reached to cup her chin. He lifted her face, but she didn't want to look at him. "If you told my father, for example, Lottie, he'd make sure we never saw each other again. He's already suspicious about your mother, I'm sorry to say, he thinks she's not taking proper care of you.

"And if he felt strongly enough about it, he'd try to have you ... separated from her. So that you could be with people who'd do a better job."

She jerked her face from his hand. "*Mommy* does a better job than people."

"Yes I know love, I know how you adore her, and I'll try to convince him that you must all stay together. And I'll help as much as I can, I'll see to it you have proper food and dentist visits and so forth. I long to take care of you."

He was looking at her the way Daddy used to. She suddenly had a clear memory of Daddy hoisting her up, high above him, so that everything looked far away, but she knew she would always be safe in Daddy's arms and that he'd never let her fall.

"Never let me fall," she repeated to herself in a murmur.

"No, I never would. But if my father knew the way I love you, I wouldn't have the chance to help your family. D'you know what I mean?"

She nodded slowly.

114

"So I wanted to make sure that you didn't ... talk about us."

"Because I'd never see you again. That's why I didn't tell." Even though Polly had wanted her to tell Mr. Eswyth. Polly had shouted her head off in that horrid barn.

His eyes widened. "You *do* love me, Lottie."

She wondered, suddenly, why Polly had fallen silent. She hadn't heard her since the barn. She looked under the bed where Polly looked a bit neglected. She reached under, dusted her off, and asked her, "Would you like to try on this lovely red sari?"

"Red is the colour of brides in India, I think," he said. "Or perhaps it's a funeral colour, I can't remember. I know it's a lucky colour in China."

"We didn't get to China yet. Miss Dowd says we do Greece and India first."

He lay down on the floor, propping a pillow under his arm to lean on as he watched her play. "If we lived in India, I'd marry you."

Marry him? She looked at him again. He was smiling now, the haunted look gone from his eyes. He looked happier than she'd ever seen him. *Marry* him? She waited for Polly to shriek in horror. But Polly lay stiff in her hands, draped in the sari, eyes closed. One of her new gloves had come off. Lottie fixed it for her.

"But I'm ten." Soon, anyroad, and she was planning to write a letter to Daddy to ask for money for a party.

"Girls get married very young there." He sat up and took the sari doll, now half dressed in one of the white bride dresses, and did up the buttons on her back. He stood her up on the floor, next to the bobby, the only boy doll in the collection who wasn't small-sized, or a baby.

Bobby loomed over the sari girl; he was about a third again her height. He looked a proper groom, tall and dignified. Rory walked them along together. "Like this," he said. He leaned their faces into each other's with a little kissing sound that made Lottie snicker. He moved their

115

arms so it looked like they were holding each other, in a straight, stiff doll way. He lay them down like that.

"But he doesn't squeeze her too tight," she couldn't help remarking.

Rory looked up. "Too tight?" He studied her. "No, he doesn't."

He twisted the dolls round so the bride, Sari, was lying on top of Bobby. "Like this, then, so she's comfortable." Sari's nose pushed into Bobby's metal badge. Lottie reached over and turned her face so it was leaning on his heart instead, and she moved Sari's arms so they weren't stiffly pressing her above Bobby, as if she were doing a pushup like they had to do on Games Days, but rising up toward Bobby's head.

"I *lurve* ya, ducks," Rory said suddenly, turning Bobby into a Cockney, "an I sh'll make ya ever so appy, bangers n' mash or beans on toast every day, an all the choc'lates down the Waitrose." Lottie laughed. Waitrose was the enormous greengrocer's where they went shopping every month after the check came.

"An I'll ave a telly," Lottie answered, for Sari, "an a million new frocks, one for every day, an new shoes to match."

"Ow about a pony then as well, lurve?"

"Don't like them ponies. They might turn into orses, great slatherin beasts."

"Ooh, ducks, bit arsh, ain't ya?" Rory's Cockney voice suited Bobby perfectly. "They're ever so noice, once ya gets to know em."

"No." Lottie had Sari talk to Bobby firmly, like Rita told Jimbo when he wanted to bring home the stray mongrel dog from the park. "I won't ave no bloomin ponies round ere. And if I find em I shall make you take em roight out to the rubbish bin."

"Lottie!" Nell's voice came calling up the stairs. "Little Noddy's on!"

Rory looked at Lottie. "Would you like to try the piano again, after Noddy?"

116

The biggest piano in the world, right downstairs. "Mmm."

"Right then." He sat Bobby in the chair and then sat Sari next to him. "Come to find me when you're ready. I'll be in the room next door."

TWENTY-ONE

HE WAS ASLEEP when she went in, after Little Noddy was over.

He looked as boyish, asleep, as the photographs she saw on his wall; where he was on a horse, he was playing piano, and he was sitting next to a blond girl. She leaned close to look. Sara's hair was as pale as the buttercups that grew in the fairy ring down Stevie's garden, her dress as pink as the rose room. Sara's eyes didn't look right, though, she was staring like Mommy did in a mood, even though her smile was like Rory's.

"She was blind."

His voice startled her. Blind! She turned round. "I thought you were asleep."

"That's why her eyes look different."

She looked again at Sara. "Was she happy?"

"It was difficult to know how she felt about things. I tried to make her happy."

"Did you give her ... special lessons?"

"God no! She was my *sister!*" He reared up, looking as revolted as Jeremy, when Mr. Moore told him not to try anything on. He even exclaimed just as Jeremy had done: "What do you take me for?"

"I only ... wondered. If I remind you of her."

"Lottie, we have *our* lessons because we love each other. It's special that way."

He looked so shocked that she changed the subject. "How could she be in the wedding, blind? Wouldn't she knock into the people, and the candles, and the wreaths?"

"What wedding?"

"When she wore the white and gold velvet dress."

He laughed. "She didn't wear it. There wasn't any wedding, Lottie, I just made that story up so it wouldn't seem odd to Althea. I bought you that dress at Harrods."

Crikey! She'd never heard a grownup admit to a lie.

"Don't look so grave, love, it's perfect for your pageant."

Mommy had said that as well.

"But what if Mommy tells your Mum? Won't they think it's odd then?"

He shrugged. "They'll just assume the other got it wrong, I suppose, it hardly matters. Women their age are so forgetful."

"So, when I said that, about the dead girl's dress ..." she tried to puzzle it out. He *was* peculiar! "But you were bloody well pissed off at me."

"Lottie! That's nasty talk, coming from a sweet mouth like yours. Don't use that language, I've told you."

"But you were. You banged down the piano lid."

"I was fed up with how far apart we were, just after I'd made you feel good at last, don't you remember, the first time? You were so rude. You hurt my feelings."

"Well, before then, you told Jenny to try the dress on."

"I was trying to make you jealous, love, of course. Come here."

She went to stand by the bed. He was lying under a red blanket thrown across the bed, his arms folded under his head, eyes half closed. "Come up here, there's room for you to lie down, I won't squeeze too tight." He sat up and reached for her, pulling her on top of him. He wrapped the loose half of the blanket round her legs. "Give us a kiss, Lottie," he whispered. "I've been waiting."

She closed her eyes. She was thinking about how he bought the dress, how he tried to make her jealous with Jenny, how he treated her from the very beginning, and a question began in her mind.

119

Their first lesson, at the end of the summer, had been a disaster. While she was waiting for Mommy to bring him in, she'd sat half-heartedly at the new piano, straddling the bench sideways. She'd plunked at the keys aimlessly, bored, wanting to be out of the dim room and getting to China with Stevie. They were digging in Stevie's back garden rather than Lottie's because they thought the bomb shelter would fall in and block their route at an interesting juncture. By that point in the summer they thought they'd got more than halfway, and they wanted to finish before school started, so they could meet some Chinese people and tell their teachers and classmates all about it.

"They eat dogs in China, you know, we must ave a care of what's in the butcher shops up there," Stevie had informed her.

"Won't we come out upside down?" she'd wondered.

"No, we'll crawl out the ole and be right side up. It's gravity."

"Don't get there before I do, Stevie, wait till I come back from my pianer lesson."

She hadn't even cleaned her hands from the digging, and the first thing Master Rory had done was make her scrub them, hard, in the bathroom sink, standing beside her to make sure she got every bit of dirt. Then he helped her wash her face.

"There now," he'd told her, holding her hands in inspection, "doesn't that feel so much better? A pretty girl like you should always keep clean."

She took no notice, then, of the way he examined her, but she remembered looking up at him for the first time. He was all black and white, like the somehow dashing Jack in their battered old card deck: white face, black hair, white shirt, black trousers and jacket. The only bit of colour was his soft-looking pink lips. She thought she might like him because of that softness, and because he smelt like a Christmas tree and had a quiet voice. She'd thought he would be kind, even if he didn't look jolly.

But during the lesson she'd stopped thinking that. He was very strict, he criticized everything she did to the keys, and he didn't smile. She'd thought, scornfully and a bit afraid, that he couldn't be much of a teacher when he didn't even look at her hands, after the scrubbing and once he showed her what the keys were.

But she'd known this was important to Mommy, so she worked her fingers, and went slowly, and listened with her whole self when he spoke and when he played. At the end, after her tentative improvising, he smiled at her for the first time. He didn't look black and white anymore.

"Your playing is extraordinary. Quite amazing," he'd said in his quiet voice. His smile grew, in a way that made her know how much her music pleased him, and his eyes sparkled as he looked her up and down, slowly.

When he'd asked her to give him a kiss, friendly as Stevie's Da or Jimbo, she'd been happy to smack her mouth onto his pale, fragrant cheek, thinking that she'd done well and that he did like her, after all.

But he'd turned her face and showed her a different kind of kiss.

When, after the next few lessons, he'd stroked her, she'd squirmed about and giggled and tried to tickle him back, the way she and Nell always did, surprised that he wanted to wrestle with her like a friend instead of a grownup.

"Shh. We mustn't make a sound."

"Whyever not?" She wasn't used to being still, then.

"We don't want anyone to know what we're doing here."

"But why?"

He'd taken her face between his hands and looked at her with an expression more serious than anyone had since the day Mommy told them they were leaving Daddy in America, and coming to Israel. His look had alarmed her.

"They wouldn't understand. Don't tell anyone."

"Why?"

121

"It's our secret, all right? It's like a special lesson, just between us."

She'd poked at his side again then, to see would he laugh, would he tickle her back, but he took her hand away, holding it too tight.

"I need you to promise, you won't tell." He'd told her about the special school. That was when she began to be afraid of him.

This time, in his old bedroom, she didn't go to sleep afterwards. She rolled away from his side and stared up at the ceiling. "Master Rory, is there really a special school? Was that just a story as well, like Sara's dress?"

He didn't answer right away. "Darling. It's ... difficult to explain. I told you, nobody would understand the way we love each other."

"Because I'm a little gel."

"Er ..."

She sat up. "I think there isn't any special school." It was as if Polly was suddenly back in her head, speaking plainly now, as Ursula would. "I think you made that up to frighten me. To make sure I wouldn't tell."

He stared up at her. "Lottie."

"That was very naughty of you."

"I'm sorry," he whispered. He looked quite frightened himself, like a little boy.

"Don't frighten me anymore."

"I promise I won't. But you must promise as well, darling, that even though we love each other, we must keep it secret. You do realize, nobody would understand."

"Until we get married."

"Er." He shifted under her. "Until then, yes."

TWENTY-TWO

THANKSGIVING DINNER was turning out a great success. Mommy's dressing was toasted by all, with the wine Mr. Eswyth poured, even a tot for the children. Lottie ate so much that she thought she couldn't manage any sweet. Mommy had made 'pumpkin' pie out of some sort of rooty English vegetable, that everyone took a polite bite of and then left on their plate, but Mary had made an absolutely smashing dessert called trifle, all whipped cream and light sponge cake and bits of fresh fruit.

"Why did you ever leave home, for London?" Mommy asked Rory, after moaning over how delicious the trifle was.

"Music," he answered simply, putting another serving of trifle on Lottie's and Nell's plates, on either side of him, and then helping himself.

"He left at seventeen for the Conservatory." Mrs. Eswyth added, "After that he came back at holidays, and then that time when Sara got so ill."

"We tried to convince him to go to university," Mr. Eswyth said. "But it was only ever music, and I must say, lad, you've done well with it."

"Thanks Dad."

"And your other son, Colin, is it? What does he do?"

"Our Colin's in publicity," Mrs. Eswyth said. "He says he's 'in the new media'!" She laughed.

"He means the telly." Rory looked at Mommy. "He does advertisements on television."

123

"But he's not the bloke showing off the cornflakes and shaving cream. He's the one arranging all that, behind the scenes, as it were." Mr. Eswyth said. "He's with an agency."

"So both of them are succeeding in the creative life," Mommy said, a bit wistfully, as if continuing the conversation they'd begun yesterday. "You managed that, somehow, even out here in the country." She stared down at her coffee cup.

Mr. Eswyth glanced at his wife. "We've a few suggestions for you, dear, as regards raising creative children all on your own. We can chat after dinner.

"I say." He pushed his chair back. "I heard a lot of practising going on this afternoon. Let's see what our musicians can produce for us in the way of entertainment."

"Can we watch the telly?" Lars and Nell were in heaven, a telly nearby at the ready, in a little room to itself. "Secret Agent is on."

"How ever will their lot, their generation, raise its children, if they've the telly on in the background all the time," wondered Mr. Eswyth as Lars and Nell hurried away.

"I should think they'd raise a right lot of idjits," Mrs. Eswyth said stoutly. "Dreadful clamour! We only bought it so that he could have a look at the occasional cricket match." She collected the coffee things on a tray. "Take the coffee to the music room, there's a love," she told Lottie.

Lottie carried the tray into the grand piano room and set it carefully on the table in front of the couch. As she went back to the dining room she heard Mr. Eswyth speaking, and his tone was so somber that she decided to stop at the doorway to listen.

"... regular visits. I know our National Health system can seem a bit daunting, so many forms and offices and so forth, but it's really quite decent care. I think you'll find it will make a deal of difference in terms of her overall developmental progress, not the least of which will be her confidence that she's being well looked after."

If he was going to suggest that Mommy have 'other people' look after them, Lottie would get her satchel ready, and Mommy's too. They could leave after the Eswyths were asleep tonight. She knew, now, exactly how her hands could put Rory to sleep quickly. The Arkwrights could steal back over the moor, past the ponies, and walk beyond to where there was a road; Rory had described the terrain to Lars on their way out this morning.

"The others seem fine, a bit on the thin side, but they're at the time of greatest growth so we'd expect them to be thin. Is shopping a difficulty, without any car?"

"Sometimes, although we've been so grateful to Rory for the times he's helped us with the heavy stuff. But sometimes the check doesn't come on time, and sometimes it's less than what we need!" Mommy gave a little laugh.

Lottie felt a jolt of disapproval, a strange feeling to have about Mommy; but Lottie herself wouldn't have let loose even one bloody hint about the check, even if Master Rory said they were family now. Stevie's family made do with beans on toast, and would never have dreamt of whining about not having money.

"That's difficult, then, seeing as it's not possible for you to work here."

"But with the children at school during the day, mightn't there be something part-time, in a nearby shop, perhaps?" She could tell Mrs. Eswyth was trying to be helpful.

"She wouldn't be able to get a work permit, dear, she's an alien."

"She needs to concentrate on writing during the day," Rory's quiet voice added.

"Ah, yes, the writing. What's your book about, then?"

"It's really a long narrative poem, about the life of St. Paul."

125

This seemed to bring the conversation to a halt. After a long silence, during which Lottie flattened herself against the wall of the adjoining hallway, lest they all come trooping out, Mrs. Eswyth said finally, faintly,

"That ought to be ... of interest, in some circles."

"Not much of a quick money-maker, though, I fear," Mr. Eswyth summed up shrewdly. Lottie heard the sound of the bottle being uncorked once more, followed by the gurgling of what must be another round of wine poured into the glasses. "I say, Althea, normally I don't think I'd be quite so blunt with a lady I'd only just met, but—"

Lottie thought he'd probably be just as blunt with anyone, actually.

"—your situation does seem rather to call out for some strong advice, and I hope you won't mind my offering it, only in the best of spirits, of course, I can't possibly presume to know exactly how it is for you.

"And I wouldn't be so bold as to speak up like this if I hadn't seen that child's appalling molars and the way she reacted to my attempt to pat her head. I suspect someone's mistreated her."

The bottle thudded conclusively onto the table top. Mommy gasped.

"You're an intelligent-seeming young woman. Yet you've chosen to bring three school-age children to a country where you cannot work, and you're completely dependent on your ex-husband, is it, and perhaps the kindness of your parents, and of friends, for survival. London is a harsh city when one has no money, we all know that, and I'm sure the school fees and so forth are significant, since you can't possibly be sending these children to the local comprehensives, not in the neighborhood where Rory says you live.

"You've spoken with us, eloquently dear, and Rory has as well, of your need for the creative life for yourself and the children: Lars is to be a composer, Eleanor a ballerina, and little Lottie a pianist. You've quite devoted yourself to that, and it's totally admirable. Evelyn and I were saying that to each other earlier, how impressed we are with you and with these marvelous children of yours. You've done much better than I'd have expected, under the circumstances.

"But your primary concern must be for their physical and emotional well-being, since their creative energies can't be sustained unless they're well fed and protected. The way that little girl ran off today, and stayed out on the moor for hours ... and only because I started to pat her head! She was like a puppy that's been beaten, cringing away from human touch. I know animal behaviour. That child is *suffering*."

A strangled sensation crowded Lottie's throat, and noisiness filled her head, as if her ears were being stuffed with cotton wool dotted with tinny little radios. She shook her head, fiercely, so she could keep listening.

"Charlotte?" Mommy asked, faintly. "I don't ... I can't imagine ... Rory, have you noticed that, about Charlotte?"

"No. She's quite affectionate with me." His voice, though soft, was very clear. "I think she'd gotten a bad fright from Airy, I'll never forgive myself—"

"—As if it was your fault! You couldn't possibly know Airy'd bolt like that," Mrs. Eswyth said in his defense. "You're an expert horseman."

"—I shouldn't have had her on with me. That's always a risk, I knew it, but I wanted to save time."

"Nevertheless, hers was an extreme reaction. I should think a thorough evaluation would be in order. She seems so young for her age. I should want to find out how it's going for her at school, with friends, see whether there may have been some contact that's been less than ... savory, shall we say."

"I didn't put her in school right away. She spent most of the year at the neighbors' house, playing with their little boy." Mommy's voice was taking on the high tone of a mood. Lottie longed to rush in and get her away from this too-close conversation, get her away from this train of thought. "I thought it was a good thing, to acclimate her to England, they were together day and

127

night, along with his sister and his uncle. She picked up their accent."

"A little boy? Not likely. At her age, sexual exploration between boys and girls isn't as common as in younger children.

"She's such a comely child." He went on, slowly, "It's a dreadful shame to think this, I know, but lovely girls, and even attractive boys, are sometimes the target of … interest, from unhealthy men, if they're not closely kept."

She heard gulping, heard the clunk of a glass being set down again.

"You remember, Evelyn, the shock we had about that tutor of Rory's—"

"Dad. Must we go into *that*." His voice was barely audible.

"In any case, Althea, I'd feel remiss if I didn't express this: I think you should consider letting the children's father know about your true circumstances here, or perhaps even consider returning to America so that he can help keep an eye out, so to speak."

The silence that followed this was deeper than the others.

Finally Mommy's high mood voice came again. "That really isn't … possible."

Mrs. Eswyth spoke up. "I can understand why it might seem difficult, to go back, if this was a statement of independence, dear, how going back might seem like defeat, especially since your husband, recently remarried—"

"We're *supposed* to be here," Mommy said, a bit more firmly.

"I think perhaps Althea's had enough advice." Rory sounded cool. "Eleanor's just about to take her Eleven Plus. Not a good time to make a move."

"Not right away, Althea, that isn't what I meant. But if, in time, you're still finding it rather a bit much, why then perhaps it's a sign that—"

"It's a sign that we have to go on to Israel," Mommy said softly.

"Sorry, did you say ... Israel?"

"The Holy Land, yes. It's where we're headed. It's where He wants us."

Now there came the sound of a chair being quite definitively, leavetakingly scraped back. Lottie had to scurry into the music room; she heard Rory's voice but could not understand what he was saying. She sat at the piano and heard his 'now' quite clearly in her head, however, and she began to play, as carefully as she'd ever done.

She did her scales again. Then she did 'Jesu Joy of Man's Desiring' that he'd taught her after 'Claire de Lune.' Then she tried a lovely new one he'd been showing her for the last few times, 'Pachelbel's Canon.'

When he'd played it, showing her how, she wanted to close her eyes, it was that beautiful; but she kept them open to watch his fingers on every ringing note. She tried closing her eyes now, though, imitating the way he played, just to see could she hit the right keys without looking.

The measured tune, a bit like scales itself, seemed to rise up from the heart of the piano into her fingertips and flow into a swelling river.

There was a bass line that wandered slowly up the river in a straight path, and a melody line that circled round it, winding, stopping in sunlit pools and dappled glades, dipping into the water, climbing out onto the banks, always coming back to the path.

She felt water prickling at the edges of her eyelids; she blinked it back and kept on, sure there would be such relief in the finishing of this good song that she might well never have to feel that burning of tears again.

At last she picked her way, very slowly, to the last notes.

She let them ring out, let all the majesty of the grand piano take them to their final resonance in the corners of the room, before she let her hands drop and lie in her lap.

Then she was able to hang her head down, resting it, and let relief swoosh out. *If I can do this then nothing else blooming well matters.*

When she opened her eyes, and swiped at her cheeks with the backs of her hands, she realized there was a sensation behind her of listening, of an audience.

She turned round. There were the Eswyths, Mommy, and Rory—standing at the doorway, looking at her with similar expressions of amazement.

"Oh, Charlotte." Mommy's voice was hushed, but not moodlike.

"Jolly good teaching, son." Mr. Eswyth approved.

Rory sat down next to her on the bench and took her hands in his. "I'd like to hear you try that on my grand in London. You are *absolutely* ready."

TWENTY-THREE

IN THE NIGHT, she felt the bed sink when he joined her. Afterwards, turning over half in dreams, she wondered why he'd gone, why he didn't just sleep beside her, after all, if they were going to marry; it was rather nice, being cuddled close in the dark. But she was so tired; the thought faded, and she slept.

The sun was shining once more this morning, on the dolls still scattered about the carpet. She had a long playtime putting them to rights and setting them back inside their case, exactly as they'd been before. Even though he'd said she could have any, or at least as many of their dresses as she liked, she didn't want to take them.

"No new clothes after all. You'll just have to make do," she told Polly.

"As will you," Polly replied. "I've seen what's been going on in this bed."

"You're not allowed to be rude to us, Polly."

"Ye don't want to hear what I might have to say, missy, and that's the plain truth of it." The doll had taken to imitating Mary.

"He loves me," Lottie declared. "We're to be married."

"It'll be a sorry day when you reap what ye shall sow, missy, a sorry day—"

"None o your beeswax, dolly-bird, now shut ya face."

"Are you talking to yourself again, with that doll?" Nell bounded in and snatched Polly. "Ha ha ha! I'm the wicked witch of the west! I shall turn you into a frog!"

131

Lottie grabbed the winter doll out of the case and waved her threateningly at Nell. "I am the Snow Queen, and I rule this room," she said in Sara's hollow voice. "Put Pollyanna back under the bed where she belongs."

Nell looked up in astonishment. "Does she belong under the bed now?"

"I can't bloody well sleep with the loikes o'them!" Polly was talking out loud now, for the first time, in front of Nell. "The carryin on! The gigglin and shakin!"

Lottie frowned at the doll. "That's nasty talk, coming from your pretty mouth," she told her. "I've told you not to use that kind of language! However do you get these dreadful ideas!"

"Lottie," said Nell, leaning close, "what are you talking about? Did you hear the Eswyths, in bed? Were they ... doing it!"

"What are *you* talking about, Nell? Doing what?"

Mommy's head poked round the door. "Mary's making oat cakes with clotted cream! Come on down quickly!"

Oat cakes? Clotted cream? They stared at each other for a moment after Mommy left. Then Nell made a retching noise, and Lottie got the giggles. They rolled about, gasping and holding their stomachs. "Clotted cream!" one would say, and the other would moan, "Oat cakes!" and that would set them off again.

"I say," came from the doorway, "are you making fun of one of our cherished Dartmoor traditions?"

They jolted up to look at the speaker, whose tall frame lounged against the jamb. "I'm Colin Eswyth, sent to fetch you for a lovely meal, for which you're obviously ungrateful. Wretched Americans. No taste whatsoever." The twinkle in his deep blue eyes, just like Mr. Eswyth's, belied his sarcastic slow drawl. He took a step into the room, surveying them. "Hallo! You girls are as pretty as everyone says! Who's who?"

He was dressed in a raincoat like the one the Secret Agent wore, and his hair was shiny black like Rory's, and

132

his grin was as genuine as Stevie's. He looked a roight bloke. But Lottie wasn't ready to smile.

Nell did, though, jumping up and announcing, "I'm Nell! And this is Lottie. We weren't really making fun, it's just the words sound so silly—"

"Oh I know, I heard it all the way upstairs. OAT CAKES! CLOTTED CREAM!" His sudden shout brought fresh chortles from Nell. "You've put me right off my feed, I must say, damned shame, I'd been looking forward to it the whole drive."

His grin swept over both of them again. "Lovely Lottie and Elegant Eleanor, I'm to tell you to get dressed and come down. You can eat blooming cornflakes, as far as I care, more OAT CAKES for me and Lucy!"

"Who's Lucy?" asked Nell.

"She's my fiancée, but don't be upset, you can be my other one."

Nell giggled.

Colin told Lottie, who still regarded him without a smile, "Not you, Primrose, I heard you're Rory's prodigal sweetheart, so don't be flirting with me like that."

She let her hair slide down to hide her face.

"Ah yes, it's always the shy ones, still waters ..." He turned away, wittering on as he went down the hallway. "Hurry down, dollies, before it's time for lunch, clotted cream with ham, ooh."

Nell grinned at Lottie. "Aren't they great, I wish we could stay here with them forever. This is the happiest I've been in England. I love this family."

Lottie looked at Nell's glowing face.

"Come on! I don't want to miss a minute." Nell hurried away.

Lottie put the last of the dolls away and closed the case.

The door clicked shut.

Locked up tight.

She stood in front of the case, hands behind her back, swaying back and forth, giving them another survey. It was like a toyshop, indeed, as he'd said.

"Take any you like, he said you should," Polly suggested. "That little boy with the kilt. Or the one pushing the pram. Or just the pram itself, so cute, he'd let you take them all as long as you ..."

Polly was lying down. She was the kind of doll whose eyes closed unless she was upright, but Lottie fancied she could see her eyes open, gleaming maliciously.

Lottie's foot swung out to give Polly a kick, and she went spinning under the bed. "That's where you belong! Stay there!"

She whirled away out of the room and ran down the hall, down the stairs.

She stumbled into the kitchen and almost tripped over Rory, who was sitting backwards on a chair near the doorway, arms dangling over the chair back, laughing. Two grownup girls were half-sprawled on the table, doubled over in laughter. Nell was laughing too. Mary was smiling as well. She caught Lottie's bewildered eye.

"It's our Colin, Lottie, he's always been ever such a clown."

Colin gave Lottie an exaggerated wink. "They're just slow, Primrose, they'd laugh at anything, given enough OAT CAKES. Pack of loo-OO-oonies." He waved his finger round his ear, to indicate how loony.

One of the girls, the one with dark hair, held out a slim hand to Lottie over the table, and smiled through watery eyes, still giggling.

"Hallo, I'm Lucy, I'm the one loony enough to actually think about marrying this nutter. You must be Charlotte."

Lottie gave her hand the littlest shake.

"And I'm Annabel," drawled the other girl, who was as blond as Lottie. She blinked huge blue eyes at her, but didn't offer a hand. "Friend of the loonies here for years, I'm afraid, bad taste."

"It's a wonder you keep turning up, now Colin's taken," Rory said, looking up at her from under his long fringe of hair. His mouth curved half-smile, half-sneer.

Lottie thought his remark sounded rude, but it made Annabel laugh.

"P'raps I've set my cap for *you* again, Rory," she told him. She reached over to flick his hair aside. He jerked his head away, but his mouth stayed in its crooked smile.

"Nonsense, Annabel only comes for the oatcakes. She's actually yearning for Mary here, nursing a secret pash all these years," Colin said.

They all laughed again. Lottie stood on one foot, then the other, not knowing where to put her hands or where to look.

"Lottie, try an oatcake," Rory said suddenly, as if he'd just noticed her. She shook her head. She would have liked to get cornflakes, but she felt shy in front of all these strangers. She hunched her shoulders so that her hair fell about her face again.

"My word," Colin murmured. "She's a sort of ... presence, I daresay ...a bit ..." He came close to her and she backed away to the door. "No, Primrose, don't be so *boringly* shy, I just want to have a look at you."

As he walked round she felt the prickles of his scrutiny like measles all over her body. Then he looked at Lucy. "Wouldn't she make the perfect Dandy's girl?"

"Mmm, no, she's more ... Alice in Wonderland? Long hair, dreamy eyes, that wistful look ... rather nineteenth century, rather ... erotic?" Lucy's gaze on her suddenly sharpened.

"Nonsense! That can't be the campaign, at least not in England!" Colin laughed. "No, picture her with shorter hair and a sharper expression. I see a wholesome Dandy's girl, clean, modern, wanting only the best, the very essence of consumer purity. Standing next to Mummy in the shop, basket on arm, earnestly looking up—" He suddenly reached under her chin and lifted it. "Can you speak, Primrose, can you say 'Mummy, why ...'?"

She had to stare right into his bright eyes. She said nothing.

Colin's hand dropped.

135

Rory laughed. "You needn't listen, love, he's always rabbiting on like this, trying to rope everyone into his adverts." He looped his arm round her waist, pulling her close, next to the table. "Try this. It's good." He spread what looked like a pancake with red jam and a spoonful of what looked like whipped cream. He held it up to her mouth.

After the first bite she took it from him to finish the rest.

"Here." He held out the mug in front of him. "Milky, lots of sugar, just the way you like it." She drank, grateful to wet her dry throat.

Colin was watching. "This is brilliant. Even better than Mummy. She's with her ... uncle, since you're too young to be her dad ... but perhaps you're her older brother! So you're at the shop together and she wants to buy some. So you tell her—"

"Put a wet sock in it."

"—no, Rory, be nice, you tell her, Well, love, it must be Dandy's. And she says, Why? And, after a breathless pause, you answer." He began to pace the kitchen. "Or, no. *She's* the one answering. *She* must say—"

"Say what?" Mommy came in from the outer door, the one that led to the garden.

"Mrs. Arkwright, your daughter, she's perfect for my new campaign. Would you consider allowing her to lend her talents toward the artistic interpretation of a rather grand new sweep of commerce in the land?"

"Artistic ... interpretation?" Mommy looked bewildered, but hopeful.

"Sweep of *commerce*, Althea," Rory repeated in a dry voice. "That's the phrase you need to remember." He added, "Mind you, there's money in it, might be one way out of your straits. For the time being. As long as it doesn't take time from her piano."

"I ... don't understand."

"He wants Lottie to act in an advert, on the telly." With all the grownups in the room, it still somehow fell to Nell to explain. "It's ever so exciting."

136

Lottie could tell she didn't really think so.

Perhaps Nell wanted to be Dandy's girl.

"I don't want to do it," Lottie declared.

"You do speak!" Colin tilted his head. "Whyever not, Primrose?"

"I don't like people looking at me," she muttered, wriggling close to Rory. "But Nell doesn't mind, she's a grand ballerina, not shy at all. Choose her."

Colin turned to study Nell. "Hmm, perhaps, perhaps, another vision of loveliness, more Anne of Green Gables than Alice, but ... *she's* old enough to be in the shop alone! Yes! Mummy sent her round the corner to collect a few things, and she's keen to ask the greengrocer why it's always Dandy's. Or, even better, he asks her. "

He walked over to Nell and circled her as slowly as he'd circled Lottie. "Don't laugh, my dear, it's quite a serious endeavor."

He faced the rest of the people in the kitchen, flinging his arms wide. "And the burning question of the day will finally be answered!

"Lucy ... pray tell, dearest love, why is it *always* Dandy's peas?"

Lucy stood. She cleared her throat. She stared out above everyone's heads. Her nostrils flared as she breathed in. She raised her arms and held them out like Colin's.

"Because ... they're not just *picked*, but *chosen*," she answered, slow and clear, stiffening even her fingertips in the manner of an oracle: as if celestial voices were speaking of peas, through her. Miss Dowd had read a Greek story about the oracle.

Mommy laughed, and clapped. Mary and Annabel joined in.

"Not just picked, but chosen!" Nell cried, eyes shining. "I'd love to be the Dandy's girl!"

Rory leaned his head on Lottie's shoulder, rolling his eyes up at her as if they now shared more than one secret.

TWENTY-FOUR

ANNABEL INSISTED ON BEING TAKEN to see the little horses' meadow, so they saddled up, even Nell and Mommy. In spite of Rory's insistence that she would be on the gentlest horse, that he would lead her so carefully alongside, Lottie refused to join them.

She wandered instead into the piano room and let her fingers just rest on the keys. She wondered how many other fingers had rested like this; long ones, thin ones, fat ones, lazy ones, old shaky ones.

Sara's, perhaps, even if she was blind.

Lottie closed her eyes, imagining she was blind Sara.

She let her fingers meander along as they found the 'Canon' again, lingering in here still from last night, and others as well. Some her fingers made up as they roamed and some were ones he'd taught her. She had no notion of time passing. It was a surprise to be called to lunch.

The meal was loud, with Colin and the big girls joking and nudging the children. Lars seemed to find Annabel more fascinating than the prospect of telly, as she divided her attention between him and Rory, on either side of her. Lucy spent her time drawing out Nell, coaching her on how to be a Dandy's girl.

"Sorry to spoil the party," Rory said when he'd finished his coffee. "I've a concert tonight, must get back on the road. Need to practise."

"Can't you practise here?" asked Colin. "On the old piano?"

Rory's mouth twisted as he shook his head, as if to say *not bloody likely*.

"I thought we'd visit the pub later, Althea and the kids would love it," Colin went on. "Billiards, bit of darts—"

"Don't they have school tomorrow?" Mr. Eswyth asked.

"We can get them back tonight, I've plenty of room in the Bentley. They needn't go right now, surely, it's only just gone two."

Mommy looked from Colin to Rory. "We'll come with you, Rory, you shouldn't have to make that long drive back alone."

"Very kind of you, Althea, but if you'd rather stay the afternoon it's perfectly fine with me. Colin's right. There's no need to rush off just because I have to go. Unless perhaps one of you would like to see my concert. I've a guest pass for this evening's performance."

"What a fine opportunity!" Mommy exclaimed. "Lars, would you like to go?"

Lars, perhaps anticipating an afternoon with Annabel, shook his head.

"Or Lottie, maybe, if children are allowed to use your pass, Rory?"

"Mmm, not a bad idea, exposing her to a concert. She'll need to get used to it." He smiled at her. "Would you like that, Lottie?"

"Watch you play?"

"Yes, actually, I've a solo this evening."

"I like watching you play."

His smile deepened. He looked over at Mommy. "Are you sure that's all right with you, Althea?"

"He used to take Sara, when she was well enough to sit still and listen," Mrs. Eswyth told Mommy. "Lottie will be fine there, I'm sure."

"I think it's a wonderful opportunity for her," Mommy said.

"Right then." Rory pushed his chair back, and put his hands on the back of Lottie's chair. "I shall bring her back to the flat at about ten thirty, I know that's late, but I won't be able to get away before then."

139

"We'll see you off," Annabel told him.

Lottie went up to fetch her satchel. She dragged Polly out from under the bed. "You'd better look sharp, missy, you've no idear what you're getting yourself into," Polly began, but Lottie stuffed her into the satchel headfirst so her voice was muffled. Downstairs, she took her coat off the hook in the little cloakroom, and was about to go back into the dining room, when she heard a soft voice. Annabel's.

"—ever call me in London, when you know how much I'd like to see you?"

Lottie peeked into the kitchen. Annabel and Rory were standing just inside the door. Their arms were around each other. Annabel put her face to his, so their lips touched. "You used to like me when we were young, remember our games?"

She heard his little laugh. "That was a long time ago."

She kissed him, Lottie could hear the soft sound of her kiss even though she could only see Annabel's back, and she could hear how Annabel's voice got low. "They'd be even more interesting, now we're older."

She saw his hands squeeze Annabel's shoulders.

She pulled her coat tight round her own shoulders.

"I've ever such a busy schedule just now, Annabel," he said. "And you know I've no interest in your social circle."

"I don't see why not. My circle would adore you. We could add to your fan base, so to speak, call it career advancement."

She saw, as he backed away from Annabel, how he smiled. "We'll see."

"I shall call you, then, Rory," Annabel told him as they left the kitchen. "We're not going to let you stay a hermit locked away with your piano all the time."

"We'll see."

Lottie put her arms in the coat sleeves, but her fingers wouldn't work the buttons. She felt as stiff as Polly, stiffer even, unable to talk. After a moment she followed them out to the front walkway, where everyone was standing now.

"Goodbye!"

"Good luck with the concert, break a leg."

"See you soon, sweetie."

Swift hugs from Mommy and the Eswyths while she stood still. It was like playing statues. She climbed into the front seat and held her satchel on her lap.

"Ready darling?" His quick smile. "Right then, we're off."

The scenery flew past, grey and brown, with flashes of white cloud and a few scraps of blue sky showing. The radio played more Beatles songs, ones she hadn't heard, as well as a lot of other music that sounded so different to what he'd been teaching her to play, sounds that she couldn't help but listen to, even as she sat frozen beside him.

"You're awfully quiet, love, what are you thinking?"

She let her eyes move sideways, to take in his profile.

As if sensing her gaze, he reached over to squeeze her leg. "I'm so happy you decided to come with me. We can finally be all alone. And I've been wanting to show you my piano, to let you try it, you'll be amazed at how you'll sound."

"You should have brought Annabel instead."

"She's not a bit musical."

"But she likes kissing."

He shot her a puzzled frown. "She's very kissy, yes, always has been—"

Polly seemed to speak up from the satchel. "You should have kept on with her then, mate, instead of starting with me."

His eyes widened. "Lottie—"

"She'd make a proper girlfriend to you. You wouldn't have to pretend all the time, as you must with me."

"Pretend what?"

"That we ... that you're just my tutor."

"I don't understand."

"Then you're *thick*."

141

"You're angry because she kisses me?" He laughed. "You're a better kisser than she was, at your age, you're better at everything than she was or will ever be, I'm quite sure. So you've no need to be jealous."

Jealous? The very idear. He was a right idjit. She didn't feel jealous, whatever that meant exactly, but ... *I don't know how I blooming well feel.* She hugged the satchel tight, to make sure Polly didn't start talking again. She looked out the window. He brought the car to the side of the road and stopped it.

"Look at me." When she still didn't, he reached to bring her chin up with a firm hand. She closed her eyes. "You're being very silly." She felt his lips move onto hers, felt his hands tighten on her arms. She pulled away.

"All right then, don't kiss me," he said finally. "But don't be jealous of Annabel." He turned the key to start the car again.

"You said you want to marry me."

His hand dropped from the key and he turned to stare at her. "Well ... er," he said slowly. "I want to keep you with me. I want us to do what married people do." He leaned toward her again, and now she let him hold her. "When I didn't see you, those last weeks, I felt ... so sad. This weekend with you has been just what I wanted. Didn't you like it?"

"I didn't get any dolls." Her voice was muffled in his coat.

"Whyever not?" He laughed, and let her go. "That's what we went for!"

"I didn't want to take Sara's things."

He stopped laughing.

They drove without speaking then, until the fields disappeared and the buildings began. Soon they were going through city streets again. He stopped in front of a tall building, got her out, took her up in a lift just like the one in Grandfather's office, to a flat that was one large, light-filled, squarish room. There was a piano even bigger and blacker than the one in Dartmoor, shinier, with whiter keys. Everything in his flat was shiny, in fact, every surface gleamed and there was a fresh scent in the air.

He showed her to a little cream-coloured bathroom. After she washed her hands and came out, he sat her on the bench.

"Now," he told her.

He was right about the piano. Even the simple scales sounded like bells, not the old iron church bell but bright silver bell-ringer bells, each one crisp and pealing, it made a shivery feeling run up her back. She played until her hands cramped.

"Now you know." He lifted her, but instead of taking her to the bed in the corner he bundled her into the armchair where he'd been listening to her play. The chair was still warm from him. "Listen, love, this is a concert preview, you can tell me if you think I'm any good."

The sound he made was so dreamy she had to close her eyes. It ran up and down like the wind on the moors, the way it parted the grass for the ponies, the way it swirled round the formation where she'd hidden yesterday, making a moaning noise like the sirens who sang that Greek bloke onto the rocks, in the story Miss Dowd told them. It was even louder than the ocean tune he'd played the first night in Devon. It was the music of the moors. The music of the pixies that he'd heard when he ran away from his tutor, Mary'd said, to hide in the same stone tower, like the runaway boy, Jamie, that Lars had found in the park that time.

After some time the pealing faded.

She heard him go into the bathroom.

She heard him pad toward her.

"Lottie. My darling love." His arms came round her, and now he did carry her to the corner bed, and laid her down on the white counterpane. This time he took off all her clothes; she saw he had taken off his own as well, and wore only a long bathrobe. She tried to squirm away; she didn't want him to see her naked, but he was stronger than she, and his hands were quick, and soon he was making waves splash through her and she closed her eyes, dizzy.

"Let's try doing what married people do." It was a whisper. He shifted so that he was leaning above her. She felt something poking into the place he'd just made warm. It hurt, waking her into resistance. She wrenched herself away, but he pulled her back, rough, and the poking began again, getting harder, turning into stabbing.

"NO!" She found the strength to push him off.

He fell back, panting, and then grabbed her once more.

"Come on darling, help me—" he slid her on top of him, but she felt the same stabbing stretch, a stretch that ripped into a scream.

A ringing screamed along in her ears.

It was a telephone's shrill ringing.

"Hush, Lottie, stop that crying!" He lifted her off him and bundled her into the coverlets. "Let me answer the phone, please, hush now."

She curled herself into a tight ball. It was sticky wet between her legs and she rubbed them together, trying to twist the pain away, sobbing into the pillow. She must be bleeding. She turned up the counterpane, fearful, relieved when she saw there was no blood, only a watery kind of film. Still, it hurt as much as when she'd cut herself at one of the American picnics, where the rocky stream was; she'd fallen on her leg and had to have five stitches. After the throbbing ebbed a bit she looked out at him.

"Latimer!" He sounded and looked frightened, standing stiff by the phone table, clutching the receiver in one hand and his robe in front of him. "I know, you told me you'd call, only it's—rather a bad time, actually, I just got in from the country."

Bloody feckin ell, he'd just tried to kill her and he was wittering on as if arranging a tea party. *Not kill you,* whispered a voice; strangely, it was Nell's friend Valerie's voice, from the time she'd heard them all talking about boys. *He was trying to make a baby with you. That's what married people do.*

144

"I told them to put one aside. You've only to pick it up at the box office."

She saw his hand rake back his hair. His fingers shook.

"That's all right. I shan't expect you before then."

He put down the telephone and dropped to the floor. His robe crumpled round him. He put his head in his hands, and she watched it sink lower and lower, as his shoulders shook. She knew boys didn't cry but this looked awfully like. Perhaps the baby-making thing hurt him as much as it hurt her?

Curious, and a bit sympathetic, she pulled on her discarded dress and crawled over to him on hands and knees like the baby he wanted to make. She put a hand on his shoulder.

His head flew back as if she'd slapped him.

"Lottie." He cradled her on his lap, and rocked her back and forth. She felt two hot drips on her back: yes, he was crying. After a moment he picked her up and laid her on the bed again.

"I'm sorry, love," he said in a thick voice. He swiped at his face with his forearm. "I hurt you. I know you weren't ready."

He wrapped her in the counterpane and patted her head. "Have a sleep."

She curled herself around the sting until it ebbed away.

When she woke, he was dressed in a suit even more serious than the ones he usually wore, with a big ribbon-like belt round his waist and another that he was tying round his neck, in front of a mirror by the door. She watched him. He didn't see her. He was frowning at the bow he was fastening.

We did the baby-making thing. The enormity of it didn't allow any other thought.

Polly spoke up from the satchel. "And he'll want to try it again, mark my words. Look sharp, missy, because this isn't India. He *can't* marry you."

"Shut up! Shut ya feckin face!"

145

He whirled round. The ribbon slid like water to the gleaming wooden floor.

"No, not you, I'm talking to Polly."

"My word! Your language!" He looked confused. "You're talking to ... Polly?" He looked round as if to find Polly. "What on earth was she saying?"

"This isn't India. You can't marry her."

His mouth was a perfect o, a surprised musical note, as he stared at her. She got out of bed, fetched the ribbon, put it in his hand.

"So you can't do the baby-making thing with her. You mustn't try again."

Now his eyes were equally round o's.

"I'm only saying, mate, she's naught but a lass."

"Oh Lottie." He sank to his knees and put his arms round her. He held her tight, she felt his face pressing against her front, it seemed he was shivering again. She touched his shiny hair, flicking it the way Annabel had done. She felt him swallow.

She was suddenly hungry. "Can we have tea?"

His chest rose and fell with a big shaky breath. "Yes. They usually have tea for us at the concert hall. I'll just finish dressing." He stood up. "I forgot I'd promised my friend Latimer the guest pass. You can stay backstage, you'll still be able to see me play, do you mind not sitting in the audience?"

She shook her head. He looked hard at her, once, before tightening the ribbon again round his neck.

TWENTY-FIVE

THERE WAS PLENTY OF TEA: thin sandwiches of different sorts and a huge tray of cakes and a giant silver urn filled with hot tea that came out of a little spout on the front. She filled a plate, and sat in an armchair in a cavernous area, from where she had a clear view of the stage.

Thick velvet curtains surrounded the grandest of pianos—lit by a single white beam, like God sending lightning onto the Ten Commandments for Moses to read.

The weekend's pianos were compounding for her like the three dogs guarding the copper, silver and gold in 'The Tinder Box:' as the story became increasingly complex, each dog had eyes bigger than the next, more ponderous, more terrifying in their dreadful stares. The soldier tamed them by spreading the old witch's apron for them to sit on. She wondered how it was that Rory so easily tamed the pianos, especially this final one: it loomed, massive, like the last piano ever made.

His fellow musicians were all dressed up: the ladies wore floor length glittery black dresses and the men wore black suits like Rory's. There weren't any other children, though, so nobody really took any notice of her old purple coat, that Mommy had given her money to buy from the used supply at school, and her faded cotton dress that hung underneath. Rory seemed to understand that she didn't want to be introduced. After a bit of chat with the others, he came to sit next to her.

147

"Sure you'll be all right here alone, darling, while I'm playing out there?"

She nodded.

She could tell it was time for the concert, by the hush that followed the noises of people gathering and sitting down. She heard a few musical notes from what he told her was the orchestra pit: she could hear, but not see, people trying out their instruments: a violin, a flute, a drum. Then there was a moment of absolute silence.

Rory put his finger to his lips, winked at her, and stood. He walked round to the front of the curtains. She heard everyone clapping as he made a polite little bow before sitting at the bench. He closed his eyes. She leaned back, sighed, and closed hers as well. He played his moor music again, and the sound seemed to shimmer beyond the walls, bolstered and buoyed by the other musicians.

She didn't realize she was falling asleep until she felt the plate sliding from her hands. She clutched at it with slippery fingers, anxious that it not fall with a terrible clatter to the floor.

But the concert was over, anyway, she could hear the sounds of people chattering and laughing and rustling.

Her tea, in a cup on the floor next to her, was cold, and the air felt cold too. She leaned to put her plate carefully onto the floor. She tucked her legs under her, as best she could, huddled inside her coat, curled her frigid fingers up into the sleeves. She didn't mean to close her eyes. She didn't mean to fall asleep again.

He woke her with gentle shaking.

"Come, darling, it's late, they're closing the hall." Opening her eyes, she could see someone behind him, someone in a raincoat like Colin's, and she thought for a moment it was Colin, bringing Mommy to take her home. But when the man came into view, glass in hand tilting brown liquid, she saw it was a stranger.

"Christ, Eswyth, she gave me a fright! That long hair, I thought she was your sister, come back to haunt you."

Rory glanced behind him. "Sara wouldn't haunt me." Then he smiled at Lottie. "Lottie, may I present my friend and teacher, George Latimer. Latimer, this is my student, Charlotte Arkwright."

"Your ... student! What's she doing here?"

"This is her first concert, so behave, Latimer."

Latimer came closer. "Did you sleep through the whole thing dear? I understand perfectly, mind you, I've always experienced Eswyth as a powerful narcotic." He stared at her. "Who is this picturesque wild waif? Wherever did you find her?"

"That's a question for the ages Latimer." Rory knelt beside her and laughed, looking deep into her eyes. He smelt of sherry. "Wherever did I find you, Lottie love?"

"In Lars' room. At the piano."

Latimer guffawed as if she'd said something terrifically funny. He ruffled Rory's hair and a little of his drink sloshed out. "I say, old son, won't Lars be looking for you to put her back?"

They both laughed once more.

"Can I have some sherry?" It might make her feel warmer. It might help to clear the cobwebs in her head, where bits like insect wings were stuck fast on the strands: the soreness between her legs, and big Bobby and Sari, and the dogs' eyes from the soldier's story, that reminded her of pianos but she couldn't remember why. She was so cold.

Rory's eyes and smile widened. He sat on the floor and laughed again. "Some sherry! My word. Of course, darling." He held his glass out to her, but it was empty.

"You've taught her rather too well, Rory," said Latimer in a dry voice. He took a bottle from the tea table and poured, looking at her with what seemed an unkind sort of curiosity. "Here you are, Sleeping Beauty, have a drink."

She sipped it and closed her eyes, so she didn't have to see Latimer, so she could enjoy the warmth sliding down her throat and the sweet taste as she licked her lips.

149

"What a sensuous little vamp. She makes it look delicious."

"She makes everything look delicious," Rory murmured. When she opened her eyes he was looking at her in that way he did, chin in hand propped on the edge of her chair, even though Latimer was hovering right beside him, staring at her as well.

"Let's spirit your Sleeping Beauty away before the cleaners' shift begins and we're caught pouring sherry down her throat." Latimer turned, slipping the bottle into his raincoat pocket. He looked over the tea table. "Nothing much left, we'll find a pub that's still open, once you send her back to her enchanted castle. I'm famished after that exhausting performance of yours. As always, your music takes everything out of one."

Rory unfolded himself from the floor, a bit unsteady, with obvious reluctance. "I should take you home, love, I suppose, though I can't think *why* I told Althea I'd have you back tonight—" he gulped down the last of the sherry. "I'd much rather have you sleep with me. At my flat, I mean," he amended quickly, glancing at Latimer, who was walking away. "Come along."

Lottie got up and followed them out into the dark street, where a thin wind sliced at her bare legs. She bent to wrap the coat ends round her knees, and when she looked up they weren't there anymore. She stood still, looking in the direction they'd gone.

As soon as she began to feel frightened, Rory came bounding round the corner.

"Darling! You should have kept close!" He lifted her up and carried her down the street, staggering a bit, to where his car was. Latimer was already in the front seat.

"Can I have, do you have a blanket?" Her teeth were chattering.

Rory stripped off his coat, wrapped it round her, and bundled her into the back. "You should have a proper coat, and boots, and a hat and gloves—"

"Like the winter doll."

150

"—we shall have to take you to Harrods and get you fitted out for winter, that's right, just like the doll. Perhaps I'll take you shopping, for Christmas," he said, climbing into the front and then accelerating away. "I'm turning the heat up, love, are you warm enough now?"

"Yes."

"You can go back to sleep if you like. I'll take Mr. Latimer home, and then you."

"All right." She curled up on the seat, head resting on the sleeves of his soft coat. It had his Christmas tree scent.

"Dolls, is it, old son, is she your new dolly then?" Latimer said quietly.

Lottie suspected this wasn't a proper thing to say, but Rory answered him, just as quietly, "You can't begin to fathom it, mate," in Bobby's Cockney voice.

She opened her eyes.

Rory was smiling at Latimer, with his gleaming look.

"God, Eswyth, you're a veritable Pan." Latimer touched Rory's hair again, and his hand stayed, smoothing the back, the way Rory rubbed her neck. "You just draw us all like flies to honey, don't you, draw everyone in: men, women, children."

"This time I'm the one being drawn."

"However did the agency assign you? Mind you, I can see she's a winsome lass, under all that hair, but so ... unkempt. Not the sort we're used to teaching."

Lottie smoothed her hair back, wiped the remains of tea from her mouth, brushed crumbs away, under his overcoat.

"Her Mum's rather a ... I suppose you'd call her a beatnik. She's American. Fancies herself a poet. They live somewhat a bit ... on the edge, as it were."

"How can they afford you?"

"I'm donating my time, actually. Don't tell the agency."

"Rory, no, that's a terrible mistake."

"But Charlotte is a genuine musical prodigy."

151

"Her accent is atrocious. Where on earth do they live?"

"Near Hammersmith. She hasn't been properly schooled, I gather, since they left America last year. Her Mum wanted me to correct her speech, as well as teach piano. But as soon as I heard her play I was completely lost to her. I could listen for hours."

For hours? He could listen to her play for hours?

"Hours, Rory? In Hammersmith! That's a first. It was like pulling teeth to get you to accept any pupils! You haven't the patience of a flea!"

"She's unique. I've never heard anyone like her. A completely intuitive musician. Intoxicating."

"Intoxicating, is it now?" Latimer's low chuckle was an older echo of Rory's. He moved his fingers in Rory's hair. "Why don't you try someone who could give you real pleasure?"

Rory laughed. "Since you always see right through me anyway I shall confess: I'm infatuated with her."

Latimer chuckled again. "Christ in a nightdress you're drunk!"

"Shush, Latimer, don't wake her. I am drunk, indeed—"

"Pull the other one, it's got bells on."

"—but I'm telling you the truth."

"About this ...scruffy child?"

"Shh. Yes. I'm head over heels."

"Rory, darling, you're deluded as well as drunk, you're being taken in by the appearance of innocence. That's always a risk."

"She is innocent."

"She's a she, they're none of them innocent," Latimer said, dry. "Look, I'd never presume to give advice in this kind of situation, you know me, live and let live. I'm a true believer in bohemian values. You could call me a beatnik as well."

"And I sense a 'but' emerging."

"That's right, a huge one. You're risking the most extreme consequences if you take this seriously. Surely you know it."

"There will be no consequences. Nobody knows how I feel except the two of us."

"And now the three of us."

"You'd never breathe a word. You love me."

"True enough, though forever unrequited, I fear. But what's to stop her from talking? What makes you think she understands your ... interest?"

"I told her it's private, just between us. She's in love with me too."

"You're barking mad! Children don't fall in love."

"I'm as sound as can be. I've never loved anyone the way I love her."

For a few moments there was only the humming of the Mini's motor.

"And so it's happily ever after, then?" Latimer resumed. "Except you'll have to go to live in some Arabian land where child brides are legal. Mind you, it won't be all milk and honey, I daresay there won't be a concert hall in sight—"

"I've only to wait until she's older, here—"

"Rory." Latimer's voice got heavy. "You don't know what you're saying."

"I do, very well. This weekend was the happiest of my life. I never feel alone, when I'm with her. I want to be with her all the time."

The car slowed, then stopped. Lottie felt as though they'd been talking about some other girl. They seemed to have forgotten she was there. She closed her eyes and pretended to be sleeping. The men kept talking, rapidly, with a quiet intensity.

"Look, Rory love, I've found you attractive since you were fourteen, but I knew enough never to cross any line when I was your tutor, not like that other unscrupulous swine your father told me about—"

"—he wasn't an unscrupulous swine."

153

"Taking advantage of your family's distress over Sara's illness! When your parents had to leave you alone with him, all those times taking Sara to hospital, with Colin away at art school."

"He was good for me."

"He was monstrous!"

"No. He taught me ... gratification."

"—d'you mean ... you actually ... *enjoyed* it?"

"Yes, after a bit of confusion." Rory's voice rose, in defiance. "I think we underestimate how intensely children can feel pleasure, if they're initiated carefully."

"Good God, he sounds an outright criminal! No wonder your father was so careful vetting me, when he hired me!"

"I had no say when Dad threw him out."

"But, Rory, surely you know he was wicked to treat you, his pupil, like a lover. Acting on an attraction to someone so young is morally wrong. An outrage. You can't think of this child in that way. You must understand that."

"It's not wrong when we love each other."

"Oh my word." She heard a huge sigh. "You really think you're in love, when she's, what, half your age? You think you can wait for her to grow up, all those years?"

"Only three. The age of consent is thirteen, in Scotland. In some counties."

Latimer fluttered a hand in the air and spoke in an exaggerated high voice. "Scotland, is it, well then, bless my bloomin plaids! In *some* counties!" Then his hand dropped and he said, roughly, "You're talking *rubbish*."

"Tisn't rubbish," Rory said, with a hint of the anger she'd heard once before.

"Let me tell you something, lad, something I've wondered, about you. I suspected, when I caught you and Annabel in your room that time. And I wondered, as well, about what the burden of Sara did to you, the way your parents relied on you to keep her happy, and the way she died so soon after you left —"

154

"—leave Sara out of this." Rory's voice sounded menacing. "I won't listen."

"—and the way you've never had any regular girlfriends, or even boyfriends," Latimer went on. "I know you don't want to listen, but I shall tell you what I fear for you, anyway. Waiting ten years, or even three, isn't what you're really thinking of. You want her now."

"God yes, of course I do—"

"You're not hearing me, Rory, and perhaps I'm risking more of your anger by saying this, but if you're serious someone must say it to you: you *only* want her now."

There was a short silence.

"And I shall want her forever." Rory's voice was so low she could hardly hear him now. "I shall love her and care for her, forever."

Latimer said, in a slow frightened voice, "Rory, please, tell me you haven't touched her."

Lottie didn't want to hear any more. "I say." She yawned, sitting up and rubbing her eyes. "Are we home?"

Both men turned round to look at her. Rory had the shocked look in his eyes, the straight mouth, from the moor. Latimer's sneer had vanished; he looked horrified.

"Hallo, Sleeping Beauty," he said, moving his mouth into a pretend smile. "We're just taking you home now."

"Latimer, this is your flat."

"Don't you want to get another drink, a meal?"

Rory didn't look at him. "The pubs are closed. I'll see you Wednesday."

Latimer touched his shoulder. "Rory, I'm sure it's just the drink talking, let's sort this out. Take her home now. I'll come back to your flat."

Rory shrugged his hand off with a sharp jerk. "I'm tired."

"All right then." Latimer got out, slowly, and leaned in to look at him and Lottie. "Straight home?"

"Goodnight." Rory revved the engine and Latimer jumped back.

155

Lottie looked out the back window and waved, a little, because Latimer appeared so lonely standing by himself under the lamppost outside his flat.

"Filthy old faggot," Rory muttered.

He drove so fast then it seemed they were at her building in no time.

He got out and opened the car door for her, and followed as she walked into the vestibule and up the three flights. They had never seemed so long, nor the hall so dingy, nor the light, when she opened their door, so dim. But Mommy was there, holding out her arms, and Lottie ran into them and felt her hug even through Rory's thick coat.

Mommy slipped it off her shoulders and wrapped it around Rory, in as big a hug as she'd given Lottie. "Thank you Rory, for everything, it's been ... so wonderful. The best Thanksgiving ever!"

Lottie thought his eyes couldn't look any blacker. "Althea," was all he said.

"Won't you come in, have some tea or sherry, tell me all about the concert!"

"It's too late." He looked down at Lottie, with the same frozen expression, standing still as the statue she'd felt she was, earlier. "Charlotte. Goodbye."

She couldn't tell what he was thinking, but he looked, just then, even lonelier than his friend Latimer. A sensation of unfamiliar pity, like gagging, rose in her. She reached up to hug him, but when he didn't hug her back she dropped her arms.

"Goodbye, Master Rory."

TWENTY-SIX

LOTTIE THOUGHT SHE'D NEVER be able to sleep, with so many jumbled impressions she couldn't sort them out. But she slept well, somehow, because when Lars woke her the next morning she felt eager to see the girls at school again and tell them all about the weekend. The Devon part. She needn't tell what had happened in Rory's flat yesterday, nor repeat his conversation with Latimer. She'd pretend she never heard any of that.

But the dolls! They'd be wanting to know about the dolls, and she hadn't brought a single one. She pushed at the top bunk with her feet, making the springs squeak, jostling Nell.

"Nell. I don't know what made me think I didn't want them, I was so stupid at the weekend, but I didn't bring any of the dolls with me."

Nell's face appeared upside down, hair dangling over, and grinned at Lottie.

"Ah, but I did! I went up after you'd gone, to see which ones you'd picked, and when I saw them still there I knew you'd forgotten. I got even more than twelve, the Eswyths said we should simply keep them!" She nodded to two great shopping bags standing in the corner. "Aren't they the best family in the world! I love them!"

Lottie blinked.

"And we brought all kinds of food, Mrs. Eswyth practically emptied her larder, and Mary sent loaves of bread."

In the kitchen, they foraged for food in the bags piled on the table, ripping into the fresh bread and tearing off chunks to eat on their way to school.

Nell was full of being the Dandy girl. "And I'm to have a screen test this Saturday, and I'm to get a lot of new clothes, and a hair cut, and they'll pay me, Lottie, we won't have to be waiting for the bloody check all the time and we can have a smashing great Christmas after all!"

"Not just picked—"

"— but chosen!" The walk to school had never seemed so short.

Ursula, Wendy and Jenny came home with her. They came chattering up the stairs and into the girls' room to examine the dolls.

"Oh! Just look at how cunning this one is!" Wendy held up the doll with the pram in both hands, one for the mum and one for the baby in its carriage. "But she can't be a princess, she's already married, and a mother."

"And this one, she's lovely, Lottie, you should bring her to school." Jenny unwound Sari's sari. "Miss Dowd would like her."

"This one's her husband," Lottie told them, bringing big Bobby out. "He buys her all the chocolates down the Waitrose."

They found this as funny as she did. "But he's huge, Lottie, and she's only a little girl. They can't be married. He can be her daddy."

"They live in the Arabian lands. That's where girls marry when they're our age."

"No! When they're our age! Who told you that?"

"Mr. Latimer. He was Ro- Master Rory's piano tutor. I met him at Master Rory's concert last night."

"You went to a concert! Was it at the Symphony?"

"It was a big hall, but I didn't see it from the front. I waited backstage for him."

Ursula sat back, dolls forgotten, and gave Lottie a frank stare. "Jolly good on you, Lottie, you are sophisticated," she said approvingly. "For an American."

Lottie looked at her, not sure if she was joking or being *sarcastic*, a new word Lars had started using, to explain to Mommy the way he was talking lately. The way Ursula was looking over her spectacles just now ... Lottie pounced.

Ursula struggled beneath her, laughing so hard she started to gasp, and she cried, "Lottie, stop, stop!"

"I'm tickling you to death," Lottie said, and she poked Ursula again, on her chest, but Ursula shoved her off with a serious push.

"Don't touch me there, Lottie, that's where I'm growing, don't you know?" Ursula rubbed herself. "It's ever so tender just now."

Lottie stared at her. Her hands unconsciously went to the tiny bumps on her own chest, where he liked to stroke her, where she sometimes felt an odd twinge. She wondered would Ursula's feel different; they looked a bit bigger than hers.

"So ... you're not so sophisticated, after all, Lottie, didn't your Mum tell you about what's going to be happening to us in the next few years?"

"Is it to do with the baby-making thing?"

Jenny put in, dubious, "We're not supposed to do that until we're married, of course, but I gather that we'd be able to do it before then."

"But we mustn't. It's wrong," Wendy said.

"Is it wrong if they love each other?" Lottie picked up Bobby and Sari and made them kiss and hug. The others giggled.

"My Mum said it's only all right if they're married," Jenny concluded.

Lottie walked the couple around the way Rory had done the other day. Ursula, laughing, began to ha-ha ha ha the wedding tune. Jenny and Wendy picked up two other brides and walked them behind, making them bow to an unseen audience. They laughed so much they brought Mommy to the doorway.

"Girls! Won't they make fine princesses?"

That reminded them to get the rehearsal underway. Lottie ran down to fetch Stevie next door, and they finished stringing up twelve princesses under the rigged curtain. Stevie tried out a number of princely lines that were pronounced satisfactory. The gauze Mommy had strewn over the backdrop looked like the clouds on the moor, Lottie thought, and the blue was just right for the magic river.

They took a tea break—Mommy brought out the rest of the vegetable pie, which the girls were too polite, or too hungry, to refuse—and kept on into the late afternoon. When Lars came home, he was pressed into service for a few final scenery touches.

"I daresay we're ready, Mrs. Arkwright, shall we do it this weekend?" Ursula put on her coat. Lottie was surprised it was past seven o'clock. "We've only to review the music with your tutor. Will he come tomorrow Lottie?"

"Yes." He usually came on Tuesdays and Thursdays.

"Let's have it on Friday, since Nell will be so busy on Saturday," Mommy said. The girls were excited at the prospect of seeing Nell being the Dandy's girl on the telly. It was like knowing someone famous. "Tell your parents, if they'd like to come, and the other kids. Lars and Rory will help clear out the furniture, sorry, we won't have many chairs, but it's not a terribly long play and some people can stand. I'll have drinks and snacks. It should be fun!"

Mommy looked so happy that Lottie ran to give her a hug. She felt a rush of love for Mommy, to have persisted in putting on the play, to have stayed out of a *silence* mood the whole time they were rehearsing, and to be able to give a party, their first in England.

"Sweetie!" Mommy hugged her back. "We have a lot of work to do, but I think we can do it, I can stay up all week if I have to!" She laughed.

"Now that we have the dresses, you won't need to."

"Oh, there are a lot of little things I need to get ready. I'm so glad we have Rory. I could never pull this off without his help."

"Was your Master good, in concert?" Ursula asked.

"Yes." She wasn't going to admit that she'd fallen asleep.

"Was he the only one playing?"

"There was an orchestra, in the pit. He was the only one on the stage."

"Gracious, he must be extremely talented." Ursula sounded just like a grownup.

Mommy looked around, with a little laugh. "Without him here, after the weekend we had with his family … it feels as if something's missing."

Lottie looked at where Bobby and Sari lay together near the fireplace.

"I should think he's frightfully busy." Ursula finished tying up her scarf. "My dad knows one of the Symphony musicians, a violinist. It's a frantic life, my dad says. Practise, and teaching, and finding jobs where they actually pay him to play music." She looked at Mommy. "It's a wonder your Master Rory can spare the time here."

161

TWENTY-SEVEN

THAT KIND OF FRANTIC LIFE must have kept Rory away that week: he didn't come on Tuesday, and by five o'clock on Thursday, when he wasn't there for the final rehearsal, Mommy took Lottie aside.

"Charlotte. I need you to go to Mr. Singh's and ask to use the telephone." Her fingers were shaking as she handed Lottie a paper. Her eyes were blinking rapidly, and her voice was thin. "This is Rory's number at home. Tell him he has to come tonight, no matter how late. If he isn't home, call his agency, this number, and tell them."

"No." Lottie put her hands behind her back. "Mommy, you do it."

"Charlotte." Mommy took a deep breath. "Please. If I talk to him, I'll get so angry that I'm afraid I'll—I can't understand why he's letting us down this way!"

"But he didn't know it was for this weekend—"

"Just go!"

Frightened by the *silence* voice, which hadn't been heard in so long, Lottie ran down to the second floor. She knocked.

Mr. Singh was a small Indian man, exotic to the Arkwrights because he wore a turban. Passing by his flat on the stairs was an occasion of sniffing, when they stopped to notice—there was usually an enticing scent, of cooking or of sweetness like soap.

"Miss Lottie?" As usual, he stood with his hands together.

"Please, can I use your phone?"

162

"Certainly." He led the way to a telephone table just inside the door.

She looked at the paper. It came to her that she did not have to talk to Rory. She could tell Mommy that he was out, or the agency was closed. It was only a game really, the play; nobody took it as seriously as Mommy. Of course, Ursula would look over her spectacles, that way she did, but Lottie felt sure they would remain friends even if the play could not be done.

And, for that matter, he didn't have to be present, for the play to go on. Lottie could do the music. She could play all sorts of music now. It didn't have to only come from ... him. She could be in charge.

"Isn't working?" Mr. Singh put his head round the corner. "Not at home?"

Lottie looked at him. Her hands had gone behind her back again, and had crumpled the paper so tightly it was damp in her palm. She opened it. The numbers swam.

"You need help with numbers?" He came over and took the paper. He ran his finger around the dial and Lottie watched it spin back into place after each number. It would be so easy to put her finger in one of the holes, and stop the spinning.

Mr. Singh spoke. "Hallo sir. It is Miss Charlotte Arkwright who is wanting to speak to you." He handed the phone to Lottie, with a little bow, and went back into his front room.

She held the receiver to her ear. Her mouth didn't bring out any words.

After a moment she heard his voice in her ear, as low as if he were lying next to her, but sounding as formal as when they'd first met. "Charlotte?"

"Hallo."

"Why are you calling me?" She hadn't noticed, until now it was so absent, how much affection was usually in his voice when he spoke to her.

"We have the ... we're doing the play tomorrow."

Silence.

163

"Mommy told me ... Mommy says you're to come round right away."

She heard a sigh.

"She can't do it without you." She didn't want, in the end, to risk having Mommy's impending mood get worse, not now. "So, please? Would you come?"

Another sigh. "Look ... can I ask you a serious question?"

"Mmm?"

"Do *you* want me to come?"

She twisted the snaky black line coming out of the phone.

"Charlotte, if you want to see me, I'll come. But only then. And it won't be ... I'm trying to find you another tutor."

"Another piano tutor?"

"Yes."

"But I don't want another tutor, if I don't have you." She couldn't imagine watching anyone but him tame the piano. If she couldn't watch how he did it, she'd have to bloody well do it on her own.

Now she heard him breathe in, sharply. "Lottie." Now the affection was back. "Thank you for that."

"Mommy can't do the play without you."

At last he said, "All right. I'll come." Then he asked, "Do you need anything at home, food, or milk, or coal?"

They were still polishing off the bags from the weekend. "No."

"Then I shall see you in twenty minutes."

When she told Mommy he was coming, Mommy beamed as if she'd never worried. She put out her Kent, swept papers off the kitchen table, took a bottle of sherry from one of the weekend bags. She collected the tea things, from the girls' room, and announced to them that final rehearsal would begin as soon as he arrived. When she came back in, a few minutes later, Lottie saw she'd put on lipstick and combed her hair.

"Let's look sharp now, girls, for Rory!" She laughed in a giddy way. "Get those princesses ready."

But Rory, when he appeared, didn't look sharp. He had dark circles under his eyes, dark hair growing on his chin, his clothes were rumpled, and he smelt of sherry: a lot of sherry. The children looked at him, surprised and disapproving. He looked back at them without a smile, not meeting Lottie's eyes for more than a sullen second.

Mommy took his arm and led him into the kitchen. They heard her speaking to him, low, and heard his mumbling reply.

"I think he's been drinking whiskey," whispered Wendy, wrinkling her nose.

"Not whiskey, no ... ale, more like," suggested Stevie, with an educated frown. "Sheets to the wind, anyroad."

"It's probably sherry, that's what they drink at the concert hall." Lottie added, without quite knowing why, "It's what I drank there with him."

Now they stared at her disapprovingly as well, all but Stevie, who grinned.

"He looks ill," Ursula said. "If he can't do the tunes, we should leave them out, or can Lars do them, Lottie?"

"I can play, if he can't."

"Then we don't need him. Why is he here?"

From Lars' room next door, they heard a tentative beginning of the music, as if someone were coughing in the morning to wake up. Then it grew stronger, more measured. They looked at each other, shrugged, and began the final rehearsal.

They got through the whole story in forty minutes. Rory came to lean on the doorjamb once it was over. He asked Ursula for her review.

"The music was all right," she told him, eyeing him critically. "But you're to make yourself a bit more presentable tomorrow. Our parents are coming."

He glanced round at all of them, looking longer at Lottie, his scrutiny as cold as the day they met, before he made her wash her hands. "Right then," he said at last. "Tomorrow, children."

165

She told Polly about it later that night. *He doesn't like me anymore.*

"Well thank me lucky bloomin stars!" Polly exclaimed. "You're well shot of im."

I miss him.

"I know what you miss, missy, and you can do that on your own, no muckin about with some sort of baby-makin rubbish."

But why doesn't he like me anymore? He's put me in Coventry. Coventry was the deliberate silence English children used when they were excluding someone from their group. Pamela used it from time to time on some of the unfortunates at school; Lottie felt lucky to have been spared.

For once Polly had no ready answer.

"Mummy?" Nell interrupted her thoughts. "Why is it always Dandy's peas?" She didn't care about the play anymore; she was practising for her screen test.

"Not just picked, but chosen," Lottie answered automatically.

"I'm so excited I can't sleep. But Colin said I must get a lot of sleep. But my eyes just won't stay closed." She leaned over the bunk to peer at Lottie, in the low light from the banked embers in the fireplace.

"Did you finish your maths?" Lottie remembered to ask her. They had started taking turns reminding Nell of the day's schoolwork; she was that distracted. But the schoolwork was to prepare her for the Eleven Plus. She couldn't be allowed to forget it.

"Bugger all." Nell slid off her bunk and climbed to the floor. She switched on a lamp. "Sorry, Lottie, I forgot again."

Lottie turned away from the light.

166

TWENTY-EIGHT

MOMMY DIDN'T SLEEP that night, either, apparently; in the morning she was still drinking coffee at the kitchen table, an ashtray full beside her cup, her pages stacked under her elbow. Her face looked grey, but she smiled when the girls came in.

"I've made oatmeal. I want us to start eating oatmeal every morning. Especially on a big day like this for you, Lottie, with the play tonight, and for Nell tomorrow with her screen test. Oatmeal every day."

"What about the snacks for tonight, Mommy?" Lottie asked. She hoped Mommy remembered, otherwise it'd be Saltines and marmite and Spam. Or oatmeal!

"Rory promised he'd bring an assortment from the caterer that does his concerts."

"Do you think he'll remember?" She'd decided, late last night, that if he didn't like her anymore, then she didn't like him either, if she ever really had. *Bugger him, anyroad.* "He was sheets to the wind yesterday."

Mommy didn't even seem to notice her language. "We can phone to remind him, from Mr. Singh."

"Colin says we must get a telephone of our own. He says the agency and the studio and all the other people will want to get in touch with me." Nell spooned sugar onto her oatmeal.

Mommy looked into space. "I don't know ... I suppose we can ask Mr. Lowell." Mr. Lowell was their landlord. He was not very nice, when the check was late.

In the cloakroom at school, Lottie reminded everyone about the play.

167

"My Mum's bringing those little cakes you like." Wendy smiled.

"Mine's bringing a box of chocolates," Jenny said.

"My Dad wonders can he bring a bottle, he thought it's all right for him to offer a drop to everyone?" Pamela sent Lottie a challenging look. "I told him Master Rory and your Mum drink sherry."

Ursula elbowed her. "Did you tell him Lottie drinks it too?" She imitated Stevie: "She's a roight ruddy rummy. Sheets to the wind." They moved into the classroom as a group, laughing. Miss Dowd had to raise her brows.

Lottie realized she hadn't been alone, that week, to take anything from the cloakroom pockets; but she didn't feel as hungry as before.

When they came to her home after school, they saw that the girls' room was cleared of the desk, and of their things usually strewn about, and a huge red-patterned carpet was laid onto the floor. Mommy and Rory were bustling in the kitchen, where trays like those that had been backstage were crowding the narrow counters.

"Here, help me take this into the play room, or should I say, the theatre." He picked up one end of the kitchen table. Lottie, who was nearest, picked up the other, and they shuffled it down the short corridor. They pushed it against the wall. Rory covered it with a cloth draped over his arm. "There. That should suit, as a buffet." He stood back and looked at it.

He was as shiny as he'd been for his concert, no sign of yesterday's scruffiness. He met her gaze for only a brief second before turning back to the kitchen. He was still keeping her in Coventry. *I don't care,* she reminded herself. She didn't follow him. She looked around the room, enjoying its new appearance. Even the bunks were covered with colourful spreads.

"Coo-er, posh!" Stevie exclaimed when he came up.

"Mr. Singh brought them," Mommy told them. "I invited him to the show." She was dressed up, her hair neatly curled and her lipstick on. But there was a look in her eye like the one that had been in the big horse's, when

168

he'd thrown his head back, and Mommy's fingers were deep yellow and trembling. Lottie wanted to fetch her a Kent before she exploded. But Mommy's smile, though shaky, was bright.

Lottie noticed that Rory was watching Mommy just as carefully as she was; as carefully as Lars and Nell would have done, if they'd been paying attention. He took her wrist, as if taking the string of a wayward balloon, and held it until she looked at him. "It will be fine, Althea," he said in his quiet voice.

And it was. His and Lars' music was lovely, the girls' and Stevie's delivery was crisp, and the dolls and scenery looked grand. The production was declared a success by the small group of parents in the room. Pamela's blond, boisterous father poured round the drinks, and everyone toasted the performers. Even Rory's wide smile appeared once more, when he and Lars and Stevie took a little bow as the 'background' players: the suggestion of princes. Mommy's giddy laugh blended in with everyone else's as they mingled afterwards, eating and drinking.

"Splendid party, Mrs. Arkwright, and a fine job with the girls," said Ursula's mother, as she stood at the door.

Lottie had been a little worried about Ursula's parents, she could admit, now that it was all over. Ursula's father hadn't come, but her mother was as straight-up-and-down as Ursula, with the same spectacles perched on her no-nonsense nose. She wore a smart-looking grey suit, in contrast to the other mums' pretty frocks. She'd only sipped at one small glass of sherry. Her gaze was clear as she took Mommy's hands in hers.

"Ursula has enjoyed this so much, I wanted you to know that, and she's expressed no end of admiration for you. Your writing, and your finding such a famous piano tutor, and, I gather, you've done it all on your own."

"Thank you." Mommy held onto her hands. "That means a lot to me."

Ursula's mother turned to Rory, who was standing behind Mommy. "Mr. Eswyth. It's an honor to meet you.

169

Thanks for inspiring the girls." She took one hand from Mommy to reach toward him.

Ursula nudged Lottie as they watched the exchange. "She's going to have him tutor me as well, she's that impressed with him."

Lottie stared at her. Ursula looked back, and a little frown appeared between her thin brows. "What? He can still come to you, you needn't be jealous, he can manage us both. I'm sure he's a capable teacher, when he's not drinking."

Mind he doesn't touch you, Lottie warned Ursula, so loudly in her head that she expected Ursula to answer. But perhaps he wouldn't touch Ursula. Perhaps Ursula gave off such an air of crisp awareness that he wouldn't dare. Whereas she, Lottie, must have obviously given off quite a different sort of air, an air that said *go ahead, she'll never tell; you can do anything to her and she'll like it. She'll love it.*

She hadn't realized she was shivering until Ursula came closer and took her arm. "Lottie. It's all right!" She repeated, low, "He can tutor both of us."

Rory turned away from the door just then. His gaze flicked briefly between the two girls before he passed, as if to dismiss them, on his way back into the 'theatre.'

Lottie told Ursula goodbye and wandered into the kitchen. She sat on Mommy's bed, feeling so tired suddenly, so she crawled under the covers. She wouldn't be missed; the small group that was left seemed to be settling into the 'theatre' to make a night of it, as Stevie's Da would say.

She was sorry Stevie's Da hadn't come. His brusque kindness would have soothed Mommy, at least as much as Rory's protective watchfulness. But Rita and Jimbo were chummy representatives; they made fast friends with Pamela's dad.

Lottie was woken by someone sitting on the bed with her. The room was dim and the flat was quiet. She turned and put her arms up, instinctively reaching, but he didn't hold her.

She opened her eyes. It was Jenny. She was bent over, taking off her socks.

"Sorry Lottie, didn't mean to wake you," she whispered. "Your Mum said I should sleep with you." She opened the covers and slipped next to Lottie.

Perhaps she was still half asleep; perhaps she still thought he was beside her; perhaps she knew very well that it was Jenny. Lottie's hands reached over to pull Jenny, who was a bit smaller, close to her. She kissed her before Jenny had a chance to move away. Then she kissed her again, like he did, and ran her hands into Jenny's hair the way he did, and down her back.

Jenny pulled away and laughed. "You're daft, Lottie," she whispered. "Have you been at the sherry? Master Rory let me have a sip of his."

"This is how he kisses me," Lottie whispered back, and kissed her again. "And then he does this." Jenny laughed, wriggling away, as Lottie pushed her hand into Jenny's knickers, to show her.

"Lottie! That tickles!"

"No, stay still, it feels nice, just wait."

Jenny lay still. Soon she breathed hard, the way he did, the way Lottie herself did, and finally she sighed. Afterwards she turned to Lottie. She giggled once more. "Who does this to you? Is it Stevie? Is he your boyfriend?"

Lottie looked at the ceiling. In the faint light from the stove she saw a twisty-looking crack in the plaster that, she realized, had the shape of the stone tower she'd hidden in last weekend. The tower Rory had hidden in when he was just a pale-and-dark boy, running from his tutor, his tutor who he didn't think was an unscrupulous swine after all; listening to the moors.

She thought of Stevie's bright eyes, red face; his endearing rascal's grin. He was like a Disney cartoon animal, all cheek and charm. Rory was like a black and white sad old film. "Yes," she told Jenny finally. "It's Stevie."

TWENTY-NINE

NELL'S EXTRA MONEY meant a trip to Harrods, their first visit ever to the famous shop, where Mommy raced round like a mad person picking out Christmas presents for everyone they knew in America and England.

Colin arranged for Lottie to see the same dentist as Nell, so she was fitted out with a little pair of plastic brackets to wear at night. "No more chewing on the taps," the dentist told her. He gave her vitamin tablets to take every day.

Mommy, Nell and Lottie spent a long afternoon at the beauty parlour recommended by Colin's agency, getting themselves 'done.'

Lottie's hair was washed, combed fiercely and, finally, cut, for the first time ever; in an excruciatingly uncomfortable session. Her hair scattered about the floor like the straw the miller's daughter wept over before Rumpelstiltskin came to spin it into gold. As Lottie stared down at it, a bit teary, wondering could she spin it into a wig for Polly, the hairdresser, a cheerful smart-smocked girl, swept it away with unsentimental efficiency.

"There! Doesn't that feel so easy now!" She whirled Lottie to face the mirror. "Aren't you much prettier this way, lovie, we can see your face!"

She was disappointed her hair wasn't curly like Polly's after all. It did look nice, though, still long, shining onto her shoulders like a front-row girl. "It's all right," Lottie said, scrambling out of the chair. She felt itchy all over. The girl gave them a bag of shampoos to use at home.

Rory did not come again, nor did another tutor. Mommy said, distractedly, surrounded by wrapping paper at the kitchen table, that they could look into more lessons in the new year. She said Rory was too busy just now with the Symphony season.

The school pageant took place the last Friday before Christmas break. Lottie stood on the table in the white velvet dress, hands neatly pressed together for prayer, and looked out at the assembly hall. The table wasn't as wobbly as she'd feared, and the audience gazed at her kindly. Miss Dowd had praised her new haircut. She closed her eyes, opened her mouth, and sang away.

Mommy clapped hardest when the pageant was finished, clapped so long that everyone looked at her. Colin, standing next to her with Nell, slung his camera over his shoulder, and gently reached for Mommy's hands, to stop her.

Lottie said Merry Christmas to her friends. She took the atlas from her desk and handed it to Miss Dowd. "I found it."

"Thank you, Lottie. Do you know how you're getting to the Holy Land now?"

"Perhaps we needn't go after all," Lottie answered, glancing toward Mommy, who was talking to Colin at the back of the classroom.

Miss Dowd followed her glance. "When will we see Nell's adverts on the telly?"

"Colin says, watch on Boxing Day. He's got her doing another sort now as well."

"No more peas?"

"Dandy's soup." Crates of it were stacked into the corners of their kitchen now, along with the peas, given free from the Dandy company.

"Things in tins," murmured Miss Dowd. "I do hope it isn't taking time from her Eleven Plus work."

"Mmm." Lottie looked away. In the excitement of the play, and the Dandy girl success, and Christmas, the Eleven Plus had been somewhat forgotten.

"Have a lovely Christmas, Lottie."

Colin drove them to Waverley to pick up Lars, and then to a restaurant, all decorated for Christmas, where they had roast beef and Yorkshire pudding again. "Not as good as Mum's, what, but it'll do," he said, pouring out the wine. "You should come down with me next week. We have an enormously glamourous party on Christmas Eve with the neighbours, ha ha, all three of them and their sheep, and then we come up to London to see a play or concert on Boxing Day, you know that's what we call December 26th, and Mum and Dad stay with me. This year I think we'll see Rory at the Symphony."

"How is Rory?" asked Nell. "He never comes over anymore."

"The less said about him right now the better. He's working nonstop, on some fiendishly difficult piece, he's become quite impossible. Of course, we don't mind going to see him in concert, where he's up on stage looking nice and behaving well!"Colin heaped more Yorkshire pudding onto Mommy's plate. "Which is why you should come with us to Devon again, and then back on Boxing Day to hear him play. It's our last chance before he goes on tour."

"Oh Mother, let's," said Nell.

"I thought we'd have Christmas as a family," Mommy said.

"Mum says I'm to tell you you're all invited and very much welcome." He tipped his glass to hers. "I hope you won't mind my saying, you look as if you could do with a rest, good home-cooked food, long lovely sleeps, healthy walks in the country air." He looked suddenly at Lottie. "And no running off again, Primrose, I heard about that stunt you pulled last time and I shall keep a close eye on you."

But Lottie was looking at Mommy. Funny, now that Colin mentioned it, she saw how yellow Mommy looked—not just her fingers but her neck and face as well, yellow-grey, and dark circles under her eyes.

She knew how little Mommy was sleeping these days; she often heard her stirring her coffee late at night and

174

smelt her Kent first thing in the morning. Often, on the kitchen table, there were pages and pages of the book, which needed to be put aside if Mommy remembered she wanted them to eat oatmeal. St. Paul must have criss-crossed the entire Roman Empire ten times by now, she imagined, at the rate Mommy was going.

"When will your book be finished, Mommy?" she felt bold enough to ask now.

Mommy looked down. One thin finger came up to twist a lock of blonde hair. "I don't really know. It's taking a different path now, one I'm not sure I see the end of."

"Does one ever, writing?" asked Colin. "Isn't it like wandering in an unknown forest, seeing everything for the first time, not knowing which path to take? Some paths seem marked, so one tramples gamely along and gets lost; others are completely obscure, yet they end up having been the right way to go."

"That's exactly how I'd describe it, at least for the papers I have to write," Lars agreed.

"Are you a writer, Colin?" Mommy asked.

"God forbid! Perish the thought. But I'm surrounded by frustrated novelists who are only doing adverts until they have the leisure to pen their life's work." He smiled. "And sparing no end of detail as they describe every bloody boring bit of it."

Mommy looked at him with such a deep look for such a long time that, returning her look, one of his brows rose in an expression that made his face less friendly. "I greatly respect the creative life, Althea," he said quietly, as if she'd asked that question. "But I don't like arty moods foisted on me. It's why I have such a difficult time with Rory. I've no patience for his everlasting artistic temperament."

"So you don't believe in suffering for one's art?"

He raised both brows now. "Suffering?" He put his mouth close to her ear, but Lottie, who was next to Mommy, heard him say softly, "Rory isn't suffering for his art just now Althea. As you must well know, he's suffering for love."

Mommy stiffened. She glanced at the children, but Colin had waved for the sweets cart and they were poring over it. Lottie looked as well, pointing at the chocolate cake even as her heart was suddenly pounding. She tried to eat and listen at the same time, as Mommy addressed Colin.

"How would I—what do you mean, as I must well know?"

Colin shrugged, and helped himself to Mommy's apple tart. "I don't think it takes a genius to suss out his current mood. He's always been frightfully romantic, deluded really, usually fixating on someone totally unattainable, or letting them get fixated on him, which is actually worse—and the way he was so devotedly *with you*, for months, and now most emphatically is not—well, it's a matter of putting two and two together." He glanced over and caught Lottie peering at him. "And since little jugs have such big ears we'll leave this topic to another time, hmm."

"All the more reason for us not to come to Devon for Christmas."

"Nonsense. Of course that shouldn't stop you."

"But if it's ... if he's somehow too attached—"

"He needs to grow up," Colin said firmly. "You must come, if you want to."

"We'll see." Mommy stirred her coffee, looking as fragile as its dainty cup, with fingers that Lottie saw tremble as her spoon clicked a little drumbeat inside the china.

Colin launched a discussion with Nell about the new campaign. Lars joined in, offering opinions. Lottie scooted closer to Mommy, wishing she could tell her that she shouldn't worry about Rory, that Rory had put Lottie in Coventry; that if he was suffering for love—whatever that meant, exactly—it wasn't anything Mommy had done wrong or should fuss over. Surely, if he didn't like Lottie anymore, that meant it was all over, didn't it?

As she told Polly, she *didn't* bloody well miss him anymore. She didn't even think about him. She didn't keep seeing the black-and-white of his hair and face. She didn't think of how his fingers moved silky over the keys, over her. She didn't thrash about, when she remembered, trying to replicate for herself what he did, thrashing as quietly as possible so Nell, who rarely slept normal hours now anyroad, would not hear her and lean over, hair flopping down, to query, "What the bloody hell are you on about down there?"

Colin dropped them back at their flat after dinner, making plans with Nell to pick her up again early the next day for more studio work.

"Bring your schoolbooks," he said, as an afterthought. "That teacher mentioned your exams again."

"As if it matters, now that I'm the Dandy girl," Nell murmured.

"It matters, Eleanor," Mommy pronounced, so firmly it was like suddenly hearing *silence* again. "Your studies are the most important thing."

Nell rolled her eyes.

Mommy sat up late again in the kitchen that night, but she wasn't writing, Lottie saw when she went in to get a drink of water. She was ... brooding, staring into space, coffee and Kent at the ready but neglected, a long ash just waiting to fall into the butter.

"Mommy." She had to say it again. "Mommy."

"Hmm? What is it, sweetheart?"

Lottie didn't know how to begin. She put her arms round Mommy and leaned close. She saw the page on the table was blank. St. Paul must have been on Christmas break as well just then. "Mommy, about Master Rory ..."

Mommy's head whipped round. "That is none of your business, young lady, and I'm surprised that you would eavesdrop that way. It isn't how I taught you."

Lottie stared.

"His relationship with me had nothing to do with his tutoring you."

177

His relationship with ... Mommy?

Mommy's mouth trembled suddenly as she looked at her. "Honey, I'm sorry, I didn't mean to snap at you. None of this is your fault. I could strangle Colin, for bringing it up in front of all of you today. It wasn't meant for you to hear."

"What?"

"I didn't mean to encourage him! But he was always so sweet, so solicitous, so understanding, and he's so ... handsome." Mommy's head drooped. "I have a weakness for beauty," she finished, in an anguished whisper. "I miss him so much."

After a moment of utter silence in the kitchen, Polly's voice spoke up.

"Well, I swan, your precious Master Rory was a bloody cad, e was, wot a turnup." Even Polly was shocked. "Wot a bloomin turnup," she repeated, for once at a loss for any more descriptive phrases.

Mommy was staring at her. "What did you say?"

But Lottie couldn't speak, and Polly had fallen silent as well.

Mommy hugged Lottie to her, hard. "I should never have blurted out this ... sordid story. It isn't what the Father wants for us. We've been led astray, we've been seduced, by money and comfort and the sins of the flesh. We're meant to achieve higher things, Charlotte. We'll begin planning our route again. We could be there by Christmas if we fly, we could get an advance from Colin."

But Lottie stood stiff as a statue again, embraced by Mommy but unmoved inside.

"I don't think she believes in Israel anymore," Polly muttered under her breath.

178

THIRTY

NELL COULD NOT TALK Mommy into going with Colin to the Eswyth's house again. Their family Christmas was quiet and relaxing, with food and new clothes and books bought with Dandy money. Lottie got five Enid Blyton books from Colin, who'd dropped off a big box of gifts on his way out of London, and she was completely absorbed in the adventurous foursome of Jack, Dinah, Lucy-Ann and Philip.

Her Boxing Day, the day following Christmas, was enlivened by the invitation of Stevie's family to come round and watch the variety shows on the telly. Lottie eagerly left the flat to join the Avery fun.

They watched 'Your Show of Shows' and 'Top of the Pops' and a special programme just on the Beatles, which Stevie's Da pronounced rubbish.

"Give me a good race, or a music hall panto, that'd be the ticket," he grumbled.

"Leave the kids watch, Da, don't be a spoilsport." Rita bustled him and Mrs. Avery into the kitchen for a cuppa so that Lottie and Stevie, left alone, could lean close to the screen and peer at the shaggy-haired youths whose voices could barely be heard over their fans' screaming.

"E looks loike Rory, that one," Stevie said suddenly, pointing at one of them. "Would you scream, Lottie, if it was Rory playin?"

"D'you think I'm daft? E's not worth screamin over."

"E's a good musician, and a roight bloke." Stevie looked at her. "Thought you liked im."

179

"I'm roight sick of earin about im." She was sick of thinking about him as well. She looked back at Stevie, leaned her face closer to his, so close she could see the depth of his bright brown eyes. "Give us a kiss, Stevie, for Merry Christmas, there's a lad."

Obediently, Stevie smacked her cheek with his pursed red lips.

"Not like that," Lottie murmured. "This way." She showed him how Rory did it.

Stevie reared back as if struck. "Blimey, Lottie, what you on about?"

"You'll see, after a bit, it feels nice." She put one arm round him and tugged him closer. She slid her other hand into his lap to do what she did to Rory. He squirmed and pushed her hand off, face blazing.

"Bloody ell, Lottie, I dunno wot's got into ya," he muttered, not meeting her eyes. He scooted onto the floor to sit. He turned up the telly and hunched forward.

What a silly get he was! She jiggled one restless leg back and forth.

Rita came back in to hear the Beatles. She sang along with them and laughed at the agonized fans who screamed, tears running down their faces, as if they were being tortured instead of seeing the band they adored.

"You wouldn't catch me carryin on like that, even if Elvis imself came round." Rita was loyal to Elvis, athough she knew all the Beatles' words. "Roight fools."

"They're suffering for love," Lottie told her.

"Coo-er, Lottie, sufferin for love is it, what would you know about that, young lass?" Rita laughed. She tugged on a lock of Lottie's hair. "Sufferin for want of a knock on the ead, smack some sense into em, that would."

"Lottie!" Stevie shouted. "It's Nell!"

Sure enough, there was Nell on the screen, standing in a greengrocer's shop. Holding up a tin of Dandy's peas. Smiling a gleaming smile.

"Not just picked ... but chosen!" They all chorused along with her.

"Run next door and fetch your mum and Nell! Tell them to come straight away. P'raps they'll show it again!" Rita was all in a lather, as Mr. Avery would say, as excited as if she were going to rush right down the shops to buy the first Dandy's she saw.

Lottie snatched up her coat and ran into a wild night that was ringing with the music of a storm. Snowflakes were flying round, big and wet from the dark grey sky, eclipsing the lights of the buildings and making the pavement slippery. She bent to make a snowball, remembering how from America, but it was wet; heavy and half-frozen, not fluffy and packable. She slapped her hands together to get it off. She picked her way carefully to her building, looking at the pavement so her worn school shoes didn't slide on the icy slush.

She didn't see Rory as he stood in her way.

"Oh Lottie." He sounded as hollow as she'd imagined Sara would, that first night in her all-white room, sliding in from the window as the Eswyths and Arkwrights slept.

Before she could think, she was folded into his damp overcoat, nose smashed against one of the buttons. His arms wrapped her as tight as another coat, pulling her into the vestibule. His fingers gripped the back of her head. She lost her breath.

She suddenly remembered Mr. Moore the greengrocer. Kick. Scream. Run away, he'd told her, that night so long ago when she'd gotten lost and met Jeremy.

She wrenched her face free, crooked her knee back, and swung at him as hard as she could possibly swing. Her sturdy new boot connected into his shin, with a satisfying thud, and he collapsed backwards onto the stairs at the end of the vestibule.

He bent over his leg. Snowflakes melted into his sliding-down hair like tiny white stars winking out in a pitch black sky. She stared down at him, locked in place for one frightening moment, before she had the wit to rush past him up the stairs, shouting at the top of her lungs, "Mommy! Lars! Mommy!"

Mommy leaned down from the third floor as she clattered upstairs.

"Lottie! What is it!"

She reached their doorway, sped past Mommy into the flat. Lottie reached past her, slammed the door shut, twisted the lock. She didn't realize she was shaking until Mommy knelt down to grip her arms.

"Lottie. What!"

She pointed her finger downstairs. "H-he's there," she stuttered through a sudden flood of sobs. "Ma-Master Rory."

"Yes, he just left, he brought our Christmas present here after his concert," Mommy said, mystified. "What happened?"

But the girl's voice vanished. She slid to the floor in a seizure of tears.

Polly had to come to the rescue once more. "She'd have kicked is bloody teeth in, were she able to reach, but as it is she got is leg. Hope it's broke into a million pieces!"

Mommy sank down beside the girl, her face beginning to wrinkle up. "You ... hurt him? You kicked Rory? Why!"

"And she'd do it again, kick is feckin teeth in! Muckin about with us! The *gall!*" She chose one of Mommy's words, to make more of an impact.

"Lottie, oh Lottie." Mommy hugged the girl close, like he'd tried to, even using the same crooning. She tried to struggle away but Mommy was strong. "Listen to me. What I said last week, about him—you must forget you ever heard that from me. Nothing ever happened between us, nothing. He was a perfect gentleman, he didn't let me even kiss him. We never got that close! It was all just ... feelings."

A perfect gentle man.

Didn't let Mommy even kiss him.

Just ... feelings.

182

Mommy left her crumpled there, turned to unlock the door, ran downstairs. Her light footfalls echoed like descending scales in the lofty stairwell.

She heard the front door being opened, heard Mommy's high voice and his answering low rumble. Heard them laughing. Heard them coming back up, slowly, with pauses, some groaning, more laughing.

She managed to scramble up and into her room. Lucky for her Nell wasn't there. She couldn't lock their bedroom door, but she could turn out the light, strip off her coat and shoes, hide under her covers and pretend to be asleep.

She heard laughter in Lars' room that sounded odd, sounded—like the telly next door at the Avery's. She heard the distinct sound of Lars' and Nell's laughter above the programme sounds. Crikey! He'd brought them a bloomin telly.

"That's done it," said Polly. "'E's a ruddy saint, there'll be no gettin shot of im now." She was wedged into the space between the iron bed rails and the mattress, just right for Lottie to lean her chin, for chewing on the metal. She'd gnawed away a little ridge there, like on the inside of her cheek, which she hadn't told the dentist about. A bit of gnaw now and then couldn't hurt, just a bit before she put on her tooth guard.

Of course, the door opened.

He shut it behind him.

He sat down on the bunk, next to her.

183

THIRTY-ONE

FAINT LIGHT FROM THE SWIRLING SNOWFALL under the lamppost outside their window shone on him. From under her eyelashes she peeped at his face: pale as the white plaster shepherd boy in the group from Woolworth under their Christmas tree; they were meant to be Jesus' parents, with a neighbor in his dressing gown, and the shepherd's animals. The spindly-legged sheep fell over no matter how often she re-arranged them. They hadn't bought the wise men; next year, Mommy said.

She felt as well as heard his massive sigh. The springs creaked.

"I'm sorry I frightened you, outside, I ... couldn't stop myself from holding you, when I saw you." His voice was as hesitant as his words, so soft she barely heard. "Too tight, again, I know."

She didn't have to speak.

"Your Mum told me what you'd been thinking, that she and I ... that you were angry because you thought I was somehow ..." he trailed off. "But you know that's nonsense, you know it's you that I love."

She didn't have to move.

"The thing is," he began again, "when I stopped coming to see you, that was ... I was trying to live without you." He heaved another sigh. "I thought I should try. Latimer told me I must."

She could feel him looking at her. She could feel the waves of his attention washing round her as if she were a boulder on a beach, over and under: even if it took a long time, eventually, the boulder would be moved.

184

"I've missed you, darling. It's been agony, only hearing about you from Colin."

But she could be as still as the boulder.

"If I thought that you felt the same way about me, why then perhaps we could still be ... close, and wait for the rest until you're ... more ready." He suddenly tugged Polly out of her lodging, so fast Lottie couldn't hold onto her. "Hullo, Pollyanna," he said, holding her up in front of his face so they could see each other clearly.

Polly looked at him.

"I didn't think about her age, in the beginning ... she enthralled me. It didn't matter to me how old she was." He looked at Polly a moment longer. "Will you tell her how sorry I am, for ever hurting her in any way?"

Polly's only a doll, you silly get, she can't really tell me anything, that was just me being a baby, pretending dolls can talk!

He tucked Polly in next to her. She could feel his hand lingering above her head, as if longing to stroke her; she could feel his warmth emanating into her skin as if he were actually touching her—even through the centimeters separating them.

But he didn't lower his hand.

"Anyway. Your Mum wants me to do the recital with you that I told you about, when we were in Devon. So, if you want to, I'll help you get ready for it. But then ... then I think I must find you another teacher, because I ... don't know if I'll be able to bear being near you." The bedsprings squeaked again as he stood. "Let your Mum know if you want to try the recital."

He walked out in an uneven way—limping, she realized, though the realization didn't bring the glee she'd have expected—and the door opened and closed once more.

Lottie turned onto her back and opened her eyes. The snow, lashing against the lamppost outside, was making watery patterns on the ceiling.

She heard the telly laughter and low occasional voices from Lars' room.

185

She heard, after some time, the sound of Rita's anxious inquiry from the hall, wondering where Lottie'd got to, and heard Mommy's happy warble, responding with the telly gift announcement. Rita laughed, and went into Lars' room—more exclamations of sweet Nell, rough Lars, smooth Rory—and then out again, she could follow the trail of voices as clearly as if it were all the kind of radio show they'd used to listen to, back in America, back before they had a telly.

Daddy's favourite had been The Shadow, an odd story that Lottie had never really understood, but it hadn't mattered when Daddy held her and Nell close on the sofa, listening and laughing and sometimes clutching them tight during the scary parts.

She missed Daddy. For the first time she actually knew, she really missed him.

I miss Rory too.

As soon as she thought this, she heard his voice out in the hall, murmuring, and heard Mommy's farewell to him. She heard Lars' door close, and heard slow separate footsteps clop down the hall and into the stairwell, downward, awkward, lopsided.

She launched herself out of bed, out her doorway, onto the landing, leaning out as far on the banister as she could, balancing perfectly without falling, arms stretched, as she and Nell had done so many times. The top of his head was just on the second landing.

"Rory."

The black hair swung upwards and his pale face turned toward her, through the wooden railing. She saw one hand clutch onto the banister suddenly.

"Rory." She liked saying his name once more, seeing how he stared at her.

"Be careful, Lottie," he cautioned faintly.

Her hair was dangling down into her mouth. She swept a strand aside with one hand, and that was enough to make her lose her balance. She tilted forward, sliding a bit on the polished banister. Rory lurched into the space

186

between the landings, stiffening his whole body, eyes wide with panic.

"Silly," she told him. "It's ever so safe, I've slid down a million times."

"Not this time, all right darling, not just now?"

"But you'd be there to catch me, righty-ho, you'd never let me fall?"

His knuckles bunched on the railing.

"Never, Lottie, I promise."

It was too much of a dare.

She let go, let herself fly down the first swoop of banister, arms out so she wouldn't lose her balance, and she careened into his waiting arms just at the juncture of the second landing.

He buckled under her airborne weight and fell back with her into the hallway. She felt his arms close about her, but he scrambled up as soon as he could and set her upright as well, away from him. He picked up his fallen coat.

"Don't do that anymore. I shall speak to Mr. Lowell, tell him that he must have some sort of—barrier—put up here."

She was close enough to see mauve circles under his eyes and the pinpricks of hair where his beard grew. He looked ill in the ochre hall light.

"Are you 'suffering for love,' then?"

The bruised look sharpened briefly. "Don't be a tease. This isn't funny to me." He hooked his coat over his shoulder. "Run back up now."

She took hold of his dangling sleeve. "I heard you talking to Polly."

"I know."

She plucked at the buttons, three in a row, why did anyone need three buttons on the outside of a sleeve? She clicked the buttons together like castanets. Clap-clap, clap-clap. One of Sara's dolls was a Spanish dancer with little castanets attached to her palms.

"I ... should like to do the recital," she told him.

187

He leaned down so his face was level with hers. His coat collapsed as he took her face in his hands. She expected a kiss, but he didn't move closer, didn't smile. His eyes fixed on her as if he'd never looked away. She felt her hand creep up the coat sleeve to hover just next to his cheek. He turned his face, slightly, to meet her fingertips.

He stayed like that while she looked her fill.

After some time, he slowly straightened. "Right then."

She watched him limp the rest of the way down.

THIRTY-TWO

THE NEXT DAY Lottie was sitting at the piano, playing her latest improvisation, when the door to Lars' room opened. She turned to see Rory, not in his usual suit but in a pair of jeans and a white jersey.

His smile was quick. "Hullo, Lottie, shall we begin?" he said, cheerful, instead of, "Now." He left the door open and raised his voice to call to Mommy. "Althea, have a listen if you like, let us know how we're doing."

"I'm working," Mommy said from the kitchen. "But I can hear you."

Rory sat facing forward with Lottie. He watched her hands on the keys, showed her how to work the pedals this time, made her do the same tune over and over. He never closed his eyes even once.

"Again, Lottie, it must become automatic." His voice was so pleasant that she glanced up at him to see was he joking. He didn't look at her. He didn't sit close, although she smelt Christmas-tree. The change in him distracted her. Finally he gave up.

"All right," he sighed, closing the lid. "You're to practise a bit more daily, please, your style needs polish."

He stayed after the lesson, having brought a take-away meal, lemon fizz and a bottle of wine. He was like someone's friendly uncle, chatting them all up as Colin would, with newfound charm; a changeling uncle who'd taken the place of the cooler, broodier Rory she thought she knew. He paid her no special attention. It was as if he'd forgotten all his wittering on, to her as well as to

189

Latimer, about love, and marriage in India or Arabia or Scotland.

Looking round the rickety kitchen table at everyone's smiling faces, Lottie felt she was the only one noticing the difference. Perhaps he'd been distantly jolly like this all along, and she was just now realizing? It was like a cartoon going backward, back to a beginning they'd never had, everything in between erased. Who could say, once the little woodpecker had exploded, that he'd ever been whole to begin with? Unless one watched the next episode. She'd never wondered about that sort of thing before they had the telly. It made her feel dizzy to think about it, now, as Rory poured lemon fizz into her glass without a hint of his suffocating stare.

"Have you maths this afternoon, Nell?" he asked.

"Oh God, don't remind me," she groaned.

"Yes, she does," said Mommy. "We agreed, every other day."

"Mums! I don't give a ruddy flying fig about the stupid exams!" She'd taken to imitating the way Colin spoke. "First of all, it's Christmas break! And second of all, I don't need to worry about secondary school. I'm going to be an actress!"

"You might become an actress, but by God you will be an educated person."

But Mommy's *silence* voice did not intimidate this new Nell. "Oh right, educated." She sniffed. "Memorizing all the English kings? Memorizing a lot of useless equations, none of which I'm ever likely to need?"

"Even if you pursue acting, you'll need to know how to balance a budget."

"Like you do?" Nell sneered. Then she looked down. "Sorry, Mums, it's just … this all seems such a waste of time."

"I don't care how it seems to you. It's the way the system works here, and I'm not going to stand for having you kept from going to college just because you didn't want to spend the time passing these exams."

"But I'll be thirteen shortly! In some societies that's practically an adult."

"You must admit, Mother, the exam is ridiculous," Lars said, taking another helping of fish'n'chips. "It condemns children to a class system that—"

Mommy put her hand onto Lars'. "But Lars, you didn't have to go through this, you don't know how England judges these things—"

"Bloody hell I don't!" Lars jerked his hand away. "I know better than any of you!" He grabbed the lemon fizz bottle from Rory and glared at his sisters. "At your age, they look at your shoes first." He poured some into his glass as Nell and Lottie exchanged startled, acknowledging looks. They'd noticed that right away about English children—indeed, they looked at shoes before faces.

Lars continued fiercely, "At my age, they only want to know about the score you got on the Eleven Plus, and which prep you came out of." He gulped a mouthful, turned his stare on Rory. "Isn't that right?"

Rory nodded slowly. "I was lucky. I was tutored at home for years, so the Eleven Plus simply came and went, for Colin and me. It was only when we ventured out into the world that we realized the importance everyone places on these things." He turned to Nell. "You must listen to your mother. In England your Eleven Plus determines your future, absolutely."

Nell looked at Mommy then. "So why are we here?"

"Eleanor."

"You heard me, Mother, why are we here? We should be in America where they don't have this stupid rule that if you don't pass the Eleven Plus your life is ruined. We don't *have* to stay in England, there's no law keeping us here."

"There is a law. A higher law. The Father's law."

Lottie glanced at Rory, whose eyes were as wide as Nell's, fixed on Mommy. Lottie knew that Nell didn't dare question this. Nor did Lars. Not out loud.

"One you can't understand," Mommy continued.

191

Rory leaned forward. "Althea, *I'd* like to understand. Tell me."

"No," Lars said suddenly. "It's only an idea."

"She needn't," echoed Lottie.

"Let me talk to her alone, children." Rory scooted his chair close to Mommy. "Althea, I'm listening." His shoulder curved, making a wall that shut the children out.

One by one they left the table, Lars with a doubtful frown at Rory, who by then had taken Mommy's hands in his. Lottie dawdled, last to leave, watching the way they looked at each other. Why should Mommy tell Rory about God's sending them to Israel? It was nothing to do with him, who did he think he was, to insist?

"Go on, let me have a word with your Mum now."

Her persistent stare must have alerted him to her opposition; a quizzical wrinkle formed between his eyes as he looked back at her. But, "go on, Lottie," he repeated, his gentle tone not hiding his impatience.

She kicked at his chair as she shuffled out of the kitchen. He didn't take notice.

In their room, she flung herself onto her bunk.

The top bunk squeaked as Nell thrashed above her, turning around. "Father's law my ...! Pull the other one, it's got bells on."

"Nell, don't you believe Mommy? That God talks to her?"

"I don't know what I believe. But don't tell her I said that, you little maggot."

Lottie shot both feet up onto Nell's mattress, bouncing her up and down with such force that her sister grabbed the railing to avoid being thrown out onto the floor.

"Maggot!" she repeated, but laughing, so Lottie had to laugh along.

Nell peeled back the thin mattress to peer at Lottie through the metal springs. She pursed her lips, ready to spit. Lottie shot her legs up again. This time Nell did fall, clutching at the mattress as she careened over, twisting so

192

that she landed with its padding protecting her from the floor, a move honed by much practise.

Nell sprang up and attacked Lottie in her bunk, but after a brief tussle, she heaved her mattress back and climbed on top again: neither had the energy to keep fighting.

"It isn't *fair*. Colin says, if I were a little older, he'd be able to get me ever so many other kinds of jobs ..."

Lottie had heard this from Nell for weeks now. She went back to reading The Peninsula of Adventure. It was the most exciting book so far in the series, so real she felt she was one of the Adventurous Ones, watching the birds, sailing the waves and feeling the encroaching threat of menacing criminals. The friends used their own pluck to get themselves out of scrapes. They slept outdoors, on bedrolls made from blankets, and they made campfires and ate things out of tins. Only rarely did a grownup appear, to help them out of trouble, and then leave them alone. They had a trusty Alsatian dog named Fear to protect them.

"I wish we had a dog," she interrupted Nell.

"You aren't even listening to me!"

"If we had a dog he would never let anything bad happen to us."

"Nothing bad ever happens to us anyway. Our lives are not that interesting. Except, perhaps, for having to leave America and Daddy, and live here."

"If we didn't live here, you wouldn't have met Colin."

Nell's springs squeaked again. "I know. But the Eleven Plus is so boring!"

"But don't you want to go to university one day?" She didn't really care, she wanted to keep reading, but she'd heard Lars ask this once and it had shut Nell up.

Nell had obviously come up with an answer. "Colin told me he only went because he wanted to meet girls, and Rory went to Conservatory instead, and look at them. They're both wildly successful."

Lottie opened her book again, but her attention was broken. She twisted on her bunk, feeling the springs

193

stretch beneath her. She wanted to sneak into the hall to hear what was being said in the kitchen. What gave Rory the right to interfere? It was none of his beeswax. Yet he'd banished the children effortlessly. For the first time, she saw Lars and Nell as being a bit wet. But that meant she was wet, as well.

"I'd like a big ferocious dog who bites intruders." She was thinking once more of the ever-larger dogs in 'The Tinder Box,' which made her remember the ever-larger pianos, the day of Rory's concert.

"Mr. Singh wouldn't let us have one. He's afraid of dogs."

"He's not the landlord, what does he have to say about it?" Lottie twisted again. Her new pink jersey was itchy, pulling at her neck, and she unbuttoned its collar with impatient fingers. "We can get an Alsatian from the pound, for my birthday present. I'll name him Terror." She stood, too hot suddenly to lie down anymore. "He can sleep right here at the foot of my bed. He won't let anyone in."

"I'd rather have a dog like Happy," Nell said. "He's a sweet old thing."

"I want one who can bite off someone's hand. I want one who can rip out someone's throat."

"Those Enid Blyton stories are giving you insane ideas, whose throat do you want ripped out? Who do you need to kill?" Nell leaned over the side and sneered down at her. "Pamela? She's your only enemy that I know of. Everyone else loves you, since they don't know how annoying you are, they only see a pretty little girl."

"Bugger off!" Lottie stomped out of the room and slammed the door behind her. She marched into Lars' room and, ignoring his protests, began banging on the keys. She used the pedals to make her playing even louder. She stiffened her fingers and played like Terror howling, like Terror snarling as he stalked his victim, hackles raised, teeth bared, nose wrinkled in awful menace, ready to slash into soft flesh.

"Gracious, what a noise!" Rory had come in and was standing beside her. She pounded harder, to drown out the amusement in his voice. When he laid his slim hand on her forearm, she shrugged him off with a violent jerk of her elbow, not letting her hands leave the keys.

"Shut UP!" Lars shouted. "It's time for Secret Agent!"

Lottie unhooked the piano lid and let it fall down with a jarring clang, a hurt sound that would have made her wince, if she wasn't thinking of Terror's fangs snapping satisfyingly shut around a slender wrist.

She made a snarling face at Rory. "What did she say about Israel, then?"

He frowned at her. The theme song from 'Secret Agent' started from the telly in the corner, and Lars turned it up. *"There's a man who lives a life of danger, everyone he meets, he stays a stranger..."*

"Shall we talk about it outside, Lottie, perhaps go for a walk?"

Lars glanced up from the telly, eyes narrow. "You can talk to her perfectly well right here, Rory."

"Later, when your programme's over, we can all have a chat about it, hmm, Lars, would that suit?"

Lars' frown moved from Rory to Lottie. "Don't be long."

She could pretend Terror was walking stiff-legged beside her, ready to spring. As they went downstairs the song followed them: *"And every move he makes, another rule he breaks. Odds are he won't live to see tomorrow ..."*

THIRTY-THREE

OUTSIDE, GREY MIST hovered thick on the ground.
"Not very nice walking weather, after all." Rory turned up his coat collar. "Let's go for a drive instead, or perhaps you'd like to sit in a teashop."

She'd never sat in a teashop.

"Or perhaps this is the day to get you some warm clothes. We could go to Harrods. It's open for another two hours at least."

"Without Mommy?"

"Your Mum wouldn't mind, I told her I'd help her out with that."

Now that they were outside, she realized she didn't want to go to Harrods with him, or to a teashop, or for a drive. It was so foggy she couldn't even see to the end of their row of houses. Suddenly she wanted to go back inside, she wanted to finish The Peninsula of Adventure, in her bed, hearing the telly in the next room.

She turned back to the vestibule, but he caught her arm. "I thought you wanted to know what your Mum and I discussed, just now."

He watched her thinking about it. "Come on, here's my car."

She hadn't been in it since his concert.

She sat stiff in the seat next to him, wrapping her arms tightly round herself, trying not to remember that day and that final ride home, when she was lying in the back covered by his coat as he and Latimer talked in ever-louder whispers.

196

When he turned up the heat she had to unwrap her arms a bit.

"You do need those winter clothes," he said. "We shall get them this week whilst you're still on Christmas break." He turned on the radio to something quiet and tinkly. "I never got round to asking you, when we saw one another on Boxing Day—did you have a nice Christmas?"

"Mmm."

"And when do you go back to school, a week from next Monday is it?"

"Mmm." She wondered why he was talking like someone's mother.

"Right then, we shall get everyone outfitted at Harrods, make sure you're all ready for the winter here."

"Will there be a lot of snow?" She didn't remember snow when they'd come, nearly a year ago now.

"Not much, really, in London. But they're predicting a killer fog, a smog, they call it. See, it's in the air already. It's supposed to be very dangerous for old people and children. You must cover your faces when you're outdoors. We shall buy thick scarves."

Cover their *faces*? "Blimey," she blurted.

"I wish I could just take you to Devon for the whole winter, it's so much cleaner than London. But Nell's got her exam, and Lars can't very well leave Waverley. It's a bit complex." He accelerated as they got to the high road, and switched on the wipers, which cut no swath into the gloomy fog. "I told Althea to let me take you, since you're the youngest and the most vulnerable to the smog. Perhaps you can help me convince her."

"You mean ... we'd go to Devon instead of going to Israel?"

He left off peering out the window to give her a quick smile. "Lottie. You're old enough to know, that's just a fancy of your Mum's, that Israel nonsense."

"But God told her to go."

"I know she believes that, she told me all about it just now, but I'm quite sure that isn't how God

197

communicates. It's real to her, obviously, but it doesn't mean you're actually going to walk there, and settle in some ... collective farm, and grow olives, and listen for Jesus on the wireless."

Olives? Jesus on the wireless?

"Some kibbutz, what an extraordinary idea, with three children in tow!" He gave a little laugh, the kind Pamela gave when she thought Lottie was being silly, a nasty sort of laugh that made Lottie frown at him. "In any case, it's a simple matter of making your Mum see reason, and I'm sure that if we work together, all of you as well as Colin and me, we can succeed in doing that. I shall talk to each of you in turn, and then I'll have another chat with your Mum."

He sounded like Ursula all of a sudden, when Ursula was in charge of a school project. But this was a project doomed to fail, she was sure.

"Mommy would wonder why we're trying to make her change her mind about God." She tried to explain. "She gets ... upset, when she thinks God's plan isn't working out." She remembered Mommy's sadness on the moor, when she concluded they had to make their own path. But she'd brightened when Lottie had suggested leaving for Israel direct from Devon. "We're better off using the map to get our directions in order, and packing our bedrolls and tins, and booking our ship's passage."

She felt Rory looking at her, but she went on, "I should think a dog would be useful, to help lead the way through the mountainous areas and the deserts once we get there. A ferocious dog named Terror. We can get him from the pound." She needn't tell him that Terror would make short work of him, at her command, if she liked. "He'd protect us against thieves and ... intruders." She thought of what Fear did, for the Adventurous Ones. "He'd sniff out explosives in caves for us. Perhaps even gold."

"Come now, Lottie, *really*," he said, as if she were some sort of half-wit. She could almost hear Terror's low growl. "That sort of talk just isn't on, don't you see? I

198

think you're not quite understanding your Mum's state of mind. She may talk about this Israel idea, but she isn't really going to carry it out. It's a wonder she even got to London! I'm amazed that her family, and your father, allowed her to bring you all here, even though I know how persuasive she can be—but it must have seemed utter madness to them. Of course, *I'm* glad she got this far, to bring you to me."

His hand suddenly patted her knee, startling her. "I'll get you a puppy, sweetheart."

She swung her knees away. "No. I want a big, frightening, horrible-looking dog."

Rory drove on without speaking. The tinkly music played. The lights of the city buildings loomed out of the grey, reminding her of the ship they'd passed once on the way over, in the middle of the ocean, sliding past like a floating skyscraper and blasting its long hooting horn. It was the loneliest sound she'd ever heard.

He stopped in front of a cosily lit curtained window. "Go in, love, find us a table, don't wait out here," he told her as he fed coins into a meter at the curb.

She stood just inside the door, uncertain, feeling suddenly grubby when she noticed how the few ladies at the tables were dressed, so nicely; there were no other children. At least she was wearing her new pink jersey. She straightened its neck. A black-uniformed lady came toward her, holding out a large square page. "You've your pick of spots today, Miss, the weather's kept all our regulars away."

"Can we sit by the window?"

"Of course, right this way, is your Mummy joining you?"

"No," Lottie began, when Rory came into the tearoom.

"Oh it's your Daddy then, lovely, we don't often see that."

Daddy? Lottie watched him approaching. None of her friends' fathers looked like him. The ones she'd actually spoken to were a bit grumpy, in rumpled clothes,

199

with tired faces; except for the Twelve Dancing Princesses night. Usually they were polite, but sometimes they told the girls to be quiet, or to leave the telly. Rory, when she really looked, had an altogether different sort of face. She wondered how the lady thought he could possibly be anyone's Daddy.

"Cream tea, two cups, we'll share the sweets." Rory handed the page back to the lady without looking at it.

"Right away sir."

Lottie looked round the room, liking the feeling of being wrapped in its prettiness while the fog boiled outside, wondering could she come back here somehow with Jenny and Wendy and Ursula. How they'd enjoy this! A fire blazed in the corner. She heard violin music in the background.

"Lottie." His serious tone jerked her attention to him. He was sitting forward, hands clasped on the tabletop, studying her with the sort of expression Headmistress used when some schoolyard transgression had occurred.

"Do you know what I mean, about your Mum? Do you understand that when she talks about going to Israel, she's only meaning she wants a change? Perhaps you don't realize how tired she's getting, managing everything on her own."

"We do a lot as well. We try to help her."

"Yes I know, you're all quite amazing, but it's wearing her down. So when she wants a little rest from worrying about school fees or doing the shopping or Nell's exams, or when her St. Paul poem isn't going well, or when for example she was hoping ... for a deeper friendship with me ... why then she goes in her mind to a place where she thinks life will be easier. She calls that place 'Israel'."

"It's a real place, I found it on the map, I know exactly how to get there." Israel. Is real. She played with the words for a second, letting them drown out what he'd said, about the deeper friendship. "Israel's as real as can be, it's as real as England."

200

"Er ... quite." He sat back as the lady brought a silver tray with their tea, a cunning assortment of tiny cakes, and napkins as flowery as Wendy's Mum's.

"Would you like to pour out, for your Daddy?" The lady was smiling at her, but Rory's brows lowered in a sudden scowl.

Lottie took the teapot and pretended to be Wendy. "Yes, thanks, it looks ever so lovely." She poured a neat stream into his cup. "Here you go, Daddy. Lemon or sugar?"

She didn't look at his face, but she saw his chest heave up in a great intake of breath. "I'll have a short Glenfiddich as well."

The lady looked at him a little more closely, and her smile grew puzzled, as she glanced again at Lottie. "Very good sir."

He sat back then, watching Lottie, as she poured her own tea and stirred in cream and sugar. She sipped a bit, the way she'd learnt, and broke off a dainty piece of cake.

She heard him sigh again. "As I was saying, the Israel idea is a non-starter. You mustn't give it another thought. Your Mum does need help, more than you children can give her, more perhaps than any of us guessed. Although I daresay my Dad suspected." He accepted the glass handed to him, this time by a portly man in a suit, and drank a mouthful. Then he stirred his own tea. "Lottie."

"Daddy."

His hand snaked out to trap hers, next to the cake plate, and the heat of his palm clamped down like one of her too-tight mittens. She tried to pull away but he held fast.

"Stop being silly." His gaze held the black-ice warning. "I'm trying to help your family, but I can't do it if you're ... under this same ludicrous delusion as Althea."

Terror would crunch his hand into bits.

But then how would she ever hear him play again?

201

But she could play on her own now, she was starting to feel it in her fingers. She tried to make her eyes as icy as his, as she narrowed them on his face.

Abruptly, he laughed at her, and took his hand away. "That's all right, love, you needn't worry about this anymore. I'll see to it she gets the help she needs." He sipped the glass of Glenfiddich. Its smell wafted rich and comfortable to her across the table. "You just get ready for the Conservatory recital, and leave the question of 'Israel' to me."

She let her teaspoon clatter.

She leaned forward to hiss at him, "It isn't yours to question, it isn't any of yours! It's only mine, and Lars' and Nell's. And Mommy's. We can manage on our own."

"You poor darling," he murmured. "I'm so sorry I left you alone all these weeks. I should have stayed close, to keep you safe, to protect you properly." He reached again across the table, deep into her hair, his strong fingers spread, stroking up with his thumb to her forehead and down with his little finger to her neck. Terror lay down under the table and folded his paws onto his nose. "I'll take better care of you now, Lottie, I promise."

THIRTY-FOUR

OUTSIDE THE FLAT, he sat for a moment after turning off the car. "I might not be here on your birthday, as I expect I'll still be on tour, but I've brought you a present." He tilted his head. "Open it."

She turned to see a large box sitting on the back seat. "Go ahead, lift the flaps."

She knelt, to lean over the seatback, and undid the corners. There in a nest of paper padding lay a record player and, stacked next to it, a shaft of records. She flipped through: classical music, pianists from around the world, and the Beatles' first LP. She could not contain her startled excitement: "Coo-er!"

"I knew you'd like it."

"Thank you." She looked to see if he expected something more. But his smile was serene as he watched her, serene enough that she allowed her own smile out, timid though it felt.

"Let's try it, shall we, see how it sounds." He got out, lifted the box and records easily, and carried them upstairs.

Nell pushed next to her, crowding Rory as he plugged it into the wall socket in their room, next to the doll shelf. "Wizard, Rory, first the TV and now this!"

"It's really for Lottie, so she can hear a range of pianists."

"But I'll hear the Beatles! And Cilla Black, and Frankie Avalon, and—"

"You're going to be studying, I thought." Lottie turned to see Lars at the door, arms folded, signifying disapproval. "You got that for Lottie?" His expression, settling on Rory, was cold.

Rory's back was to Lars as he bent over the record player. "It's her Christmas and birthday present."

"That's a pretty expensive present for a little girl."

"She needs exposure to a lot of musical styles, she's got to realize what a difference it can make—" Rory put the needle onto the record he'd selected. A cascade of minor-key notes filled the room. "She needs to go to more concerts, as do you, Lars." Rory stood, walked over to Lars. "I'll bring you some records as well, old son, don't look so glum. You can share this."

"You shouldn't spoil her like that." Lars' arms were still folded.

Nell turned from the pile of records to make a face at him. "What's it to you, Lars, what do you care? Are you jealous because it's not in your room?"

"I just think it's ... too much."

"You've already got the piano and the TV in your room, and now you're acting like you're the boss all of a sudden—"

Lars interrupted Nell. "Where did you take her, Rory?"

Rory slid his arm round Lars' shoulder. "We went to a teashop and talked about your Mum. I told you before we left, Lars, that I'd want a word with you, and Nell. You must realize how dangerous this Israel fantasy is becoming." He spoke quickly, and quietly, eyeing past Lars as if Mommy might be right there in the hallway, listening to him, instead of having her afternoon nap; Lottie had plainly seen that she was asleep, when they passed by the kitchen.

Lars closed the door and stood with his back to it, his pale face looking even more careworn than usual, like a little old man's.

Nell stared at Rory as if he'd just told them Mommy had three heads.

Once again, the thought came to Lottie, *they're both wet. They're both ... helpless.* She turned the volume wheel on

204

the record player and the music softened to a tragic background lull.

"I know this is all rather ... difficult, but we're better off talking about it now, before it's too late." Rory looked at Lars and Nell in turn, with the Headmistress' straight-mouthed, level-eyed demeanor. "I've told Althea I want you to go away for a bit, at least until your school starts again. I've even thought that I should have a solicitor make me your guardian here, since your Dad's in America."

In the Adventure stories, guardians were always a child's enemy, wielding their power only for their own benefit, invariably wicked.

"We don't need a *guardian*," she told him, "we need a guard *dog*. Mommy's not as bad as all that!"

Rory folded his arms and tilted his head slightly so that he was looking at her in a narrow sort of way. "But Lottie, even you must admit, she clearly needs a complete rest." He turned to Lars and Nell. "You two wouldn't want to find yourselves on the eastbound tube one morning, next stop Tel Aviv, just because Althea said 'now'—would you?"

Nell shook her head.

Lars scowled.

Now, Lottie heard inside herself, and in her mind she was sitting on the bench next to him while he faced backwards; starting her scales, feeling his warmth lean closer, his scent grow sharper.

"And yet, in her current state of mind, that's entirely possible. I fear it may be only a matter of time before she takes the notion to simply set off, on her own if the mood strikes—"

"—she did that already," Nell blurted. "Last fall, she left."

Rory's Headmistress face fell and his own black-ice look burned on Lottie. "You never told me," he said in a near whisper. "She left you here alone?"

"The bobbies brought er back, see, she'd lost er way." She heard her voice, small and weak, sliding back into the

205

Cockney accent that used to sound so brave. "She never meant to worry us, loike, she'd just got it wrong that time."

The room was silent following this addition. She risked a glance at her brother and sister. Lars stared at the floor, red blazing the tips of his ears and outlining his cheekbones, as if he were suffering a crushing shame. Nell's pushing-out lips and slitted eyes told Lottie to *shut UP about the ruddy bobbies, tell-tale maggot!*

"But Nell, you were going to tell im, before, you were ready to tell im ..." she broke off, confused, realizing it didn't matter: *she'd* betrayed Mommy now, in the worst way because of telling about the bobbies, to the very person who should never know. His slow satisfied nod confirmed this.

"Children." Rory reached out for them, his arms stretching impossibly long to enfold them all, his strong hands wrapping around their heads and cradling them to his chest like a trio of footballs. Nell's soft hair crowded into Lottie's nose but smelt sweet. Lars' new chin stubble prickled her forehead.

"Children, you've been so brave, carrying this secret all alone for so long." Rory rocked them from side to side so they swayed precariously; Nell and Lars leaning into him off-balance, Lottie snug against his heart as usual. "I shall take care of you now." Lottie swayed harder, rocking deliberately astray, and wriggled out from under his suffocating embrace.

She edged close to the doorknob, keeping an eye on them. She saw Nell's arms tighten around him, and Lars' push away, as Rory bent to kiss their foreheads.

Lottie wrenched the door open and dashed down the hallway. Mommy was awake now, sitting at the kitchen table swirling her coffee with one hand, making notes in the margin of her St. Paul poem with the other, a frown of concentration on her face. It was so ordinary a scene that Lottie felt suddenly cartoonish in her haste, skidding to full stop beside Mommy's chair.

"Rory wants us to go away from you!"

"Yes, he told me, it's a very sweet idea. A little holiday will do you all good."

Now she was turning from a cartoon into a statue, again. "No, Mommy," she heard her voice begin, in a tiny squeak, "don't let him take us—"

"Only for a few days, Charlotte, he knows I'm at a critical juncture with my book right now, and he very kindly offered me a break. You'll have fun in Devon."

"We're not in your way," Lottie said, hurt crowding out fear, pushing her closer to Mommy in a clumsy thrust that jogged Mommy's coffee hand. Coffee slopped over the rim of the cup onto a St. Paul page.

"Now look what you've done!" Mommy swiped at the splotch with an impatient gesture that spilled more coffee. "You see, you are in my way. I'll be able to get so much more done without worrying about all of you."

Lottie reached for a napkin to blot the stained page. "Don't let him take us." Her squeak wobbled into a whine. "Please, Mommy—"

"Charlotte." Mommy took the napkin and finished mopping, not looking at Lottie. "I'll miss you too, but it's just for a week, just so I can finish by the deadline."

"What deadline?"

"Rory found a contest for me to enter. Poems are due mid January."

"I shall stay with Jenny or Stevie."

"You couldn't practice at Jenny's or Steven's," Rory said from the doorway. Nell and Lars stood right behind him.

"I could, Jenny got her piano for Christmas."

"Don't be contrary, love." Rory seemed to glide, past her, to take her own place, wedging to stand closer to Mommy. He smoothed back a lock of Mommy's hair, watching the children, smiling, warm light sparkling from his eyes as if he were revealing a huge treat. "We've got it all worked out. Your Mum can have her time alone to finish her work, and you can have a holiday in Devon."

207

"Thanks, Rory!" Nell launched herself at him and he staggered back a little, chuckling, quickly encircling her with his free arm.

"There, Lottie, you see, Nell's happy with my plan. Surely you can show a little enthusiasm for your Mum." The sparkle in his eyes seemed to challenge her.

"I'm staying here. I won't be a bother."

"Can you be very quiet, then, can you live here like a ghost?" he teased.

"I shall sleep next door, at Stevie's flat, Mommy needn't see me."

"No, Lottie," Mommy said.

"Then I shall sleep in the bomb shelter."

"The ... *bomb* shelter?" Rory repeated.

"You don't know it!" Now it was her only secret from him. "It isn't yours!"

"Good grief!" Lars snorted. "Don't be so dramatic. I can keep an eye on you, Lottie. I don't want to go to Devon either."

"But I'd like some time alone," Mommy said.

Lars frowned at her. "Let Nell go. I can make sure Lottie's quiet."

"Just because the baby didn't like the big bad horses!" Nell sneered. "You have to spoil everyone's time!"

"Don't be so mean! I just want to stay here for a bit, enjoy my new record player, and all my books, and see Jenny's new piano."

"Bring your books. And we've heaps of records there, whatever you want to hear, new ones for you as well, Lars, I should think you'd love to come," Rory said. "And Lottie, you can invite Jenny, to keep you company while Nell and Lars go riding."

"But *you'll* keep me company, Rory, you'll be right next to me?" She dared him to deny it. "If I get frightened again, in the night, you'll come to sleep beside me?"

"Not this time, love," he countered, glib as if he'd anticipated her challenge, dismissing her provocation with a careless grin. "I shall take you down there but then I've

208

got to get ready for my tour. It's eight countries, you know, I've so much to do before I go. Colin can bring you back."

"So ... you won't be there?" asked Lars.

"Eight countries!" exclaimed Mommy. "Rory, tell us all about it!"

He proceeded to tell them. A sigh Lottie hadn't known she was holding blew out of her. Good, she thought, he won't have time to go to a solicitor if he's going on tour; he can't kidnap us just yet.

She could work out how to get them out of his clutches. It was no different, really, than the time the Ones had gotten Prince Rakham of Badlandia away from his evil uncle by hiding the prince in with the traveling circus performers.

THIRTY-FIVE

DEVON WAS DIFFERENT WITHOUT RORY.

Lottie didn't stay in Sara's old room. She slept in the rose room that had been Mommy's last time. The weather was too bad to take the horses out, the Eswyths said, so instead the children played records and watched telly and beat one another at the old board games stacked in the den cupboards. It was the first time in a long time they had played with each other.

Lottie spent hours reading the Adventurous Ones, storing schemes in her mind in case she might need them in future, if Rory found his solicitor. Every morning, for two hours, she practised for her recital on the old piano that once she'd thought was the biggest in the world.

Every afternoon they bundled into bulky clothes and tromped up the moor to the stone curvature where Lottie had hidden in November. The snow floated past them slowly, so they could stick out their tongues and catch the flavorless flakes. There was never enough to build a snowman, but it was pretty, flying about before sticking in the crannies of the natural rock gardens surrounding them. They stayed out for the hour proscribed by Mr. Eswyth, flapping their arms and marching about to keep warm, then rushed down the hill as soon as Lars' watch allowed them, into the warm kitchen where Mary always had something delicious for their tea.

Every evening in the big room where the fireplace was, after their telly favourites, they had a running game of Monopoly with both Eswyths and Mary. At the end of the week Mary, having proven a canny player, impoverished everyone as she swept up every remaining property and scrap of paper money.

"That's done it, I'm all in," exclaimed Mr. Eswyth, throwing his hands up and tossing down the last of his bills, the white ones of practically no value. "Mary, remind me to put you in my will. We could use a financial wizard in the family."

Mrs. Eswyth chuckled. She still had a few pink and peach dollars left, and had hung onto her flats in the purple slums. Even so, she was obliged to turn everything over to Mary in the next round. She laughed along with the rest of them.

"The pixies promised me great wealth one day, and it seems they were not wrong," Mary said, collecting the bills and cards and sorting them back into the box. She shot a sudden keen look at Lottie. "They're not singin to ye anymore lass, now, with Rory away to the continent. They're missin him. They dunno what to make o' ye."

This sounded so peculiar that Lottie had no answer.

"E were a good Monopoly player my Rory," Mary continued, complacently folding up the stiff board. "Taught me everthing e knew."

Mr. Eswyth's bark of a laugh rang out. "He was, too right, I remember it well! One could never get the better of him. He annoyed Colin no end!" He looked at his watch. "Evelyn, time for Rory's call, he told us, it's Friday."

Lottie felt a chill shiver right through her. She had forgotten about the telephone. He could easily find a solicitor that way, whether he was in England or not. She leaned toward Mrs. Eswyth. "Can I say hullo to him, please?"

"I'm sure he'd be happy to hear from you." Mrs. Eswyth got up and reached a hand for Lottie to take. "Come along into the study."

"Just like that Annabel," Mary muttered, as Lottie went past. But that couldn't be right, it was Sara she resembled, wasn't it, Sara who had died. She put Mary's ramblings out of her mind as she followed Mrs. Eswyth into the study.

Promptly at nine o'clock the telephone rang.

"Hallo?" Mr. Eswyth said loudly. "Rory, is that you? Where are you now lad? Holland is it?" He listened a moment. "I'm not shouting." In a bit he continued, "We're all well and the children are fine. Mother is here waiting to talk to you, and young Lottie has joined us to tell you hallo." He turned his broad grin on Lottie, and handed her the heavy receiver. "Say hallo, lass, be quick about it, this is costing Rory a fortune."

"Hullo," she said hesitantly.

"Lottie, love, how sweet of you, thanks for coming to the phone." He laughed low in her ear, happy, as if he was just next to her playing with Bobby and Sari once more. "Do you miss me then, are you thinking of when we were together there?"

"Um," she said, looking at the beaming Eswyths. She pretended to be Ursula. "I just wondered, Rory, had you found the time to see the solicitor you mentioned?"

There was a compound silence: on the phone, where Rory didn't answer, and in the study, where both of his parents looked at her, inquisitive.

"Is everything all right?" she heard Rory ask at last, the happiness leached from his voice. "I spoke to Althea yesterday through Mr. Singh. She sounded fine, she was just finishing her poem. Are you well, darling, do you need me to come to you?"

A curious irritation washed through her. "Of course not, everything here is perfectly lovely. Only I did wonder, since you said that before, about being our g—"

"—don't say it," he broke in. "My parents haven't an inkling of what I have in mind. They wouldn't understand, darling, please say no more about this now. I haven't had time to fix it yet, I've been traveling every day. But I promise you I shall arrange it as soon as I'm back in London."

When she didn't answer he went on, "Lottie? Angel, don't be afraid. As soon as I can, I'll make sure I can keep you safe with me forever."

Wordless with dread, she handed the receiver back to Mr. Eswyth.

"Rory?" he bellowed. "What did you say to the child, she's pale as rice pudding, don't go frightening her with your tales of the moor ghosts, there's a lad—"

Mrs. Eswyth leaned over to pat Lottie's knee. "He's always so convincing, our Rory, you needn't pay him any mind. Just divide everything he says by six!"

Lottie stared at her. Divide by six?

Mrs. Eswyth took hold of the receiver then. "Hallo!" She bent her head. "Hang on, dearest." She unfastened her large gold filigree earring. "There now, I can hear you perfectly, tell me all about Amsterdam."

The Little Dutch Tulip Girl, Lottie thought. The Little Boy with his Finger in the Dike. She saw Rory, bending to the massive wall, poking his finger through, feeling on the numb tip, for countless hours, all the cold push of the mighty sea, ruining his piano skills forever. She slipped her own forefinger into her mouth, warming it, the way he liked to water her fingers.

"Lovely!" Mrs. Eswyth was saying. "I knew you'd be a smashing success. Play on then darling, but be sure to get your rest and proper food. I know, it's all very exciting, but you must pay attention to your health."

She loves him, it occurred to Lottie, *she loves him as much as Mommy loves me and Nell and Lars*: but Mommy rarely talked to them in the sonorous, soothing way Mrs. Eswyth was using.

"Mind the damp as well. It's bitter here, you can't begin to fathom it, snow every day and the wind just slicing into one." She listened for a moment and then her voice got serious. "Of course we know about the smog in London, the news is dreadful, you were right to send these children to us." She sent a look to Lottie but Lottie stayed put, somehow stuck to the conversation as if she could not leave while Rory was still talking. Mrs. Eswyth

213

turned away from her. "That's right, love, old people who had asthma or lung disease, and so many babies, it's a shame."

Then she turned back. "She's right here, I'll put her on." She handed Lottie the receiver again. "He wants another word."

"I want to wish you a happy birthday. I've got you a present from each country. We'll celebrate when I come back, I'm not sure if I'll be there for your birthday or not. And have no fear, Lottie, I shall arrange to become your guardian as soon as I can."

"Don't," she managed to choke out. "There's no need, it's all right."

"I know the idea of change frightens you, because you've already been frightened for so long," he said slowly. "I want to see to it that you're never frightened again. I want to keep you, and Lars and Nell, and even Althea, safe for always."

The bulky black receiver felt slippery in her hands all of a sudden. She lifted it toward Mrs. Eswyth. "So don't worry, darling," his voice leaked out, "and have a smashing birthday party next week—"

"—we didn't know it was her birthday! We'll have Mary make a special treat before they go home," Mrs. Eswyth was telling him as Lottie stood and walked out of the study. "Yes, she's practising every day, she sounds ever so proficient—"

She passed Nell and Lars, watching telly in the den, and passed the hallway to the kitchen where she could hear Mary putting away the supper dishes and singing to herself in a high eerie voice, no doubt some pixie song. Lottie paused for a moment, caught by recollection of the odd thing Mary had said before. *Just like that Annabel;* presumably Mary meant Lottie, since she was looking in an unfriendly way at Lottie as she said it.

But I look like *Sara*, she thought, as she climbed the stairs, it's Sara I remind him of. As if to confirm this she walked down the long upstairs hallway into Sara's room. She didn't turn on the light; it was as pristine in thin moonlight, blotted by passing clouds, as when she'd stayed there before.

The cupboard in the corner still loomed dark over the white quiet. The glass of the doll case reflected oddly inside, where the dolls stood waiting, eyes open, some with their arms out as if they thought she would play with them. There were spaces where the ones Nell had taken used to stand; no one had re-arranged them into a new family. For the first time since Boxing Day, looking at the dolls' empty faces, Lottie thought of Polly. She wondered, for a moment, why she didn't play with Polly anymore.

But only for a moment.

She felt, in that curious way one sometimes does, that she was actually *here*: bare toes digging into the carpet, eyes moving about inside her head, hair brushing her cheeks, the scratchiness of her pink jersey prickling her forearms, her stomach warm from supper; and her heart pounding, anxious, reacting to his vow to keep her safe. The quiet was complete: none of her usual music filled her ears.

She gave the dead girl's room one last look before going to the one next door.

She turned on the small lamp beside his bed. She lay down on his red blanket and looked at the ceiling, where a wobbly crack skated across in the shape of a shoreline, which he must have stared at for years. She tried to listen for the sealike moor sound outside, the sea she'd heard before, but there was only the ticking of a clock on the nightstand. She turned to look at it, as he'd probably looked at it every day and night before he left this house. Its face illuminated, faintly, the doily beneath it, a doily she imagined Mrs. Eswyth crocheting for him, picking out the stitches in a painstaking but happy effort. Lottie's needlework at school was knobby and bloodstained. "Some little girls just don't have a dab hand," Miss Dowd said. "Your gifts lie elsewhere."

She sat up, and slid open the drawer of the nightstand.

215

Papers were stuffed inside, so many that some had gotten wedged and she had to tug them out. There were sheets of music, printed and hand-written, his compositions she supposed, and a jumble of letters with different handwriting and sizes and colours of stamps. Perhaps he had pen-pals. She sorted through them, not really wanting to read any, not knowing quite what she was looking for, and soon pushed everything back into the drawer. Something was rattling at the very end, rolling where she stuffed the letters and music. She reached back and pulled out a torch. She switched it on and off, illuminating different corners of his room, liking its powerful, golden, oval beam. The Adventurous Ones always carried torches.

She didn't know what she'd thought she might find, rummaging through his things; like the time Lucy-Ann went looking for clues in the harbormaster's house, when she hoped to find evidence of his cheating the fishermen and instead found only the old receipts from the prior master. And the trouble she got into when the nasty scarred culprit discovered her snooping!

At least nobody knows I'm in here. She slipped the torch into her trouser pocket, crept out of his room, shut the door quietly behind her, and went down the hallway to her rose room.

Sometimes, she was learning through her reading, there wasn't any clear-cut evidence to convict the criminals whom the Ones caught and punished. Sometimes they had only their own vague suspicions to go on. Sometimes they had to act on what they simply knew was true.

216

THIRTY-SIX

JENNY RAN RIGHT UP TO LOTTIE in the windy playground and hugged her.

"You were away the longest time, I was so bored without you!" Jenny's Mum had wanted Jenny home for her grandparents' visit instead of coming with Lottie to Devon. She snatched Lottie's hand and swung it as they paraded into the cloakroom, pronouncing them officially best friends. "We got the piano for Christmas, you must come to see it right away. Today, even, Mum said I could."

"Lovely, Jenny."

The girls clustered round her in the cloakroom, admiring her new white winter coat, hat, scarf and mittens. Most of them had new things as well, but nobody's kit was as splendid as Lottie's which had come, along with new shoes, and clothes for Nell and Lars, in a huge Harrods parcel sent by the Eswyths. Lottie wrinkled her nose, hanging up her soft new scarf: it already reeked of the killer smog which Rita claimed had smothered hundreds of sickly babies.

Jenny invited them all to see the piano that afternoon, but only Wendy and Ursula were able to come along with Lottie.

"Can I try first?" Ursula asked, as they stood in Jenny's front room, touching the shiny reddish wood. Jenny's piano was a baby upright like Lottie's, only without the 'Steinway' seal in the middle of the music stand.

"Of course," said Jenny.

217

Ursula began her scales. To Lottie she sounded stiff, chopped-up, 'plunky.'

"Don't *plunk*," Rory had told her once, sharply. "Your fingers should be soft as rainwater falling on grass. If you have to plunk it means you shouldn't play piano at all. Try the drums instead."

"Rain sounds plunky, sometimes."

"Plinky, perhaps, not plunky. Not on grass. If you're to be a musician, you have to open your ears and begin to listen to everything around you!"

"I do listen, Master Rory, I hear music all the time, in my head."

The line between his brows eased. He nodded. "I know."

"What if I want to play loud?"

"Then your fingers will be strong as if … as if you're kneading clay. You'll press rather than stroke." He'd shown her the difference, his hands guiding her fingers, just lightly, just once.

"And, Master, the soft rainwater—"

"Like this, love."

He took the tips of her right fingers into his mouth and she felt his moist tongue tickling them. She'd laughed, startled, and snatched them away; that first time.

Ursula, now, was definitely plunking. Lottie wondered should she say something, but after all, she wasn't very experienced, mightn't it be rude?

Ursula finished and turned round, her face flushed and smiling. "My old tutor says I'm ready for a recital," she announced. "I shall play my piece for you, after everyone's had a turn."

"When will you do your recital?"

"I shall see what Master Rory says, when he begins teaching me next week, see if he wants me to do the same piece."

"He's … quite strict," Lottie said. "I daresay he'll make you practise ever so long for recital."

"How long do you have to play?"

"I'm doing two hours a day, sometimes longer." It was her turn to sit down. Perhaps, since it wasn't a Steinway, Jenny's piano was naturally plunky, she thought, as she ran her fingers up and down the keys, testing their springiness. She played Pachelbel, very slowly, feeling the newness of nearly raw wood just under the polished veneer.

The tune sounded sad, as if the piano knew it was torn so recently from its mother tree and now separated forever. She could just picture the bleeding tree, its heart ripped, holding out its yearning branches. Come back, come back.

As well, it seemed, as she leaned fully into the song, the keys on Jenny's new piano carried the echo of the elephant's bellow as his ivory tusk was severed from his blocky grey head. How did they get the tusks off anyroad, it must be a horrid spectacle!

She took her hands away and folded them in her lap, frowning at the keys. She wished she'd thought to ask him about the tusks; he'd have known, he'd told her everything about the wood, the metal, and the tension on the strings. Once, early in their lessons, they'd crawled behind the Steinway to look at its insides. He'd approved its construction. But they'd never talked about the tusks.

"Lottie! Whyever did you stop, you were sounding lovely. I want you to teach me how to play that one." Jenny slid close beside her, as close as he'd always sat. Lottie put her arm round Jenny and squeezed hard.

"It's your turn now, love, you must begin to let your fingers feel the keys." She put Jenny's forefinger onto the middle of the grinning row. "This is Middle C."

Plunk!

Lottie couldn't help laughing. "Softly, Jenny, pretend your fingers are raindrops falling on grass. Plinking, not plunking."

"What? How can I do that?"

She laughed harder, thinking of the wet tips of her fingers sliding from his mouth. "You should see, you

219

should just see how Master Rory shows me! You'd find it so funny!"

"I can't wait until I have him," Ursula said. "I want him to make me as good as you are, Lottie. You're like a professional already. Mum thinks you're enormously talented."

"When did she hear me?"

"The night of the play, when you took over playing from Master Rory, in your brother's room. She said she'd never heard anything like."

She'd forgotten how, suddenly indignant that he dared to play her piano when he didn't even bloody well like her anymore, she had actually moved him off the bench with an aggressive shove of her bottom, like doing the twist, the dance sensation sweeping England. He'd given her one shocked glance before standing up quickly and walking away. She'd played Pachelbel then as well, trying to calm herself, the furious churning inside her feeling like the grinding noise underneath their feet and in their stomachs, when they'd taken the aeroplane from Chicago to New York, where the ship was.

"But I sounded awful that night!"

"No, she said you were marvelous."

Fancy that.

On their way out, she and Ursula passed a heap of blankets and clothing piled up beside the doorway. "For the poor," Jenny explained as they walked by. "Mum organizes it every year for the Oxfam drive. She has us empty out all our old things."

"My Mum does it too, and this year especially, with the killer smog," murmured Ursula. "All the sickly people are at risk."

"That's a lovely blanket, that one," Lottie said, tugging at the corner of a thick stripy mass doubled up on itself. "Can I have it?" The Ones were always hoarding 'rugs,' their name for blankets, in case of sudden Adventures outdoors.

Jenny and Ursula gave each other a quick look.

220

"Of course." Jenny thrust the blanket at Lottie; it rose above her head in a heap but smelt nice, as if Jenny's Mum had just taken it from the line.

"Ta," said Lottie, pushing the top aside so she could see where she was going. She and Ursula said goodbye at the corner.

The walk home was an adventure in itself. The smog limited visibility to less than a few feet. She had to go slowly, peering round the heaped rug, hunching her shoulder to keep her satchel in place, stopping to adjust her scarf in front of her nose and mouth as they'd all been instructed to do. She wished she had the little torch she'd nicked from Rory's Devon room. She could pick out a path to follow from its strong yellow light. They'd been told that a torch could help one see through the smog if directed down toward the pavement.

Near the flat, she suddenly wondered what to do with the rug. It was too big to stuff into their cupboard, too noticeable to haul upstairs, where Nell was sure to make fun of her proud acquisition. Where could she put it?

She went round the back way, thinking she could push it under the stairs next to the coal cellar, and she noticed the heap of bomb shelter rising out of the twilight gloom. Perfect! The shelter could be her secret hideaway and nobody would ever know.

She lurched toward it, letting the blanket and bag slide to the ground, and wrapped her slipping scarf once more round her face. It was bloody inconvenient, and hot, even in the January chill. She stripped off her coat, knotted the scarf ends tightly together, and felt under the ivy for the crumbly hand-hold that opened the shelter.

She had to pull back with all her might, using both hands, and when the heavy door finally swung open, in a groaning way that pulled off a shower of dirt and ripping ivy, she fell to the ground.

She staggered up and felt behind her for the blanket. She gave it a kick, trying to get it down the short steps into the shelter, but it was so puffily bunched that her foot could not find purchase. She ended up tumbling into

221

its midst, half sliding down the steps herself, clutching the doorjamb—such as it was, nothing but a series of moldy hinges—so as not to inadvertently shut the door and entomb herself.

She and Nell had asked Lars, when they first explored the shelter last spring, why there was no doorknob on the inside, since the people who hid there twenty years ago were supposed to let themselves out after the buzzbombers had dropped their deadly payloads and gone past, racing back over the channel toward Germany.

"I suppose there was a handle here once, look, you can see where it broke off." Lars pointed out an iron stud in the heavy plaster-coated door. "They must have used it so often, poor buggers, it just wore away, eventually."

They'd stood inside the shelter watching, through the open door, a light scatter of late afternoon rainfall, beyond which a pale blue evening was emerging. Lottie now remembered how she'd thought of the beautiful song her new friend Stevie next door had just taught her:

Glad that I live am I, that the sky is blue.
Glad for the country rain, and the fall of dew,
After the sun the rain, after the rain the sun,
This is the way of life since the Earth's begun.

But when she'd started singing it, that afternoon with Nell and Lars, they'd pushed her and told her to shut up.

"Just because we're stuck here in England doesn't mean we have to sing their songs," Lars told her with an irritated frown.

"You said *buggers*, Lars," Nell reminded him, trying to twist the broken handle. "Admit it, you're getting a kick out of it here, public schoolboy, senior form."

"I'm not the most senior yet," Lars had informed her. He pushed the door open wider. "We'd better not come down again, ever, unless someone else knows we're in here, or unless we prop the door open. Nobody would hear us."

222

"Why not?"

"Because these things were designed to be soundproof, just look at the thickness of the walls and the way they even plastered the door. They had to make sure the Germans couldn't hear them, or see them, that's why from the outside it just looks like an overgrown hillock." Lars' class had been studying World War Two; most of his battleships and planes were from that era.

"And there's no way out." He looked at the ceiling, webbed and dank, just grazing his head, and touched a slit in the center. "There's an opening, see, where they got air. That's where the smoke would go if they decided to light a fire once the all-clear sounded. That was their only ventilation."

They'd stood for a moment, looking up. Lottie wondered how the children had felt, crowding inside during a bombing, huddled next to their mommy, wondering when or if they'd get out, worried about the thousands of horrid spiders sure to congregate in a place like this. "Did they take their supper with them?" she'd asked.

"Moron, they were running for their lives. They didn't care about supper."

Lottie hadn't been able to imagine not caring about supper.

Now, in yet another dim dusk, she wrangled the blanket away from her to the shelter floor. It was bare dirt, she knew, and it felt slippery as if wet, so she dragged the blanket to where she remembered the rusty metal cot was. She could barely make out the shape of its empty frame. She would bring the torch down, and buy more batteries from the shops. She still had almost five shillings left from her Christmas stocking. She could read without interruption from anyone here, if she fancied a bit of privacy; she had only to prop the door open somehow. There wouldn't be any spiders still alive in winter. Her satchel made a decent doorstop, she found, scraping it into place.

223

She saw a light go on in the third floor. Mommy must be making the potato soup. She'd been adding grated cheese lately, which made the soup a bit thicker and tastier. If Lottie got up there soon enough Mommy would let her grate the cheese. She liked seeing the thin shreds dropping though the holes of the grater.

Lottie ran up the steps, minding her head on the low threshold, and jerked her satchel out of the jamb. She trod on her coat before she remembered it was on the ground, and she picked it up, thrashing at it briefly to knock off old leaves and mud. *Why the Eswyths think white is suitable for a little girl,* Mommy had sighed; and Lottie hadn't liked to tell her that she was sure it was Rory's suggestion, from the winter doll they'd stripped naked that day in Sara's room.

THIRTY-SEVEN

"OH, LOTTIE, THAT COAT WAS BRAND NEW!"

Just her luck Mommy was in the front hall, plugging coins into the meter on the landing. Lottie tried to hug the coat to her, hiding the worst of the muddy streaks, but Mommy pulled it away.

"Lottie. How could you! After the kindness we've been shown! What on earth were you doing to get this so filthy?"

"I was gathering leaves, in the back garden, for our science project, we're to collect and press them for an exhibit—"

"I don't know what they're thinking of at that school of yours, this is no time to be outside collecting leaves, in the dead of winter, with the killer smog at large—" Mommy carried on muttering to herself, bustling the coat into the bathroom. She dropped it in the tub and turned on the taps full blast. "I think the stains will come out if we soak it long enough—" She turned back to Lottie. "Is the scarf as bad? How about the hat?"

Lottie was watching the water creep round the edges of the coat, puzzled, knowing there was something wrong with this cleaning method but not remembering why. "My scarf—" was, no doubt, on the floor of the bomb shelter, soaking into the earth. "My hat—" was sitting on the cloakroom shelf at school. "I'll just run back down to fetch them!" She took the chance that Mommy would never remember both of them. She usually couldn't keep more than one thing in her head.

225

She whirled away from Mommy's reaching hands and thudded back downstairs, out into the back garden, heaved open the heavy shelter door, pushing it back far enough not to close on her; and snatched the sodden scarf which lay, sure enough, glowing faintly on the floor like the ribbon of moonlight in 'The Highwayman' poem they were reading at school this week. Next to it lay the old canteen. She took that as well.

Upstairs, she thrust the scarf under the now-shapeless mass of wet wool in the tub and swished in some shampoo to even out the scum on top of the water. A greyish colour seeped through as the scarf added its stains to the coat's.

Lottie sat for a moment on the side, still swishing, caught by the glint of light on the copper spigot. She licked her lips and swallowed. She kicked the door closed with her foot and fastened her mouth around the spigot. The metallic taste flooded her with a sensation of ease, and she settled in for a nice long gnaw.

When the door burst open she jerked away and turned to look defiantly at Nell.

"What are you doing?" Without waiting for an answer she gave Lottie a push. "Get out, I have to take a bath, I've got the first Eleven Plus test tomorrow and I'm hoping the prefects'll see I'm the Dandy's girl and be lenient on their marking—" she made a face when she saw into the tub. "What the crikey is that mess?"

"It's my coat." Lottie tongued off the last of the coppery taste. Her lips felt wet, still coppery, so she kept licking.

"You can't wash a coat in the bathtub! You moron!" Nell turned off the water and reached in to haul up the sopping coat. "Help me!"

Lottie dragged one end, Nell the other, and they collapsed the dripping mass into the sink. Curious streaks of pink as well as grey mingled, in the tub and on the wool.

226

"Christ in a nightdress," Nell muttered, shaking her hands. She caught sight of Lottie and stared. "What's wrong with your mouth, did you lose another tooth?"

Lottie looked at herself in the mirror. Blood was trickling from both corners of her mouth. She must have snagged them on the rough copper edge, not noticing in her sucking bliss. She reached for a wad of toilet paper and dabbed at her mouth.

"Are you hurt?"

Lottie shook her head.

"Get out, then. You look disgusting. And this tub is a right bloody mess!"

Lottie wandered into her room and sat on her bunk. She felt terribly tired all of a sudden. She lay down, twisting her blanket round her, and closed her eyes. Miss Dowd had given them the devil's own lot of homework. She was ever so strict since the new term began, warning them with dire threats about the Eleven Plus most of the class would be taking next year. But a little nap couldn't hurt, surely ...

A bright light woke her, along with the noisiness of Nell's stomping about the room, grumbling. "I didn't think we'd have to do the maths first thing, I thought it would be the reading, that's easier. Now I'll have to stay up all night memorizing the bloody formulas until I've got them fixed inside my brain so tight they can't fall out—"

Lottie recognized the watery desperation, just before tears, in her sister's voice. She dragged herself out of bed.

"I'll get Mommy to fix you a pot of coffee, Nell, lots of cream and sugar, you'll be able to think better." At least that's what Mommy always said, about the combination of her coffee and her cigarettes.

"Ta." Nell sent her a grateful glance. She sat on the floor and opened her books.

Mommy was sleeping in the kitchen, so Lottie made the coffee, took the last packet of biscuits off the shelf, and brought Nell a tray, picking her way across the strewn papers and books on the floor. She sat down beside Nell

227

and poured them both a cup. "I'll quiz you on the bits you're unsure of," she said. "That's the best way to memorize."

"Thanks awfully, Lottie, you're a good sport." Nell's lashes sparkled, the frightened tears just holding back, as she picked up a biscuit.

They set to the long list of formulas.

There was no sense of time passing, except for when Nell rose to light the fire; they poured out the last of the coffee and ate all the biscuits and turned over every page of Nell's cram booklet. Nell's voice grew stronger as she repeated what Lottie quizzed. The fire crackled and sputtered and finally died out. Lottie fetched their blankets from their bunks, to wrap round them, and they went on, into the night, going over everything once again. Toward dawn Nell's voice, and then Lottie's, started to quaver with yawns.

When grey light seeped in through the bay window, Lottie awoke. Nell was slumped beside her on the floor, head on the cram booklet. Lottie shook her.

"Nell. Wake up. It's the Eleven Plus day."

Nell rolled away from her, groaning.

Lottie leaned toward her for another push. "Nell. You mustn't keep sleeping."

"Shut up, Lottie," Nell moaned. "I'm having the nicest dream."

Lars had the watch, so Lottie didn't know what time it was. It must still be very early, though, it wasn't very light outside. Perhaps a few more moments' sleep would be all right ... she closed her eyes, just to rest them ...

"Bloody bollocking buggerin hell!" Nell was screaming, throwing her book at the wall, stamping her foot, tears flying from her eyes as she whirled around.

Lars stood at the doorway. "What the crikey are you on about, you're not late—"

"I am bloody fucking well late! We were supposed to come an hour early today. The prefects were to give us a little prep first. I wanted to be there even earlier, make sure they noticed me, chat them up a bit." Nell gulped,

228

and threw her hair back. "Not just picked, but chosen," she mimicked herself in a sour snarl just below hysteria.

"Don't worry," Lottie tried, "Mommy can write you a note—"

"—Mommy can't even write her buggerin poem."

"Nell!" Lars admonished. "That's enough swearing. I'll get Mommy to say there was a ... family emergency." He turned to go into the kitchen.

"This family's an emergency, all right," Nell muttered. "Bleedin disaster area."

"That's not fair," Lottie frowned, sitting up. "Mommy tries her best. She can't help it if she's a bit ... odd. She's suffering for her art, she's got to finish just like you had to cram last night, and she wants to do her best just as you do—"

Nell considered her with a sudden, adult pity. "You believe that bollocks? That poem deadline? Rory just made that up, he's the biggest liar I ever knew."

"... Rory ... made it up?"

"He wants us with him, he can't wait to get us out of here. He told me he thinks she's nuts, and that we should leave her, and I'm starting to think he's right." Nell snatched up the little pink plastic makeup bag she'd taken to using, the one Colin had bought for her 'look-sees.'

"He'd never let me miss the Eleven Plus." She flounced into the bathroom. Lottie heard the unmistakable sound of her sodden coat being flung once again into the tub.

"Disgusting!" Nell's scornful exclamation echoed in the hall. "He'd never let us wash our coats in the bath." There followed another wet plop, the scarf, Lottie supposed, as she sat still frozen on the floor in her blanket.

THIRTY-EIGHT

MISS DOWD SCOLDED LOTTIE for not doing her work, which was still sitting in her satchel at the foot of her bunk. She hadn't combed her hair nor washed her face that morning in the rush to get to school with Nell; she felt grubby in her same clothes from yesterday as she stood, shivering without her new coat, with the other girls in the playground at break. At least she had on her pretty white hat with its jaunty green felt feather, snatched hastily from the cloakroom; where she hadn't the privacy nor, she could admit, the heart anymore, to nick supplementary treats from the others' pockets.

"Why aren't you dressed like yesterday, then?" Jenny demanded.

"My coat got dirty and I had to wash it." And she'd forgotten she had the old one.

Ursula regarded her. "I say, Lottie, I should be happy to lend you an extra coat. I'll bring it tomorrow." Her assessment grew keener. "An extra lunch as well," she murmured low just for Lottie.

Lottie walked home that afternoon with an aching head. She wanted to crawl into bed and sleep for a year, but she had to do last night's and today's homework, and manage the coat situation. As well, she must prod Mommy to go round the shops, unless she went herself now? Mr. Moore lent the children credit when they stopped for the odd bottle of milk. Lottie supposed she could make a quick detour and buy a few tins, at least. The Dandy supply was running low.

The killer smog was thick as ever as she made her way to the shops next to the park. Mr. Moore gave her a cheery hallo as the bell rang when she went in. She hung one of his baskets on her arm and piled in a large Spam, an onion and enough potatoes to make the hash that she liked. She added a tin of pineapple, her favourite, as well as a bottle of milk, and those chocolate biscuits with the layer of jam inside, those were luscious, and some bananas and oranges as well, just to get the vitamins the dentist had said were so important. She remembered to ask for batteries. She had to put the basket on the floor at the counter, it was that heavy, and Mr. Moore gave her a sympathetic look.

"Bit much for you to carry, that, unless your brother's outside waiting for you?"

She shook her head. "Put it into two bags, I can manage. It's—to be on credit, please." She didn't like to look at him when she said that, she'd caught his sorrowful glance the first time and felt guilty ever since, it was like asking to keep the shopping for free. He must think they were a sorry lot, perhaps *a losing proposition altogether,* as Stevie's Da would say. *A bleedin disaster area,* Nell had said that morning. Lottie quickly pushed away the rest of what Nell had said as she made a cheerful face for Mr. Moore, still not quite meeting his eye. "Give me the receipt, Mr. Moore please, so that we can square with you next time round."

She was startled by the smack of the packet of caramels he threw onto the top of one bag. "Righty-ho, then, Miss Lottie, you watch yourself getting home, all right?"

The bell rang again and Mr. Moore looked up toward his new customer.

Lottie hoisted her bags and trod to the exit.

A pair of black boots, pointy toes, blocked her way to the door. She looked up to see Rory standing before her: browner, longer-haired, bright-eyed, and smiling wider than she'd ever seen, as he took her in. He was wrapped in a thick killer-smog scarf and long black raincoat.

231

"Lottie! What a marvelous surprise! I was just stopping in on my way to visit you, pick up a few treats, and here you've anticipated me quite beautifully."

"D'you know this bloke, Lottie?" Mr. Moore asked sharply, as if she couldn't be trusted to recognize friend from foe.

Lottie took hold of her bag handles more firmly and stood up straight. "Yes, Mr. Moore, he's my piano tutor." She remembered his tour. "He's just come back from eight countries. Holland and so on."

Rory reached to pluck the bags from Lottie's aching hands. "Have you everything you might need, let's see ..." he took a quick inventory and glanced at Lottie, then over to where Mr. Moore stood behind his counter, arms akimbo, in his apron. "I say ... since I've the car, perhaps we can augment your supply a bit ..." He set Lottie's bags onto the floor, took two baskets from the supply near the door.

He went swiftly through the little shop, tossing in packets, as well as roots of vegetables, vines of fruits, another bottle of milk, a bulky burlap container of fireplace coal. Two bottles of sherry. He lugged his baskets onto the counter and, after Mr. Moore totted up the cost, dug into his trouser pocket.

"I understand it's on Mrs. Arkwright's credit, sir," Mr. Moore told him, stiff.

Rory stared at the greengrocer for a moment. "Nonsense." He peeled bills out of his wallet and slapped them onto the counter. "Please settle the account in full." His mouth had its 'now' shape, and Mr. Moore, humbled, counted out change.

Outside, Rory loaded their shopping into the boot of the Mini. "Everything all right at home?" he asked, as he swung in the final bags. "It is just you, alone, buying your family's food for the week, right darling, Lars isn't waiting for you in the park?"

Although his tone was light, she heard the judgment behind it.

"I only wanted a snack, but my eyes were bigger than my stomach." She'd heard Mommy say that sometimes when they went to Wimpy's. She gave a musical laugh like Agnes. "Wasn't that so silly!"

He lifted a corner of his mouth as he opened the passenger door for her. "Quite."

Sitting beside him again, in his immaculate car, brought such a choking into her throat that she could not speak. She stared straight ahead as he drove, knitting her hands together under her cardigan sleeves.

He switched on the heat full blast. "Where's the pretty white coat I had my parents send you, it's bitter this evening, and where's your smog scarf?"

She took in a breath. "It was warm this morning when we left, I didn't feel the need of them." She gave another little Agnes laugh.

"It's not okay, Lottie. You can't be out like this, in the dark, in the freezing smog, all alone, doing the family shopping."

"I was just passing by for a sweet, er, a tin of Spam, on my way home from school." That sounded odd. "I ... had a taste for Spam." Worse. "Anyroad, it isn't dark."

He glanced, pointedly, out the window, where the killer smog made permanent dusk of every day and made four o'clock in the afternoon look like seven at night. "It's just not okay," he repeated, ignoring her argument. He must have met some Americans on his tour, she thought, trying not to hear beyond 'okay.' "I'm seeing my solicitor friend tomorrow. You children can't be put at risk like this anymore."

"Mommy isn't like what you told Nell!"

He frowned. "What's that?"

"Nuts, you said, she's not nuts! She's just finishing her poem!"

Rory pulled the car to the nearest curb and shut off the engine. He stared at her. "My darling girl. I never said she was ... nuts, what a peculiar word ... I only said to Nell that Althea is seriously ill. She can't help herself being ill, any more than one can help having a bad case of

233

flu. There are doctors she can see and places she can go for a rest while she gets better. I told Lars and Nell that I thought you children would have a better sort of life if you were well cared for at home. Regular meals, decent clothing, supervision for homework, jolly outings. That sort of thing. I'd like to provide that for you, if you'll let me, whilst Althea's having her rest cure."

"Mommy's not ill! She's an artist, like you are, Mas— Rory. Like you had to spend a lot of time on your music. She has to spend it on her writing!" She couldn't seem to get the right words out, the ones that would make him change his mind. "You were very naughty to tell her a lie about the poem contest!"

"Mmm, I daresay. What about the way she hears voices?"

Voices? Lottie sputtered, "No, it isn't voices, it's only God." Then, seeing how that sounded to him, she amended, "It's like a way she has of thinking out loud, d'you never speak as if you're talking to yourself, inside your head?"

His face was, once again, cold as the shepherd boy's who bent, ever-vigilant even now, over the manger under their dried-out Christmas tree still standing in a corner of Lars' room. He looked away from her. He stretched a gloved finger to the keys dangling from their socket, where he made them jingle a bit.

"And the walking to Israel, Lottie, when the police had to bring her back?" He gave the keys a forceful flick. "That was ... unforgivable." His tone said that he, certainly, would not forgive; and shame heated her face for having told, about the bobbies. The bobbies were what made Mommy's Israel launch unforgivable; the bobbies and speaking aloud about God sending her there.

A stifling sensation thrust up into her ears as if her body could no longer contain the massive headache that had been mounting, for hours now, and must eject its unwelcome burden. She put her hands over her ears, fearful it would come bursting out and tear her open, and she tried to slow her breathing so it would subside

234

somehow. It seemed so long since she'd heard music inside.

His arms were around her faster than she could tame the headache, hugging her to him, but instead of feeling suffocated she felt, as he rocked her, a whoosh of ease, as if he were squeezing the hurt right out of her bones. As she gasped onto his coat the headache dissolved into tears, and hurts leaked away with them, all but the deepest, which she could not release.

"Rory, don't take us away from Mommy. Please, if you love me, you said you love me, remember, so please don't take me away ..." She wept further, feeling her throat nearly close. He rocked her, steady, patting her back.

"There, darling, I know this is hard. But it's for the best, you'll see, you'll understand one day soon, the best for your Mum as well ..."

Emptied, she slumped away from him, back into her seat.

He unfastened the glove compartment, took out a tissue, and leaned to wipe the tears off her mouth. Then he lifted her chin and gave her lips a quick kiss. He drew back, a puzzled little wrinkle on his forehead.

"Darling ... did you not bathe, this morning, did you not brush your teeth?" He examined her, up and down. "I told you, love, a beautiful girl like you must keep herself ... immaculate." Then he twisted the keys and the engine roared as they drove away.

THIRTY-NINE

AFTER HE HANDED HER TWO BAGS at the bottom of the flat, she ran as fast as she could ahead of him, to sweep up her sodden mess from the tub and jam it under her bunk. Then she peeled off her now-damp cardigan and dashed into the kitchen with the shopping.

"Mommy, wake up, Rory's coming up!"

Mommy turned over in her cot, smiling sleepily up at Lottie. "Sweetie.Perfect timing. I finished my poem today."

"That's good, Mommy, but about the contest, it's not real!"

"Not real?"

"Rory made it up!"

"Why would he do that?" Mommy's smile was puzzled, but not alarmed enough, and Lottie leaned forward to whisper, frantic and quick, about the rest cure—

—but it was too late. Rory had already ascended the stairs.

"I invented the contest for you, Althea, as a motivation for you to finish. I do have a friend who's with a poetry magazine, and I thought if you had something complete, you could show it to him. I thought a deadline would help you."

Lottie waited for Mommy to get angry at him. Mommy hated lies, she always said. But Mommy was smiling as she got out of bed, and she patted his shoulder as she passed him on her way to the bathroom. "You're

236

always looking out for me. You're a true friend. Welcome home."

He hoisted his lot onto the table. "Let's put this away and have a nice supper. I bought fish'n'chips before I stopped at the greengrocer's—"

"I want Spam hash." She took the potatoes to the sink, to peel them. "You needn't stay, you'll want to go home, I should think, after all those countries."

"In a bit. I want a word with Althea." He strode over and plucked the potatoes from her hands. "I'll put these away—" He sorted the shopping out, quickly, and piled the bananas and oranges into a bowl and put it on the table. He handed her the bunch of grapes. "Drape those on top, that'll be a nice touch."

He stood then, looking round the room, and she suddenly saw it as he did: squalid, ill-equipped, full of unsavory clutter. *He can't wait to get us out of here,* Nell had said. He pulled at Mommy's blanket, straightening it on her cot with a twitchy gesture that gave away his discomfort.

He set the fish'n'chips onto a big plate just as Mommy came back into the room. "Oh, Rory, thanks!" She threw her arms round him and Lottie saw, over Mommy's shoulder, how he winced, even as he patted her back.

"Let's sit down for a chat before supper, Althea." He moved to the table and opened a bottle of sherry.

"Your magazine friend," she reminded, sounding shy, sitting beside him.

"I've found a typist for you. I think it's better if she comes round here, so she can ask you any questions she might have about the manuscript ..."

Lottie left them alone, after stowing away her batteries and the tins of pineapple in a bag she'd kept aside. She'd need a tin opener as well, but she could get that later. Jack, of the Adventurous Ones, had an uncanny knack for slipping back into the criminals' caves to snag a tin opener when needed.

She was shocked into immobility, on her way down the hall, by an unearthly shrill scream.

"What! What the fucking bollocks is this! My cram book's all wet, I can't read a thing, Mommy! Mommy! There's a leak somewhere! Come quick!" Then Nell's voice dissolved into screaming again, inarticulate, hopeless, heartbroken.

Lottie knew, with a sinking feeling, that there was no leak except from her bollocking coat, seeping noxious effluvia from under her bunk. She ran into their room, threw herself halfway onto the floor, caught the end of the coat and tugged it out, in front of Nell, shrieking beside her, and Mommy and Rory, who stood silent in the hallway, no doubt appalled, as she dragged it round the doorjamb and into the bathroom again. The coat seemed to have gotten wetter, if that was possible; in any case it was a deal heavier than it had seemed just ten minutes ago.

"Eleanor!" She heard Rory say sternly, "No matter the occasion, a lady does *not* resort to swearing. I cannot countenance what I heard from your mouth."

This admonition did not take hold the way he intended.

"Oh bloody buggering FUCK all!" Lottie heard Nell's screaming response.

Lottie heaved the coat into the tub and ran cold water full blast. Now she remembered, what she'd forgotten the day before: dry cleaning, that's what coat washing was called, she remembered it from America. Presumably English coats needed to be cleaned the same way. Without water.

She sat back. She turned off the tap. There was no point in trying to ... what was their peculiar new vocabulary word, just this week? Resuscitate. She looked at her formerly lovely, formerly white coat. Its matching scarf was surely still dripping under her bunk. *Ribbon of moonlight my great aunt's arse,* she thought suddenly, and a snort of laughter shook her.

238

No doubt Rory's hopes for Nell as a lady would never be resuscitated. Another snort shook her, and another, and she could not contain her laughter, great whoops of it, rocking there on the edge of the tub. Tears began to stream down her face as, at the same time, she felt the presence of someone standing beside her.

Rory, stern-faced, folded-armed, looked at her with an awful scowl.

She could only yelp up at him, helpless, dabbing at her eyes with one weak hand and pointing into the tub with the other. "It's ... done for," she managed to gasp.

He peered into the tub. His brows rose as he recognized the mass. His eyes narrowed on her as he unfolded one arm and followed her finger with his own. "That ... was your pretty white coat?"

Gravity gripped her as strongly as levity had done. "That was it, yes, sorry Rory. I didn't mean to get it dirty."

She heard the beginning of what sounded like a frustrated exhalation, but watching him, she saw it turn into rueful laughter; not as instinctive nor as all-consuming as her own had been, but laughter nevertheless.

He raised careless palms. "The best laid plans, eh Lottie ... that coat's not supposed to be the most important item of discussion tonight, in any case."

She was reminded. She looked away from him, even though he was now smiling. "Did you get a chance to talk to Mommy, then," she said.

"Not really. Perhaps this can wait until Nell's Eleven Plus is over. That is, I shall speak to the solicitor tomorrow but I expect you won't be allowed to move to a new house with me until it's settled with your mother, and your father as well."

"A new house," she repeated. Would even Daddy agree with Rory?

"Yes, you children need to live in a house, in this vicinity so you can keep your school status, with a large back garden, and a housekeeper who will make sure you've got the right meals and clean bedrooms"—he glanced again at the tub— "and of course, clean clothes."

"What about you?"

"What about me?"

"Well ... what will you do?"

He regarded her with a half smile. "Why ... I shall live with you, and look after your family. I shall make sure you have everything you need. During the week we'll all be working hard, and at the weekend we'll find interesting things to do.

"Lars is almost a young man, he'll need a bit of freedom; I shall teach him to drive. Nell will want some guidance, but Colin and Lucy will help with that, and her Dandy success will open all sorts of doors. Althea, well, Althea must be allowed to heal on her own, in a quiet place, where she can write—she's a marvelous poet, you should know that—and where she can understand and be cured of her illness."

"What about you and me?"

"I'll help you to be the best pianist you can be, my darling love. Of course you'll do a brilliant recital." His smile grew, slowly, as his voice lowered into an intimate whisper. "And we can take our time together, sweetheart, we'll have all the time in the world, all our leisure to ... explore. I long for that."

"Do you mind?" Nell stood at the bathroom door. "I should like to wash my face." Her arms were folded, her swollen face shut. "I must get my reading prep done, and I want my fish'n'chips, but first I must have a wash."

"Right Lottie, shall we heave this lot into the rubbish?"

He'd really toss away his precious winter doll coat, chosen specially for her from Harrods? His smile, just hovering there at the edges of his mouth, so sure of itself, seemed to say, *why bother with the coat when I'm keeping the doll?*

240

FORTY

AFTER SUPPER Lottie showed Rory the rubbish bins round the back. He held the coat in an increasingly saggy paper bag. He hoisted it up and into the big iron box, where it fell with a significant plop.

"That's put paid to any delusions of elegance you might've been harboring, Lottie. I'm not buying you another winter outfit, not until you're sophisticated enough to appreciate it. From now on it's macs and wellies for you, my scruffy darling." He meant MacIntosh waterproof raincoats and Wellington rubber boots. She wouldn't mind a set, actually; everyone else wore them. He laughed. "But I will let you pick the colour."

She couldn't come up with a colour just then. She was thinking about something else. "Can I choose the colour another time?"

He laughed again. "I didn't mean you must decide right now." He rubbed his hands together. "Let's go in, shall we." He started back toward the light.

"Wait," she said. "There's something I want to show you."

He turned round. "What's that?"

"It's just a bit deeper into the garden." She stood out of the light. "I've been wanting to show you for ages, Rory. It's my secret place."

He came close, looking down curiously. "Secret place? Here in your garden?"

"Over here, come on—" she reached for his hand, still in its glove, and held on tight, as she tugged him

241

further away from the light. "This way." She added, "Darling."

She heaved open the bomb shelter door with one hand while still clutching onto his with the other. "It's just down these little steps, look, you can follow me—"

He stopped. Her hand was yanked backwards. "Lottie. Let's come back to see this in the daytime, love, it looks a bit strange, we haven't even a torch—"

"I shall fetch one, it'll be just like the time Jack hid in the cave while Lucy-Ann went back for their supplies." She turned what she hoped was her best smile on him. "Come on, Rory love, don't be wet."

"Jack? Lucy-Ann?" He closed his hand round hers again. "The Adventurous Ones. I remember them. Which is the story you're thinking of?"

"All of them, I suppose. Come along."

He followed her down the steps and bumped his head on the entryway roof. "Sorry," she said, pulling him behind her. She was careful not to shut the door after them. She could just see the blanket she'd brought down yesterday, heaped on top of the cot. She gripped his hand, as firmly as he'd ever held her. "Let's sit down here."

He worked his way in beside her, gamely, ducking under the low ceiling, pushing aside the thick wrinkles of blanket. "I say, Lottie, this is quite a relic. I've never been in one before. We didn't use them in Devon."

"I know."

"It's rather ... close, isn't it, filthy, one should think, underground all these years. Just imagine how those poor souls felt. No food or water, no circulation—"

"There is, actually, there's an opening at the top." It wasn't visible in the killer smog evening, of course, but she wanted to reassure him. "It's just above us, covered by ivy fronds, feel the air? It's several inches wide."

"Not fit to breathe." She felt him moving beside her.

"Actually, Miss Dowd says that air which is filtered through plants like fern or ivy is much cleaner than normal air."

"Ah now that's a comfort." She felt him turning to her. "Lottie, you need a scarf in London this winter, even if you're breathing through plants. Did your white one die as well in the bath?"

When he put it like that she couldn't help laughing. "Sorry."

"Take mine." He wrapped it around her face. It smelt like smog. "Is that all right, I can't see you properly." His hands stayed on her shoulders, smoothing down the scarf ends, smoothing down her back. She leaned into him, fitting herself under his arms. They sat for a few moments without speaking.

"You did miss me." He pulled her closer.

"Mmm."

"I actually cut my trip short so I could be sure to get here in time for your party."

"I decided to have it another time." Daddy's check hadn't arrived yet. "I wasn't able to invite the girls at school."

"Your little friends. How are they, did they have good hols?"

"I'm teaching Jenny to play piano."

"Clever girl."

Funny, now that she'd decided what to do, she was reluctant to act; it was comfortable just sitting close to him like this in the dank darkness. He leaned against the uneven plaster wall, dragging a corner of blanket around her.

"Are you cold, love?"

"No." She could almost go to sleep, the endless sleep she'd wanted, he was like a long warm pillow she could wrap herself round. She felt his breathing slow and his embrace loosen. Was he asleep? "Rory."

"Mmm." His voice was a faint exhalation.

She could creep away now and collect the rest of the things she needed. She gently, gently slipped out from under his arm, taking care to prop the blanket under it, and tiptoed to the door, up the steps, out into the garden. She shut the door behind her.

243

She raced back upstairs. Lucky; Mommy was in with Nell, and Lars was in his room with the door closed. She fetched her bag of batteries and pineapple, and added to it tins of Dandy's soup and peas, some of the fruits, a tomato, the second bottle of sherry and a packet of biscuits. She remembered to throw in their spare tin opener. The canteen was on the floor of the bathroom where she'd dropped it yesterday. She rinsed it out three times and filled it with cold water.

She made her way back down and out, and heaved the door to the bomb shelter open once again.

"Lottie?" She heard him yawn. "Why are we still in here? It's horrid."

"But I've brought us a dessert picnic. For my birthday."

He sat up on the cot and laughed. "Strange place for a picnic, darling."

"It's like the cave where Lucy-Ann and Jack had to stay." She switched on the torch and gave him the sherry. "I don't have an opener for that."

He twisted its top right off. "Doesn't need one. Fancy a sip?"

She shook her head. "Would you like a biscuit?"

"Thanks love."

She handed him the canteen. "Here's some water, only don't drink it all right away."

He laughed again. "This is the funniest picnic I ever had. Mind you, it's only because it's for your birthday." He took a sip from the canteen and spat it onto the floor. "Ugh, that's foul, whatever did it come from?"

"It was on the floor here, left by the people who hid last time, but I rinsed it out, so the water's fresh."

"Tastes nasty. Don't drink it." He dropped it onto the floor and it rolled out of the torchlight. "Let's go back."

"I like it here with you, it's ... special."

He looked at her, stretching back on one elbow, letting the biscuit pack fall by his side, resting the sherry on the floor. In the torchlight the brown he'd acquired on tour, and the smoke of his day's beard growth, made him

244

look as swarthy as the kind of criminal the Ones were always battling. His smile gleamed white. "You're so sweet. I thought of you every day, dearest love. It made me so happy when you wanted to speak with me on the telephone that evening when you were in Devon."

She wondered was he going to ask for a kiss, but he yawned again. She reached into her satchel for the clean composition book and pencil she'd packed. "This is for you to write out letters with."

"Letters!"

She showed him the extra batteries. "These are for the torch." She moved closer to the door, unwinding his long scarf from her neck, letting it curl off like a snakeskin.

He watched her, raising his brows a little, still smiling.

She could dash out now, but the Ones were always forthright when they caught evil-doers. She took a deep breath and stood up tall.

"Rory. I'm keeping you here until you change your mind. I don't want you to take us. I don't want to marry you or do baby-making."

She pointed to the paper and pencil. "If you need to write your agency, or your Mum and Dad, to tell them a reason why you're not at home, I'll post the letters for you if you push them through the airslit." She took another breath. "But I won't post them if you tell on me."

He slumped further down on the cot, as if stunned. He stared at her.

"I'm going now. I'll bring you more water tomorrow, I'll find another bottle or something and drop it down the airslit. Goodbye."

Before she could reach for the door, which she'd propped with a rock, he was off the cot in a flash, gripping her arm. "You will do no such thing, what a wicked idea, what an ungrateful little—" His grip tightened into a painful vise as he glared at her. "I'm sorry to say this, Lottie, because I love you, but you're being very stupid!"

She tried to twist away. "You're hurting me!"

He let go of her arm to grab her shoulders. "You're too immature to know that your Mum is *really* very ill, that she's a danger to herself, even, as well as to you. Walking to Israel! It's criminal!"

Was Mommy a criminal?

He sounds a right criminal, she suddenly heard Latimer say about Rory's old tutor, as he turned on Rory with a look of outrage, after Rory told him *we underestimate how intensely children can feel pleasure.*

Latimer thought the criminal old tutor said that, about pleasure, but she thought, now, that it was Rory's own idea. "What about what you did to me," she whispered.

He brought his black-ice eyes blazing level with hers, as an outrage like Latimer's spread over his face, and then he shook her so vigorously her head wobbled. "That's a truly beastly thing to say, Charlotte. I know you're upset about Althea, I know you don't want to leave her, but you mustn't blame me. I didn't make Althea ill. I'm trying to help her get well, in peace.

"And you know I never meant to hurt you! My only mistake, if you can even call it that, is loving you too much. Loving each other isn't wrong. There's never been an unwanted touch between us, you know that, you always like what we do, except for that one time, and I told you I was sorry. And I haven't touched you since then! I've been very careful!"

You always like what we do. She looked down. *But he wants to take us away from Mommy,* she reminded herself. *And anyway, so what if I liked it?*

"Just because I liked it doesn't mean it's all right."

She lifted her hands up to his hair, to stroke it as she'd seen Annabel do, and a look of bewilderment replaced indignation as he stared at her. She mussed his hair as best she could while he still gripped her shoulders; pulling it down over his eyes gently, she didn't want to hurt him, but when he threw his head back, to fling the hair off, his hold on her lessened for the break she needed.

She wrenched away and whirled through the doorway.

She kicked the rock out of place and slammed the door shut.

She heard an agonized howl. Oh God, had she shut him in the door?

She scrambled to the top of the mound, where the torch she'd left him, on the bed, illuminated a swath of the shelter through the ivy. She peeled a frond of it aside. She could just see him there, at the doorway, but she could not see his hands.

"Did I slam the door on you?" If he was hurt, she'd have to let him out.

He turned to her voice, looking up. He came to stand directly underneath where she was peering. She saw no blood, as he raised one slim hand through the airslit to grab at the ivy, she saw only the heat of disbelieving fury in his upturned face.

"Open the door at once." His voice sounded small and muffled.

"No." She backed away, in case he tried to snatch her hair. His hand flailed, fruitlessly; the slit wasn't wide enough for him to turn his wrist properly. "Stay until you promise to leave us all alone. You're to think about it, like Jesus in the desert—"

"Jesus in the *desert*? You're as mad as your Mum. Open the door at once."

"Not until you promise to leave us alone—"

"All right, I promise. Now let me out."

She peeped in again, to see was he smiling, but he still looked furious. "No, Rory, you must really believe it. This is your chance to have a rest cure of the sort you want for Mommy. You must have a change of heart like—why, just like St. Paul." *At last that fellow's good for something.*

"Change of heart? I'll drive away and never come back! I'd be spared no end of worry, you ungrateful girl!" He was shouting now, but if she raised her head far enough away from the hole, she couldn't really hear him. The English must have built the shelter with just this sort of situation in mind. "Let me out!"

"Goodnight, Rory."

247

"But I promised! Let me out!"

She heard him still, but very faintly, as if he were at the bottom of a well. She mussed the ivy back onto the hole as she'd mussed his hair, slid down the ivy-covered berm and stood on the ground. "Wicked child! Come back!"

She stood a moment, trying to feel whether her conscience was irretrievably stricken, but she felt nothing but a shiver from the cold. But he had his coat, and that thick blanket, and his scarf, if he stopped shouting long enough to pick it up and wrap it round him. He might be livid, he might be uncomfortable, but he wouldn't freeze.

FORTY-ONE

UPSTAIRS, MOMMY WAS STILL coaching Nell on the reading and vocabulary section of the Eleven Plus. Lottie remembered all the homework she was supposed to do and lay on her bunk to get a start. The reading was all right, they were just starting *A Little Princess* and it seemed an interesting story. But Maths were brutal. She had to agree with Nell that some bits of Maths were useless to real life: fractions, for instance, why would anyone ever need them? But she set to work, multiplying and dividing in her head and scratching answers laboriously into her comp book with her remaining pencil.

She wondered had he started on his letters yet. He'd probably shout until his voice gave out, and then he would do some smashing and kicking; that's what she'd seen Stevie do when he was angry. She hoped he wouldn't be silly enough to break the torch or the bottle of sherry; he might cut himself on the glass shards in the dark. But after a time, surely, he would settle down, fold the blanket properly on the cot so he could make a 'book' of it, and slip himself inside. He had the torch. He could write letters.

Write letters—

—and perhaps a tune or two. He was clever enough to realize that she would not waver and that he must behave.

Her eyes were more interested in watching him write a new tune than in finding the common denominators on the list of fractions in front of her. She frowned at them and began again. Bother. They all seemed to have too many sevens.

Halfway through the page, scrunching her pencil down and erasing wrong answers into strands of her hair, her fingers seemed to notice the act of writing.

She ought to write a letter of her own.

She chewed the pencil end for a moment. How could she explain to Daddy? Or Miss Dowd? Or even Mr. Avery or Rita and Jimbo? How could she find the words, that wouldn't make her seem the wicked child he called her?

Her fingers paged onto a clean sheet and began:

Dear Nana,
I need to tell you something very important.
*I don't want us to live with Rory Eswyth even if Mommy is ill and he is trying to help her. I have done everything in my power to stop him (*that bit sounded like the grownups in the Adventurous Ones*), but you must help us come back to America as soon as Nell passes her Eleven Plus.*
Love from Lottie

She ripped the sheet out cleanly, found the envelopes and stamps where Nell kept them, and tucked the letter into her satchel before turning back to maths.

The sliding of the comp book from under her face woke her. Mommy was covering her up with a blanket. The light was off, and the fire embers glowed dim.

"I can't go to sleep, I have too much work to do—"

"You need to sleep. Nell told me you were up all night with her."

"But Miss Dowd's already angry—"

"I'll write you a note, and you can stay home tomorrow and finish what you didn't do today." That sounded lovely—she could have a nice long sleep—but she didn't want to be here during the day when she'd have to be wondering about how Rory was faring in the

250

bomb shelter. And Miss Dowd would give out even more work tomorrow, and she'd get even more behind.

"No, Mommy, just please wake me up early, can you?"

Mommy's kiss promised, but Lars actually delivered, banging on their door and shouting, "You said you wanted me to wake you early, so get up right now! It's another Eleven Plus day!"

"The last one, thank the Lord," groaned Nell.

"When will you find out the results?"

"Friday at the latest, possibly even tomorrow, Mr. Gordon said, if the prefects hurry up. We're a small class so there's hope."

Mommy had made oatmeal for breakfast in honor of the final Eleven Plus day. Lottie didn't think oatmeal was transportable down the bomb shelter airslit, so she took three pieces of bread, two small apples, and a tin of condensed milk. She didn't know how to get an empty bottle and fill it with water. Perhaps she could encourage Mommy to finish up the sherry quickly; it would make a fine water bottle if she lowered it on a string—

"What are you raiding the larder for, are you having a picnic with Stevie? Must be nice not to worry about school, and exams, and play like a baby all day," Nell sneered.

"I'm going to school. I don't want to get behind."

She ran outside as Nell was in the bathroom with her makeup. The air was very damp and the smog was thick, but at least it wasn't too cold and windy. As she crawled up on top of the shelter she heard a muffled coughing that sounded as if he hadn't had a good night. She told herself not to care. She dropped in the apples first, as a sort of warning, then the tin and the bread.

"Lottie." A slice of his face, paler than ever, red-eyed, appeared just below the airslit. "How can you do this to me? It's a miserable place."

"I shall try to bring some water this afternoon."

"It's cold and wet and filthy. I can hardly breathe." Indeed, his voice was rough and scratchy. "Please, Lottie, please, if ever you were my friend, if ever I meant anything to you at all—please let me out."

She steeled herself to be firm. "Have you done your letters?"

His face disappeared and his hand shot out, snatching an edge of her wrist. His fingertips were raw and bleeding—he must have tried scratching at the door—and his nails made red rake-marks as she jerked away.

"No I have not done any bloody letters!" His voice rose to a shout at the end.

"Then you'd best start," she told him in as stern a tone as she could muster, shaking, still seeing his bloody fingertips grasping her wrist. "Because I'm keeping you here until you say you've no intention of adopting the Arkwright family."

"But you silly child! Nobody thinks that anyway! I never got to the solicitor, you know that, I was to go today—" he broke off, coughing: but he might be pretending.

"Lottie! I'm leaving without you!" Nell cried, from in front of the flat.

"NELL! NELL!" Rory boomed suddenly in a huge voice. Lottie covered up the airslit with ivy and ran for the front where she couldn't hear him.

"You're so grubby, don't you ever take a bath?" Nell made a face.

As if I've time for a bath what with Miss Dowd's new rules about work, and Rory back there going barkers, and you with your bloody exams.

At least she was adequate in Maths.

But Miss Dowd asked her to stay in at break.

She smiled when Lottie approached her desk.

"Happy Birthday, Lottie, I wondered did you bring treats to share with the class today or do you want to do it another time, after the Eleven Plus is over?"

Her birthday.

It was January eighteenth, then, and she was now ten years old. Two numbers.

Two numbers, no treats, no party, and her only presents were from the bloke she'd locked in her bomb shelter. It sounded like an especially horrid Maths problem.

Miss Dowd looked so worried that Lottie feared she'd said that out loud.

"Lottie, what is it, what's wrong?" But Miss Dowd's sweet voice sounded too like Rory's used to, before, and she couldn't listen. She ran to the toilets near the cloakroom so she could flush and flush, hiding the noise of her sobs.

After a bit she washed her face and smoothed her hair. Cheer up, she told her bedraggled reflection. Daddy's check will come soon, and Mommy will bake a cake for the class and let me plan my party at home. By then—she hoped it wouldn't take longer than a few days—Rory would see *the error of his ways,* as Stevie's Da would say, and be out of their lives. Perhaps he'd leave the presents.

She went back to the classroom, where the others were just coming in from break, and walked straight to Miss Dowd's desk.

"Sorry about before," she said. "The Eleven Plus is making us all barkers."

Miss Dowd nodded. "It's a shame, really, such pressure on the children."

253

FORTY-TWO

AND ON THEIR SISTERS, Lottie thought on the way home. It made her feel better to post her letter to Nana in the round red box on the corner, but Nell was still moaning about how awful Vocabulary had been, even worse than Maths and Reading, it would be a miracle if she passed, she'd run away and live with Colin if she failed, he could find her private tutors like he and Rory'd had, like the children of famous actors had, she was too special, really, to have to go to all-day school anyway—

"I can ask Rory about it now, there he is!" Nell cried in obvious relief.

Lottie thought her heart would slide all the way down her body and plop onto the pavement. She actually had to stand still and catch her breath. Then she ducked into the nearest doorway. "Where is he?"

"What the blimey is wrong with you? His car's here, so he must be upstairs."

His car! Bloody hell, she'd forgotten all about it. If he were reported missing, they'd be looking for his car. And they'd probably go round to all his usual haunts, as Stevie's Da would say, and they'd send bobbies up to cross-examine the Arkwrights. That's what happened on the show Mommy had started watching, 'Perry Mason.' And if it were the same pair of bobbies as had caught Mommy?

But perhaps everyone would assume he was still on tour? She had the feeling he'd gotten back from his tour unexpectedly, yesterday afternoon. *One thing at a time, Lottie my girl,* she told herself, *don't panic before you have to.*

254

"That isn't Rory's car, see, his has a long scratch on the side and that one looks brand new."

"But why were you hiding suddenly like that?"

"He ... for my birthday, he wants to give me a surprise party so I ... I must pretend to be surprised."

Nell stared, and a look of profound chagrin slowly twisted her face.

"Lottie. I'm dreadfully sorry. I completely forgot it was your birthday."

"It's all right, I actually forgot too, in all the excitement we've been having."

"If only it were truly exciting," Nell said with a grimace as they walked up to the flat. "But why didn't Mommy remember?"

"I expect she's been ... distracted, with her book, and the Eleven Plus."

"It's a good thing Rory's going to get it all straightened out with his solicitor. I can't wait to live in a nice big house with a Nanny who's a good cook, and new clothes, and regular furniture."

Lottie stopped, blocking Nell's way. "You' d leave Mommy? You'd trade Mommy for new *furniture*?"

"Of course not, you moron, Mommy would live with us too, she'd have time to write, and she could go in the afternoons to see a doctor who would help her with her moods, and we'd all be calmer and happier—"

"—that's what Rory told you? That Mommy would live with us?"

"Well, I'm not sure that he has it all worked out, but I gather that in order for him to be our guardian, officially, he and Mommy would probably have to get married."

What?

"I know, it sounds odd, she's nearly ten years older than him, but it's not unheard of, it's not as if it will matter when they're middle aged."

"He told you they're getting married?"

Nell frowned. "Not in so many words, no, but I don't think Daddy would just let us live with him, otherwise. Daddy still does have some say about what happens to

255

us." Thank goodness for that. She couldn't imagine Daddy saying it would be all right with him if Mommy married Rory. Although ... he'd married Bunny. Perhaps she should write Daddy to explain the situation, more clearly than she'd done in her letter to Nana. But with Rory locked up in the bomb shelter, who would believe anything Lottie said?

When they opened the door, in the upstairs hallway, they heard Mommy's excited voice. "Lottie? Is that you?"

"Yes," she said, glum from her wonderings.

"Happy Birthday!" Mommy came into the hallway holding a big cake, with ten lit candles. From Lars' room she heard the piano strike up the chords of the birthday song, and she was afraid for a moment that Rory had escaped somehow and was in there at the piano. But then she heard Lars' voice, and Mommy and Nell joined in.

"You remembered," she murmured. "Thanks Mommy."

"Blow out the candles! Make a wish!"

She closed her eyes and wished that everything would work out all right, that Mommy would get well and write lots of books; and that she wouldn't go to hell for being so evil to Rory, and that Rory wouldn't hate her, for she didn't hate him, that wasn't why she'd shut him up, she just wanted him to leave them alone, and stop suffocating her—

"Blow them out before they all melt!"

She blew hard, and got them all, and Mommy and Nell clapped and Lars came out to clap too. They were all smiling at her. She was sure they couldn't understand why tears started to roll, unexpected, down her cheeks.

"Sorry," she said quickly, to stop their curiosity. "I'm just a bit ... tired. It's a beautiful cake, Mommy, let's have a big piece right now!"

"Into the kitchen, then, and you can open your presents!"

Presents too? She felt ashamed to have thought no-one remembered. There were some new clothes, and two new Enid Blyton books from Mommy, even though she disapproved of Enid Blyton's 'too-glib' writing; a book of Pachelbel piano music from Lars; and a big yellow stuffed dog from Nell.

"You can name him 'Terror' even if he didn't come from the pound," Nell said.

"You said you forgot it was my birthday!"

"I did forget that it was today. I gave the dog to Mommy at the weekend, after I bought him."

"And this came in the mail for you, from Rory!"

Inside the box eight dolls nestled side by side, each in a different European costume, each delicately made, with real bits of lace and wool. There was a letter, which Lottie was afraid to open; but which Nell had no compunction about reading aloud:

Darling Lottie,

It's a great moment to be ten years old. You are at the beginning of the most exciting years of your life. The world as represented by these dolls can be a fascinating playground, full of intoxicating experiences that I want to help you explore.

Love from Rory

"What a beautiful letter!" Mommy exclaimed. "Lottie, you should keep it with the dolls, so you'll always remember how special he is." Nell smiled, sweetly for once, but Lars made a face.

Lottie could just see the top of the bomb shelter from the kitchen window. She turned her chair so she didn't have to look. She shut the box lid on the nestled dolls' reproachful faces. She was afraid they'd start chastising her, like Polly used to, afraid they'd make her feel so sorry about him that she might let him out too soon.

"And, saving the best for last, this came from your Daddy." It was another package, smaller than Rory's, with many more stamps. The sight of their once-familiar red, white and blue flag made Lottie also see, again, that wide bright sky she always thought of when she remembered America, and she heard its fanfare, sounding mournfully tinny now, far away, as far away as a blue sky.

257

Lars helped her wrestle with the wrapping. It was a shiny white plastic box, with a silver plate full of little holes, and wheels on the side that rolled up and down—"It's a transistor radio!" shouted Nell. "Wizard!"

"Smashing," Lars said, envy colouring his tone in a way so satisfying to Lottie that she forgot her prisoner in the excitement of twisting the dials and finding the children's favourite programmes. They were delighted to get the Beatles, and they danced about the kitchen singing along and laughing while Mommy looked on, smiling her gentle smile, stirring her coffee, nibbling at a piece of cake.

"He sent an envelope, too, Lottie, here."

It was a big card with a glittery illustration of a girl riding a horse.

She'd have to write Daddy that she didn't like horses anymore.

"For a Super Special Girl on her Super Special Birthday!" he'd written inside. "I wish I could watch you blow out all TEN of your candles! I send you all my love, and so does Bunny." There was the check she'd asked for, which she handed to Mommy. Her eyes were watering again.

"I asked him for extra money, for a party. I want all my friends from school to come, I mean everyone who was in our play, and Stevie next door—"

—suddenly she wondered about Stevie. She hadn't seen him in what seemed like forever, not since Boxing Day, when they'd watched the Beatles, and Rory brought the TV here. She remembered how she'd treated Stevie as he sat next to her on the Avery's sofa, how she'd tried to pretend he was Rory.

"Lottie, what's the matter with you tonight? You keep stopping in the middle of every sentence! Wake up, it's your birthday!" Nell stared at her, then over at Mommy. She whispered, "D'you think she might be getting near her monthlies?"

Mommy laughed. "She's a baby! That won't happen for a long time."

"It started for me six months ago, and I felt mad as a hatter half the time before. And since, come to that!" Nell eyed Lottie. "We'll have a talk."

Nell felt mad as a hatter?

Mad as a feckin atter, she is, the bobby had said about Mommy. *You're as mad as your Mum,* Rory'd said last night. P'raps it ran in families, and they *were* all mad, p'raps that's why she'd shut him up there in that place like a ... grave.

For the second night now.

During the killer smog.

Alone and frightened.

But she'd only seen him frightened once, that time she found him out about the special school lie.

She must empty the sherry bottle so she could get some water to him. That was the main thing when the Ones were holed up in the Valley or the Castle or the Cave, they always found water to sustain every Adventure. He did have the canteen, but he had scorned it yesterday. This evening, however, he might not be feeling quite so ... defiant.

Lottie looked over to the sideboard where Mommy kept their tins and packets. The sherry bottle stood in full view, half empty. But would it fit down the airslit?

Nell was still looking at her.

"I know about the monthlies," Lottie said hastily. "We learnt that at school the other day, but I don't think I'm having them yet."

"Not right now, no, I wouldn't think so, but you seem ... what's wrong, Lottie?"

Nell's curiosity, once needled, was limitless. If Lottie even so much as looked in the direction of the bomb shelter, Nell would be out there in a flash, haloo-ing everyone from the Averys to the Lord Mayor of London.

So Lottie yawned, trying for a bland face. "It's just I'm that addled with tiredness."

"You were a brick to help me out the other night. If I did well in Maths it's thanks to you." Finally Nell rose from the table. "Want to watch Little Noddy?"

"In a sec, yeah."

With the pretext of putting the cake away, Lottie hovered at the sideboard. Would Mommy take notice if the half bottle of sherry simply disappeared? She closed her fingers round the bottle, measuring carefully to make sure it was no wider than her hand. She slipped it under her cardigan, along with a small jar of olives, and sped to the bathroom, where she poured the sherry down the toilet and then filled it with water from the tap.

She didn't let herself think as she ran downstairs and out to the back garden.

She could not see into the shelter; no matter how she twisted her head to peer through the airslit. But in the weak twilight she saw that he'd tried to claw a bigger hole in the top: the ivy was torn to bits, and there were marks around the plaster opening as if he'd been scraping it with a stick, or perhaps the torch.

"Rory!" There was no response. She dropped the jar of olives, hoping to wake him, hoping they wouldn't break.

A rustling sound preceded his slice of face, eyes half-closed, once again appearing in the airslit. He didn't speak.

She showed him the bottle and eased it through, relieved when she felt him pull it down. She snatched her hand away quickly so he wouldn't try to grab her again.

"... oying this?" His voice was so faint she had to lean closer than she liked.

"What?"

"Are you enjoying this? Keeping me prisoner, under your control, is it *amusing*?"

Her throat tightened. "No. I hate it. It makes me feel awful."

"That makes two of us." His cough sounded deeper, more real. "It's time to let me out, Lottie. I'm getting ill in here. I'm feeling ... weak."

That's how Lucy-Ann's prisoner had tricked her once, and she and Jack had to re-catch him once she let him out. "It's too soon for you to have had a change of heart. Anyroad, you didn't write any letters."

260

"I can't. My hands are sore. I could hardly open the tin of milk. I can't even put the new batteries in the torch."

"I'll do it for you."

His hand thrust up the torch, and then the battery packet. Caps of dried blood obscured his fingertips. It made her feel faint to look at them. She quickly replaced the batteries for him. She'd have to get more, or perhaps a candle—no, that was mad, he'd set himself on fire.

"I shall bring you some more batteries, but you must write those letters, else—"

"—else what, Lottie, you know there's no point. Let me out. I do promise, I'll leave you alone, I have my keys with me and I'll simply drive away and never come back. I won't tell if you let me out now." She heard his cough diminish, as if he were in the corner.

"It's too soon," she repeated.

"It's too late really. I'm already ill. I have to lie down now."

She stayed, lying on top of the ivy-covered mound for several more minutes, but she couldn't see him and he didn't speak. A cloud shifted overhead and a shaft of sunset showed her a sliver of floor, illuminating the jar of olives unbroken on its side, and the edge of the composition book, and a fringe of his scarf where she'd dropped it last night.

"Put your scarf on, you'll feel better," she called. "I'll try to find some aspirin."

FORTY-THREE

SHE DROPPED THE BOTTLE of aspirins down the airslit the next morning, along with another tin of milk. He did not answer when she called, but she was already late for school, and she had to leave without knowing was he all right.

A biting rain threw cold drops straight through the hole as if on purpose. She covered it up with the bits of ivy he'd not managed to tear away.

At school she watched the windows as the rain strengthened. Toward afternoon it seemed to grow lighter, but her momentary relief vanished as she saw that in fact it was turning into snow. She was so distracted that Miss Dowd had to call her name twice.

"Your sister, Lottie."

Nell stood at the classroom door. She was looking down, so Lottie couldn't see her face, but immediately she thought, *he's been found. I'm going to prison.*

"You have to come home with me now."

Lottie felt everyone, as well as Miss Dowd with her serious face, watching as she collected her satchel and walked out of the room.

Nell waited until they were clear of the school grounds. She stood by the grate where Lottie had found her marble. She wasn't crying, but her face was pinched with shocked fear, and her voice trembled. "I failed."

"Oh Nell."

"My score isn't high enough for university prep."

Lottie reached to hug her but Nell moved away. "What am I going to tell Mommy?"

262

"You have to tell her the truth, Nell, she'll find out from the school soon enough."

"I can hide the notice when they send it."

"You won't be at home to fetch the post."

"I can tell Mr. Singh." Nell's surmises sounded as wild as Lottie's, as she tried to work out in her head what to do about Rory.

"He won't understand."

"I can run away and live with Colin."

"Colin would never allow that. You have to tell Mommy."

"I'm afraid to." Nell's mouth was trembling now with her voice.

"I'll help you. We'll get it over with quickly, together."

"All right."

The snow fell on them un-noticed as they marched to the flat. They went straight upstairs, in unspoken accord that an immediate confrontation was best.

Mommy was in Lars' room, smoking, watching the telly. She looked round in surprise when they came in.

"You're home early! Is it the blizzard? There was a warning on TV, six inches predicted, it's unheard of in London!"

"No, it isn't the blizzard," Lottie said, although her gaze strayed to the screen, where a stern-looking man was pointing to a map. "We've got something to tell you."

Mommy smiled, and turned off the telly, and waited.

"Well," Nell began, "the thing is, I'm not quite sure how you'll feel about it, but I hope you won't take it too badly, because it really doesn't matter at all, in the end, it isn't at all important to what I'm going to do—"

Mommy looked at Lottie, confused.

"Just tell her, Nell."

"I failed the Eleven Plus."

Mommy still seemed confused. "Nell?" She looked at Lottie. "Lottie?"

"I didn't pass to prep level! I'm not smart enough!" Now Nell did start crying, painful-looking heaves and hot-looking tears that made Lottie ache in sympathy.

"It doesn't mean you aren't smart—" Lottie began.

"Silence, Charlotte." Mommy got up and walked to stand in front of them, looming tall, her face drawn into the frightening mask Lottie dreaded seeing. "Do I need to speak to the Headmistress?"

"It won't make a difference. The results are already posted. Anyway the school doesn't do the exams, it's the ... Council. The government."

"Should I speak to the *Queen*?" Now Mommy's eyes were narrowing, and her voice, though still low and quiet, took a deeper tone. "Wouldn't the Queen make an exception for the *Dandy* Girl?"

Nell flinched.

Mommy's hand looked clawlike as she gripped Nell's chin. Lottie could see how white, then pink, Nell's cheeks became, as Mommy's fingers dug in. "The sins of the flesh come home to roost. The glorification of the physical, the gilding of a lily that never needed gilding!"

Mommy let go of Nell suddenly, with a twist that made Nell cry out, and began to stride round the room. "But don't you remember, even Solomon in all his glory? Not arrayed as such!"

"But, Mommy, you were happy for Nell to do the modeling—" Lottie had to speak up, as Nell had crumpled into a corner, sobbing, curling up on herself.

"Silence!" Mommy kept striding.

Lottie edged toward Nell. Usually the striding phase burned out quickly, but they'd never had to present Mommy with this kind of news before.

Mommy's pace became more agitated. Her frown deepened into the furrowed concentration that took her so far away from them. She stared out into the room, as if looking for someone. Or some kind of answer. Was she listening for God to talk to her? Her mouth started to move. Lottie took a risk.

"Mommy, let's have some coffee. Let's go into the kitchen and talk about it, and you can have a Kent, and some coffee."

Mommy turned to look at her as if one of Lars' battleships had spoken.

In a fearful little girl's voice, Nell offered from her corner, "I'll put the water on."

"NO." Mommy glared at Nell. "Tell me how this happened."

"I didn't do well enough to pass." Nell said, crying again. "I ... I suppose I didn't study hard enough."

Mommy's frown suddenly imploded on itself and turned into an agonized drawn-down mouth, sad eyes that leaked into a windy, empty place where she might get lost.

"Mommy!" Lottie tried to bring her back.

"Oh Nell, it's my fault. I let you down. I didn't pay enough attention." She finished, fiercely, "I'm so stupid!" She pounded her fists onto her thighs. "Stupid!" She started grinding her teeth together, Lottie didn't like to look; it was too mechanical. She was shocked when, as she looked away, Mommy's foot flew out and kicked the wall, kicked so hard that a divot of plaster spat out and caked itself into bits on the floor.

"Mother?" A cautious, suspicious voice came from the doorway. Lottie had never been so glad to see Lars.

"I didn't pass," Nell told him.

He walked across to Mother, frowning when his foot struck the plaster. He took Mommy's arm.

"Mother, we need you to sit down now. The girls will get you some coffee, and we can think things through." This was always Mommy's advice to them, when they were upset, *think things through.*

That's what Rory was supposed to be doing.

"I can't sit down, not now, not when there's so much to do."

Lars led her to sit on his bed. "What do you have to do?"

"It's as clear as sign as I've ever had," she said, her face now shining up at Lars. "This means we should leave right away. We should take Lottie's map and get ourselves going to Israel. We can use the tuition check your Dad sent you last week."

"We should use that to go *home*, Mother, to America. Not to Israel. We don't belong in Israel, we belong at home, where Nana and your friends can keep you company and Dad can see us on the weekends. Where I can play football in high school and the girls can go to summer camp. That's what I told Dad, when I wrote to him. That's what we're going to do. Go home."

He looked over at the girls, who were still huddled together. "Coffee?"

Nell unfolded herself from the corner. "What about Rory's plans?"

Lars grimaced. "Rory! He's not a Dad. It would never have worked with Rory, Nell, that was just a nutty idea."

Nell looked as if she didn't know whether to be excited or miserable. "So ... it doesn't matter, about the Eleven Plus?"

"It matters, Nell, because the Father sent it as a sign—"

"—a sign we should get out of here," Lars muttered.

"But what about ... the Dandy Girl?" Nell wondered.

Lars shrugged. "Dandy shmandy."

"When did you write to Daddy?" Lottie asked him. "What did you say?"

"Last week. I got fed up when Nell said Rory and Mother would have to get married. Heads like *sieves!*" He frowned at Lottie. "I was never as crazy about Rory as the rest of you."

A shocked little laugh escaped Lottie, and another, and suddenly she was giggling, as silly as she'd been the other night with her ruined coat. "I'm not crazy about him either! I wrote Nana, I told her I don't *want* him to be our new dad."

Lars nodded approvingly. "Of course not."

But I shall have to let him out now. "I'll ... just put on the coffee."

266

FORTY-FOUR

SHE NEARLY DROPPED THE COFFEE in her haste to get it to him. He'd be grateful for a hot drink; the snow was blowing nearly sideways and had all but covered the shelter. She set down the thermos that she'd borrowed from Mr. Singh, and scrambled to the top: to warn him that if he told on her, she'd tell on him too, so they'd be even. They wouldn't go to the same prison, but they'd be even.

"Rory!" She didn't bother trying to whisper. "Rory! I'm going to let you out, on one condition!"

There was no answer. Perhaps he was asleep, or perhaps his cough had gotten worse and he couldn't talk. The worry she'd been carrying around about him bit into her, sharply. "Rory!"

His voice finally came, low and raspy, not sounding at all like himself. "Annabel? Did you finally find me?" He coughed. "This time was too long for the game, I really stayed lost!" A hoarse laugh. "No more kisses for you!"

"It's me, Lottie, it's not Annabel."

She saw, then, yellow torchlight swinging to the ceiling. "Lottie?" he repeated, a mystified wobble in his voice, as if he'd never heard the name. "Lottie."

She saw him now, staggering up to the airslit, his face chalky but full of wonder as he turned it up to her. A tremulous smile began to split the hairy smudge around his mouth. "Lottie, darling, why are you crying?"

He kept staring up at her. He looked, suddenly, just like the lost boy, Jamie, that Lars had found in the park.

267

"Why aren't you wearing your coat and scarf?" she scolded him, through salty tears that clogged her voice.

He looked, with a petulant frown, to where she could see the end of the scarf. "It's so hot in here. I'm roasting." He began to peel off his jersey. "I have to lie down now." He walked out of sight and his voice faded. "Don't cry. I'm just having a rest."

She slid down the berm, grabbed the thermos, heaved open the door. A zoo-like smell assaulted her, how foul; she'd forgotten he'd need to use the toilet. He was flung carelessly on the cot, blanket bunched under him, clad only in his shirt and trousers. His socks and shoes were on top of his coat on the floor.

He was wheezing, his eyelids fluttering, as she approached him.

"Rory." She jostled him with her free hand. She felt heat rise from him like pavement on a summer day. "I've brought you some nice coffee, you must drink it and then you can go home."

He wheezed deeper as he turned, and his eyes opened, bleary, not quite looking at her. He sat up and started to take a deep breath, which turned into a long ragged cough. He reached for the thermos, unscrewed the lid, heedless of his worse-looking fingers, and poured the liquid down his throat. His body twisted as he gasped and choked.

"Hot! Good Christ, I'm burnt!"

She scooted away, in case he erupted.

His eyes seemed to clear, then, as he looked at her. Incredibly, he smiled. "Lottie. Did you come to scald me, since I wouldn't die here, will you have to shoot me as well, like Rasputin?" His laugh became another wheezy cough. "Then you'll have to drown me." He lay back on the cot. "Let me just have a sleep first."

She chewed on her cheek, watching his chest rise and fall too rapidly. He was ill, too ill to know himself. She remembered raving madly when she had the mumps and Mommy read aloud from *The Back of the North Wind* and she'd felt herself flying along, feeling the breeze of the

268

night in her hair as she went with the North Wind. It had been the loveliest dream, until she'd woken with her neck on fire.

He was delirious.

He wasn't going to be able to drive himself home.

She needed help to get him out.

"I'm just going to find someone to help you get up. I'm not shutting you in again." She covered him up with the frond of blanket that was draped on the floor. "Only, just be sure, if you tell anyone I locked you in, any grownups I mean, if you try to get me in trouble ... I'll get you in trouble too."

She shook him, knowing it was unkind to wake him, but she wanted him to hear. "Do you understand me?" She said it loudly. "Did you hear me Rory?"

He opened his eyes again. "You said ... you'll get me in trouble too. If I say you locked me in." He moved a hand toward her, and she quickly moved back. "S'all right, Lottie, don't worry. S' over." He turned away.

She ran out, making sure the door was well ajar, never mind the driving snow. She ran as if her feet knew exactly where she had to go: next door.

Stevie's family was just sitting down to supper.

"Allo, look who's turned up!" Rita took another plate from the cupboard. "Bangers and mash, Lottie, your favourite, sit down love."

"No, I've come to borrow Stevie, just for a bit, I've got to talk to him."

"Oh is it like that, then ..." Rita smiled.

There were startled looks exchanged, but no objections, and Stevie trailed her obediently down his back stairs to the garden gate separating their flats.

Before they went further she faced him. "Stevie, sorry about Boxing Day, when I ... kissed you, and like that."

Stevie looked at the snow-covered ground.

Her face felt very hot, but she continued, "I locked Rory in our bomb shelter because he was doing that with me, and he was going to take us away from Mommy, but

269

since Nell failed the Eleven Plus we're going back to America anyway—"

"Ang on," Stevie interrupted her. "Rory, are you saying *our* Rory, was acting like that, like you was ... his *girlfriend?*"

"Yes. I didn't know how to make him stop, so I locked him—"

"Cor blimey, Lottie, why didn't you say nuffink? I'd've told im to sod off. I'd've punched im in the gob."

"Dunno." Looking at Stevie's confused face, she wondered why she'd said nuffink, after she'd stopped being afraid of the special school. "I suppose I ... just didn't know how." It was a jumble, the way Eswyths and Arkwrights got tied together, the Dandy girl and her recital and Mommy's poem ... "I couldn't unpick the one stitch, see, Stevie, else the whole bit would unravel ..." *Not a dab hand.*

"So then ... *what* did you do to im?" He fixed her with a puzzled stare, but she pushed on ahead, trudging through thin crunchy snow.

"You have to help me get him out," she told Stevie, over her shoulder. "He's ill. Can we call a taxi, I wonder, d'you think he has any money?"

"You locked im in this moldy old heap?" Stevie shot her a reproving look as they went down the little steps. "It was bad enough in the summer. It's like a bloomin tomb ere now. I should think e'd learnt is lesson, poor bugger."

"Only for two nights."

"Two *nights!* It's a wonder e didn't freeze to death, Lottie, you're barmy!"

Rory was sitting on the edge of the cot, holding the thermos.

He looked at them with eyes that were not his, as if the killer smog had seeped in and evaporated the black ice.

"Hallo, children, welcome to my cave."

"Allo mate, are you ... all right then?" Stevie asked cautiously.

270

"I think not, my fingers are ripped to shreds, I shall have to see a doctor."

"Wot appened to em?"

"I tried to open that beastly door." His sooty gaze slid over to Lottie. "I shut myself in here by mistake, wasn't that stupid?"

Stevie shot Lottie a bewildered look. "But I thought—" He looked at Rory again, and closed his mouth in a judicious little clamp.

Rory drained the last of the coffee. "I'm off." He stood, not very steadily. He pointed toward gloves at the foot of the cot. "D'you mind, children, get these on—"

They each took a hand, careful to pull gently over his raw-looking fingertips, as he took in little hisses through his teeth. His face was greyer after this delicate operation. "Now, my shoes, and then put my keys in my hand, and help me get into my car."

They knelt at his feet, each pulling on a sock and tying tight a shoe. Lottie glanced up at his altered face, and meeting his fixed gaze, said, "We're even, then, right Rory?"

It seemed an age until he answered. "Yes, Lottie. We're even."

They walked him to his car and swept snow off the windshield as he sat warming the engine. He gave a little toot of the horn as he drove away.

Stevie looked at Lottie. "I'd say we're well shot of im. Want to come up for supper now?"

"I have to see to Mommy. She was upset that Nell failed her Eleven Plus."

Stevie's frown was sympathetic. "Blow, that's too bad for Nell. Tell her to buck up, she'll do ever so well anyway, in America."

"In America." Lottie listened to how that sounded.

"I'll come to visit you, to see the cowboys and skyscrapers."

"Yes, Stevie, do."

271

The next day, a stay-home day, Colin came to say goodbye. Nell had called him from Mr. Singh's with their news.

"Here's the name of my company's New York office. Nell, I'm sure they could help you get some Dandy Girl sort of work in Chicago." Colin handed Nell a card, and gave them each a hug. "Kids, it's been ever such fun, eh? We shall all miss you. P'raps I'll see you, next time I come to the States."

He looked at Lottie. "Can I take you to visit Rory, love? He's in hospital, bit of an accident on his tour, not serious. He did say he'd like to see you before you leave."

They came to a room whose inert occupant had pads of bandage for hands.

"Will he ... be able to play?" she whispered fearfully.

"Oh yes, by all accounts, no bones broken. He's always healed quickly." Colin looked into the hallway. "I'm popping out for a cuppa. Go on over and say hallo."

She didn't stand too close. Rory opened dull eyes, and a tired smile curved up. "Hallo Lottie. You're going back to America then." His voice was hoarse and sodden.

She nodded.

"You must keep playing. You're a fine musician."

She nodded again.

"And Althea." He coughed, restlessly, twisting his head away. "Colin has the poetry magazine information. Remind him to give it to her."

"All right."

His mouth straightened. "I do hope you realize, I never meant ...."

He waved a white mitt in her direction, as if that would complete his sentence, not to summon her but merely to stir the air. She felt his intent waft around her and fall away, as once it had enveloped and clung.

Her chest ached as she looked at him, ached like one of Rita's suffocated babies, life squeezed out. She pressed her hands on the empty space. It felt raw as his fingertips. But something might grow there again, one day.

272

Something small.
Something new.

AUTHOR'S NOTE

I heard Neil Gaiman once say that writers are like magpies; picking out the shiny bits—what's most memorable and can be used as story material—from everything they see and experience. WALKING TO ISRAEL came from my childhood in London, with certain shiny bits picked directly from that time, but with characters who took on a life of their own as soon as they got onstage.

Children who suffer sexual abuse often do not have the words to express their fear, confusion, and guilt. I am glad to have given Lottie the chance to tell her truth.

ACKNOWLEDGEMENTS

My thanks go to: My mother who gifted me with rich, deep, strange stories. My sister whose lively imagination peopled our childhood with fabulous characters and whose love of reading inspired mine. My husband who always encouraged me and who has fascinating stories of his own. My children who allowed my writing to eclipse any notion of home cooking (apologies to my eldest son who wanted me to add scenes of people eating barbecue). My writing collective—Julia Buckley, Elizabeth Diskin, Cynthia Quam—who shepherded my work from the beginning, who are the best editors, publicists and critique partners any novelist could hope for, and without whom I would never have finished a manuscript. Wells Street Press, for getting me from manuscript to publication. Other writers and artists whose generosity has moved me: Karen Osborne, Sam Reaves, Kathi Baron, Jennifer Stevenson, Marilyn Brandt, Erica Rourke (the latter three from the august ChicagoNorth Romance Writers of America). Colombia College Chicago for Story Workshop. Cherished friends: aDOORables, NapaGals, YaYas, and Ann L to whom I declared my first novel 'finished' years ago after writing THE END and running to her house all aglow. Snaps to Mary H with whom I cooked up the idea to get serious about writing on a napkin in Canada. The Oak Park community whose support has so nourished my family and me during my illness, especially Mary, Fran, Beth, Elizabeth L and both Kathy's. Finally, pulmonologist Benjamin Margolis and Sherrie Majdic, and oncologist Philip Bonomi and Irene Haapoja, whose care has granted me the time to publish. Special thanks and love to Sue.

275

ABOUT THE AUTHOR

Award-winning writer Emma Gates was born in New York and spent her childhood in England. She earned a BA in Spanish/Latin American Studies from Indiana University Bloomington, and an MBA with concentration in Arabic/Middle Eastern Studies from Thunderbird. She worked for three years in Mexico and five in Saudi Arabia. She is an international business and telecoms specialist currently living near Chicago with her family and a pair of inscrutable cats.

Playlist

I often listen to music while I write. Sometimes I choose from the era I'm writing about, from my own collection, but sometimes my favorite radio station provides inspiration which can creep in to inform the story ambiance (shout-out: WXRT Chicago).

Thanks to my brother, who always shared the best music, and to my children who gave me the very great compliment of saying how much they liked my musical taste. Thanks to the artists whose brilliance so greatly illuminates my life.

English Tea – Paul McCartney

Oh Little Town of Bethlehem – Phillips Brooks

Claire de Lune – Debussy

How Many Flowers – traditional Morris dance

Sweet Thames Flow Softly – Ewan McColl and Peggy Seeger

From Me to You – The Beatles

Jesu Joy of Man's Desiring – Bach

Canon and Gigue – Pachelbel

Ye Holy Angels Bright – John Darwall

Miserere – Cat Empire